THE WIDOW'S BODYGUARD

Karen Whiddon

HARLEQUIN®
ROMANTIC SUSPENSE™

Recycling programs
for this product may
not exist in your area.

ISBN-13: 978-1-335-62879-4

The Widow's Bodyguard

Copyright © 2021 by Karen Whiddon

All rights reserved. No part of this book may be used or reproduced in
any manner whatsoever without written permission except in the case of
brief quotations embodied in critical articles and reviews.

This is a work of fiction. Names, characters, places and incidents
are either the product of the author's imagination or are used fictitiously.
Any resemblance to actual persons, living or dead, businesses,
companies, events or locales is entirely coincidental.

This edition published by arrangement with Harlequin Books S.A.

For questions and comments about the quality of this book,
please contact us at CustomerService@Harlequin.com.

Harlequin Enterprises ULC
22 Adelaide St. West, 40th Floor
Toronto, Ontario M5H 4E3, Canada
www.Harlequin.com

Printed in U.S.A.

Karen Whiddon started weaving fanciful tales for her younger brothers at the age of eleven. Amid the gorgeous Catskill Mountains, then the majestic Rocky Mountains, she fueled her imagination with the natural beauty surrounding her. Karen now lives in north Texas, writes full-time and volunteers for a boxer dog rescue. She shares her life with her hero of a husband and four to five dogs, depending on if she is fostering. You can email Karen at kwhiddon1@aol.com. Fans can also check out her website, karenwhiddon.com.

Books by Karen Whiddon

Harlequin Romantic Suspense

The CEO's Secret Baby
The Cop's Missing Child
The Millionaire Cowboy's Secret
Texas Secrets, Lovers' Lies
The Rancher's Return
The Texan's Return
Wyoming Undercover
The Texas Soldier's Son
Texas Ranch Justice
Snowbound Targets
The Widow's Bodyguard

The Coltons of Mustang Valley

Colton's Last Stand

The Coltons of Roaring Springs

Colton's Rescue Mission

The Coltons of Red Ridge

Colton's Christmas Cop

Visit the Author Profile page at Harlequin.com for more titles.

To my family, both near and far. I love you dearly.

Chapter 1

Eva Rowson stood smiling next to her husband, Drew, wondering how it could be possible that no one could see the misery behind her facade. Now that Drew had announced his run for governor of the great state of Texas, she'd had no choice but to join him in the limelight despite the fact that in private they were virtual strangers and had been for years.

Drew had given her little choice in the matter. In fact, when he'd handed her the list of appearances he'd had his assistant type up, he'd informed her that this was what he'd bought and paid for by marrying her. While she'd had no idea what he'd meant, she knew he'd intended his remark to be insulting, so she didn't let on that it bothered her. She simply accepted the paper and turned and walked away, aware the only reaction that would please him would be her unhappiness.

She couldn't blame him. They'd married each other for reasons that had nothing to do with love. Drew had made no secret of the fact that he planned to live his own, separate life and had informed her she was free to do the same, as long as she was discreet.

Instead, she'd focused all her energy on her son, Liam. Now two, he kept her on her toes. He was the light of her life, an ever-constant source of joy that most days was enough.

Looking out over the crowd, she saw they appeared to be eating up Drew's words, cheering and clapping as if they thought he might be announcing the second coming.

Her wide, fake smile began to wobble around the edges. She sucked in a breath between her teeth, steadying herself. Heaven help her if Drew watched the video later and saw the slightest slipup.

As she stared out over the sea of rapt faces, all of whom had paid over a thousand dollars to be here, she tried not to think about how the sky-high pair of Louboutins were killing her feet. The speech part of the evening should be wrapping up soon and then they'd move on to the gala itself, which would involve food and dancing at least once with her husband while they both pretended to be an adoring couple.

Too much more of this and she thought she might be sick.

She heard the sharp crack of the gunshot a second before someone slammed into her, knocking her to the floor. Jesse, her bodyguard. "Don't move," he ordered, **physically holding her down.**

Dazed, she struggled to catch her breath, absently realizing one of her shoes had gone flying off, even as pandemonium broke out in the crowd. People began screaming and fighting their way toward the exits.

"Drew's been shot," Jesse told her, shifting his body slightly, just enough so he could haul her up and drag her off the stage. "Stay with me." They made it all the way to the back room where earlier she and Drew had sat for makeup before Jesse's words registered.

"Wait, what?" Struggling against his hold, she twisted enough so she could see the circle of people huddled over the spot where her husband had been standing. Jesse, who had until today managed to avoid touching her, kept a firm grip on her arm.

"You don't need to see that," he said.

"I think I do." Glaring at him, she tried to pull herself away but he wouldn't release her. "Let me go."

"I'm not sure if the shooter's been apprehended," he growled, his espresso-colored eyes locking with hers. For one heartbeat, two, she couldn't look away. "My job is to protect you, and by damn that's what I'm going to do."

Out in the crowd, the stampede hadn't died down. Into the wave of panicked people trying to get out, paramedics and law enforcement rushed in.

"Where's the shooter?" one of the officers yelled. No one paid him any attention, too fixated on making their way to safety. The police fanned out, some helping the crowd escape, others clearly searching.

To Eva's relief, there were no more gunshots.

"He probably got away," Jesse groused, sounding thoroughly disgusted.

"Let me go check on Drew." This time, when she

yanked her arm, he released his grip. Stumbling backward, she kicked off her other heel and hurried over to the group forming a protective ring around her husband. Paramedics had already forced their way through to him, and as she approached, she could see them trying to work their magic on Drew's bloody and motionless body.

"Stay back," one of them barked.

"I'm his wife," she replied. Unbelievably, on the fringe of people watching, she saw several raise their phones, clearly videotaping.

Ignoring them, she dropped to her knees at Drew's side. Behind her, Jesse continued to scan the auditorium, just in case the shooter remained out there and ready to take her out too.

One paramedic had begun CPR. The other held Drew's wrist, searching for a pulse.

"Is he…?" Swallowing hard, for whatever reason Eva found herself glancing over her shoulder at Jesse, as if he could help her find the word.

"Let us work, ma'am," one of the EMTs said tersely. Two more men appeared with a stretcher and they loaded Drew up on it. Eva stood frozen, not sure what to do, when Jesse took her elbow and led her after the paramedics.

The crowd parted for them. Again, she couldn't help but notice all the raised cell phones. She wouldn't be surprised if some of them weren't already livestreaming on social media.

None of that mattered right now.

Outside, Drew had already been loaded up into the ambulance. Instead of immediately leaving, it sat idling. She supposed they were trying to stabilize him before they set off for the ER.

"This isn't good," Jesse murmured. It was then that she realized what he meant. Could it be possible the reason the ambulance wasn't rushing to get to the hospital was because Drew was already dead?

Staring in stunned shock, she watched as the ambulance finally drove off. No lights or sirens. "Does that mean he's…" Words failed her.

"I don't know. Come on." Jesse steered her to her car, a silver Range Rover. She'd come in her own vehicle, making Jesse ride in the passenger seat. She hadn't wanted to travel with the group of people who made up Drew's entourage. She wondered where all those people were now.

"Keys, please." Jesse held out his hand. Numb, she dug in her purse and handed them over. Moving woodenly, she settled into the front passenger seat, robotically securing her seat belt.

Though so far she'd managed to ignore Jesse, the bodyguard she assumed Drew had assigned to her out of spite, she couldn't actually do that right now.

"Are you all right?" he asked her, nothing but concern in his tone.

She decided to answer honestly. "I don't know." She actually wasn't sure how she felt. While she didn't love Drew and had in fact asked him for a divorce, she wouldn't wish this on anyone. Not even her worst enemy.

"I refuse to assume the worst," she declared, lifting her chin and staring straight ahead. Jesse didn't need to know any of the particulars of her complicated marriage. She actually wondered why he'd even accepted the job offer from Drew. What kind of man agreed to become a bodyguard to the woman who'd broken his heart?

Jesse drove fast but safely to the hospital, able to keep the ambulance in his sights. He wasn't sure what to make of Eva's reaction. Maybe she'd gone into shock. The woman he'd known for years had always been demonstrative and dramatic, quick with a tear or a smile or a hug. Now Eva seemed to have become smaller somehow, withdrawn, as if she did all of her living in a place no one else could ever visit. Yet none of this even slightly diminished his desire for her. He doubted anything could.

Jesse had been in his new position as Eva's personal bodyguard for three weeks, which worked out since the ATF had gotten leads that Eva's husband, Drew, had been laundering money for the Mexican drug cartels, along with the Brothers of Sin's help. Rumor had it that Drew had his own huge stash of dirty money hidden. They'd been trying to figure out a way to get someone undercover near him when Raul, head of BOS, had sent Jesse to become his daughter's bodyguard.

Eva had, of course, kept her distance. Jesse tried not to watch her too long, though he found that once he did, he had the same trouble dragging his gaze away. She was still beautiful inside and out, and kind, with a soft, sexy voice and the same sensual grave to her movements. But she rarely laughed, and her self-composure made her seem almost robotic. He didn't like it. The idea that marriage to Drew had done this to her tore his heart. And worse, there wasn't a damn thing he could do to change things.

From what he'd seen, Drew and Eva didn't have a close marriage. Part of him had been glad to see Eva's uncharacteristic lack of passion. Because late at night, when Jesse couldn't sleep, her passion had been all he'd been able to think about.

Finally, they pulled into the hospital parking lot. The ambulance sat in the ER bay. By the time Jesse parked, he felt sure Drew's body had already been unloaded.

Inside, they were directed to a waiting room, despite Eva's insistence that she be allowed to see her husband. She dropped into one of the metal-and-cloth chairs with a little huff, her arms crossed and her expression inscrutable.

Jesse took a seat next to her. He didn't speak, as he wasn't sure what exactly to say. He could offer words of comfort, but would she even want to hear them coming from him? Once he and Eva had never had a problem relating to each other, but these days neither of them seemed able to bridge the distance.

Which, of course, was how it should be. After all, Eva had left him for another man. She'd moved to Anniversary, met and married Drew in a whirlwind courtship, and had gotten pregnant. Her son was now two. Until he'd accepted this job offer to become her bodyguard, Jesse hadn't seen or heard from her in nearly three years.

"Why won't they let me back there?" Eva muttered, so quietly she almost might have been talking to herself.

Instinct had him aching to put his arm around her and pull her close, but since he no longer had that right, he didn't. "I'm sure someone will come out soon and tell you what's going on."

As if on cue, a harried-looking woman in a white lab coat came through the double doors. "Mrs. Rowson?"

Eva jumped to her feet. "Yes?"

"I'm Dr. Linwood. Please come with me." The doctor went to a door with a brass plate reading Family Consultation. Opening the door, she led the way inside. When Eva followed, Jesse went right behind her.

Inside, a slightly scarred dark wooden conference table occupied the entire room. The doctor took the chair nearest the door, gesturing that they should sit as she closed the door behind them.

"Mrs. Rowson, I'm sorry. Your husband didn't make it."

Jesse braced himself, aching for her. Surely now Eva would begin wailing, carrying on about the unfairness of life, swearing and pounding the table in her grief.

Instead, she frowned and gave a collected nod. "I suspected as much," she said, looking away. "Thank you for letting me know."

Damn. Jesse wasn't sure how to react to Eva's stiff composure.

Even the doctor seemed disconcerted by the new widow's lack of grief. "He didn't suffer," she offered. "The gunshot wound to the heart killed him instantly."

"I see." For a moment, Eva looked down. When she raised her chin again, her expression had settled into one of steely resignation. "I'll need to make funeral arrangements. I'm sure the funeral home will contact you once I have."

Dr. Linwood nodded, her gaze fixing on Jesse briefly before returning to Eva. "Again, you have my deepest sympathy. Please let me know if there's anything else I can do."

"Thank you." Both Jesse and Eva stood, watching silently while the doctor left the room.

Eva's eyes were dry. Heart aching for her, he wondered if she would cry later, when she was alone. The thought made him sad. They'd once shared everything. He wouldn't have minded helping her through what must be overwhelming grief.

"I'd like to go home," Eva said, checking her watch. "I've left Liam with his nanny and though he's only two, I don't want him seeing this on the news. I need to tell him myself."

He nodded. As they walked out into the main hospital lobby, a crowd of reporters rushed up to them, all talking at once, trying to shove microphones into Eva's face. There were huge cameras and smaller ones, flashes going off, in short, a sort of pandemonium.

Eva's stride faltered. Without thinking, Jesse put his arm around her shoulders and turned her into him, hiding her face. He tried not to think about how good she felt, how well she fit. She wasn't his and hadn't been for a long time. He was only her bodyguard. He hustled her through the crowd, and out the doors. Judging by the commotion behind them, the reporters were hot on their heels.

"Keep your head down and keep walking," he said, releasing her. He felt the loss of her body next to his far stronger than he should have.

Amazingly, they made it to her car. Once inside, they were able to back up before the throng of people reached them.

He drove off to a blur of flashes and raised cameras.

A quick glance at Eva revealed her sitting hunched in the seat, both hands over her face. *Now* would come the weeping. Jesse felt almost relieved. For a few moments there, he'd come to believe that the woman he knew and had once loved, had completely vanished, replaced by a patrician statue.

But no. Instead of wailing or crying, she straightened her shoulders and put her hands neatly in her lap. When she finally spoke, her measured tone betrayed nothing, not the slightest hint of grief or pain or any other emotion. This made his chest ache.

"What are you doing here, Jesse?" she asked, exhaling in a sigh.

Now? She wanted to talk about this now? He swallowed, deciding to stick to the facts even though she already knew them. "Your father asked Drew to hire me. Raul wanted someone he trusted to look after you. You know as well as I do that he never liked Drew."

"Smart man." Her enigmatic response told him nothing. "Do you think Drew had any idea of our prior relationship?"

"Didn't the two of you discuss it?"

At first, she didn't respond. He kept driving, alternating his attention between her and the road. He'd tried not to think of their marriage, since the thought of her making love with another man tore him up inside. When her father, head of the motorcycle club Brothers of Sin, had given him the orders to go work as her bodyguard, at first Jesse had believed the older man was punishing him. Though for what, he had no idea. Everyone in the club knew how much Jesse loved Eva, even though she'd broken up with him when he'd refused to leave Brothers of Sin behind. What she didn't understand was that Jesse couldn't. Not now, not yet. And he wasn't even able to discuss this with her.

Rather than punishing one of his top men, Raul Mendoza had simply decided to use Jesse's feelings for Eva to his advantage. Though he did business with Drew Rowson, Raul didn't trust him. Especially not with Raul's precious daughter. Even if Eva refused to have anything to do with the club, her father or Jesse, Raul still worried about her.

As did Jesse. Even more so now that he'd been around her and her husband for three weeks. His real bosses had jumped at the chance to investigate Drew, whom they considered even bigger fish than the head of BOS. Once again, Jesse had no choice in the matter.

Secretly, the thought of being around Eva made his every nerve come alive. Even if she'd married another man, even if she clearly cared nothing for Jesse, who'd once sworn to love her the rest of his life. Jesse guessed Eva didn't understand that he always kept his oaths.

Riding in silence, they finally arrived at the gated community in Anniversary, Texas. Eva punched in her code and the huge iron gates swung open. Houses in this part of town were owned by local celebrities, CEOs and other high-profile people. A former president even lived nearby.

Eva sat, her back ramrod straight, her gaze straight ahead, as if pretending Jesse was nothing but her chauffeur. Her feelings remained a mystery. These days, the vivacious, passionate woman he knew had been taken over by an efficient, bloodless automaton. Jesse wondered how hard she'd had to work to bury herself and if there was any chance she'd find her way back.

But then again, what did it matter? In the end, she'd hate him all over again, only for a different reason.

Pulling into the long driveway that led to the two-story McMansion, Jesse parked the Range Rover in front of the garage. Eva hopped out the second the vehicle stopped, barely waiting for the garage door to open.

Shaking his head, Jesse followed her, locking the car with the remote. The first time he'd seen the antiseptic, impersonal elegance inside this house, he'd known Eva hadn't had anything to do with its decorating. He couldn't understand how, in two and a half years of marriage, she hadn't put her personal stamp on a single room.

Even the nursery. Instead of the typical bright colors most people associated with infants, her son's room had been done in black, white and gray. Depressing as hell, as far as Jesse was concerned.

Of course, what did he know? He wasn't an interior designer or a child psychologist. Maybe a monochrome color palette was the newest thing in child development. If Liam were his kid, Jesse knew there would have been airplanes or bunnies or something. Normal baby stuff.

Despite his complicated life, at heart Jesse considered himself a simple man. He knew what he deemed important and comported himself accordingly. Sometimes, it was the only way he kept himself sane.

Inside the house, he stood in the antiseptic, modern kitchen and eyed the curving staircase. Knowing Eva's routine, he figured she'd gone immediately to see her son. Though she and Drew employed a full-time nanny, Eva appeared to enjoy lavishing attention and time on Liam. At least she hadn't changed in that area. For as long as Jesse could remember, Eva had loved children and babies.

Halfway up the stairs, his cell phone vibrated. His *other* cell phone, the untraceable, generic one he switched out every few weeks. He didn't answer, knowing there'd be no voice mail. Only one person had that number and he'd return the call later, when he had zero chance of being overheard.

Continuing on to the baby's room, he glanced inside. As he'd expected, Eva sat on the floor, watching as her two-year-old son played with his plastic truck.

Kara, the nanny, had retreated to the background, having taken a seat in the rocking chair. Eva's silky dark hair fell like a curtain around her face, until she brushed it back from her shoulders with an impatient gesture.

He wondered how she'd tell the boy his father had died, or if she'd even bother. Jesse wasn't sure how much the toddler would comprehend.

Right now, Eva appeared serene and beautiful, as if the horrific event of a few hours ago had never even occurred. Any other woman would have fallen apart. Even one who'd grown up around a tough bunch of bikers like Eva had. He didn't understand it. She'd been standing right next to her husband when he'd been gunned down in cold blood. She had to process the emotional trauma of that sooner or later.

Didn't she?

Eva knew Jesse stood in the doorway. One of the curses of having him here was her überawareness of his every move. Larger than life, handsome as sin, he looked every bit the stereotypical biker, except for the fact that he'd cut shorter his now spiky blond hair. Even now, when she'd chosen another man, the sight of

Jesse sauntering into a room made her insides quiver. He was her first love, only love, and now her enemy. She had no idea what Drew had been thinking when he'd hired Jesse Wyman to be her bodyguard. It was like handing the fox the keys to the henhouse.

Or would have been, she amended. If she'd been any other woman. That part of her life was over.

Her cell phone rang. Glancing at it, she saw the call was from her father. No doubt he'd heard the news.

"*Mija*, I don't have time to talk," he said, instead of his usual greeting. "I've heard about what happened to Drew and I've been told your life is in danger. Come home, where me and the club can protect you."

"No."

"Eva, listen to me—"

"Dad, please stop. This has already been an upsetting day. I'm with Liam now. I don't need any more stress."

"Do you want to leave your son without a mother?" Raul asked, his voice harsh. "If you don't listen to me, that's what's going to happen."

She'd had enough. "You sent me a bodyguard," she reminded him, refusing to give him the satisfaction of letting him know how much his choice of men bothered her. "How about you just let him do his job?" She ended the call, turning to find her son standing uncertainly in the doorway, watching her with wide eyes, his lower lip trembling.

"Mama?" he asked, his expressive little face crumpling in reaction to her harsh tone, about to break out in sobs at any moment.

"Shh, it's okay, sweetheart," she soothed, picking him up and cuddling him close. She caught a glimpse of Kara leaning against the wall playing on her phone. When the nanny realized Eva was watching, she shoved the phone into her pocket and started forward to no doubt retrieve Liam.

"It's okay," Eva forestalled her. "I'll call you if I need you."

Kara nodded, drifting away, and disappeared in her room, glancing sideways and fluttering her eyelashes at Jesse as she passed him.

Carrying Liam downstairs and into the kitchen, Eva settled him in his high chair and got him his favorite snack, along with his sippy cup and milk. This cheered him up immensely and he happily occupied himself with his snack.

Exhaustion settling over her, Eva turned and eyed Jesse, silently standing just inside the entrance. As always, he managed to look dangerously sexy, without even trying.

"That was my father on the phone," she said.

He smiled. "I figured as much. How is Raul?"

"He wants me to come home, back within the bosom of BOS," she said, not bothering to keep the bitterness out of her voice. "He thinks I'll be safer there, with all the Brothers watching out for me."

"He has a point." Jesse's steady gaze met hers. "How do you feel about that?"

"You know darn well how I feel about it." Her sharp tone made Liam frown. She took a deep breath, trying to settle herself down. "My father says my life is in danger."

Jesse's eyes narrowed. "Raul is usually right about stuff like that. You know he loves you. If you do as he asks and go back to the club, you won't have to worry about protection."

"Is that what you think I should do?" she asked, surprising herself. But then again, whatever had happened between the two of them, Eva knew she could always trust Jesse. He and she might stand for different things, but he'd never once lied to her.

"Do you really care what I think?" he asked, crossing his arms. "You haven't spoken two words to me since I got here, until today."

Dipping her chin, she acknowledged the accuracy of his remark. She thought of Drew, of the way he'd jerked backward when the bullet hit him, right before he fell. Though she'd been waiting to feel something other than shock, she still felt empty inside. Dry-eyed, as if her new reality didn't seem real.

Even though she'd asked Drew for a divorce and he'd turned her down, threatening to take Liam if she tried, she knew she ought to feel something. Sorrow, that his life had been cut too short. Worry, that someone had murdered him in cold blood and might be after her and her son. Something, anything other than the echoing hollowness that had crept through her blood, making her grow more numb day by day.

Could she even come back from that? She had to, for the sake of her son.

Inhaling, she met and held Jesse's gaze. "Tomorrow I've got to go see about making funeral arrangements. I'd like to leave Liam with Kara. Will you make sure there's extra security here at the house? I can't risk someone trying to get to him."

"Consider it done," Jesse replied. "I just need to make a few phone calls."

"Sounds good." She turned her back on him, hoping he'd go take care of whatever he needed to do. She didn't like the way Jesse was the only person who could cut through the numbness. Especially since he could never ever be part of her life again.

Chapter 2

Jesse left the room and, true to his word, made the necessary phone calls. The Anniversary Sheriff's Department promised to have extra officers patrol the neighborhood. The security company already did monitoring, and they'd make sure someone watched the outdoor cameras 24-7.

And finally, a quick call to Raul ensured that a couple more Brothers of Sin were on the way, just in case Eva needed them. They'd be Jesse's backups as her bodyguard. Since she wouldn't go to them, Raul would send them to her. Jesse knew Eva wouldn't like that, but once they were here, there wouldn't be much she could do about it.

Though he hadn't said anything to Raul, Jesse hadn't liked what he'd found after coming here. Instead of living a blissfully happy life with her new husband, from what he could tell, Drew and Eva lived completely separate lives. They not only slept in different bedrooms, but they ate their meals alone and not at the same time. If they talked—and he could count on the fingers of one hand the words he'd ever heard them exchange— it wasn't the kind of honest, tender conversation two people in love would have. Jesse should know. There had once been a time when he and Eva had shared numerous discussions at all hours of the day and night. He could listen to her talk for hours, marveling at the way her brown eyes flashed with passion.

Jesse might not have Eva's affection any longer, but he would never forget the animation that lit up her face when she spoke about something important to her. All of that was gone, replaced by a subdued shadow of the vibrant woman Jesse had known and loved. He'd been furious at first, battling the urge to grab Drew by the collar of his overly starched shirt and demand to know what he'd done to Eva. If he'd been able to do such a thing without jeopardizing his mission—and Eva—he would have. Instead, he'd controlled himself and stayed in the background where he belonged. From there, he'd simply observed.

Right away, he'd discovered that Eva wasn't herself. It was like she'd been…muted. All of the vivid, vibrant passion that made her extraordinary had been leached from her, leaving behind an automaton of a woman who softened only when she interacted with her son.

At first, when he'd arrived to become her bodyguard— a particularly cruel act on either Raul's or Drew's part— he'd believed her reserved demeanor was an act she used to keep him at arm's distance. He actually couldn't blame her. After all, she'd ended things with him and gone off and married Drew. No one wanted or expected their ex to show up three years later as their new bodyguard.

The woman he loved was gone. What had happened, when it had occurred, none of that was relevant. What mattered now was whether she could ever come back. While he knew he shouldn't care, he couldn't help but mourn Eva's disappearance. He could understand if she'd shut down after witnessing her husband be murdered in cold blood. But she'd been different since day one, long before Drew's death.

Jesse had yet to see Eva grieve.

One thing he did know for certain. If she'd once loved her husband, Jesse seriously doubted she did in the end. Knowing that made him ache to ask her why she'd gotten married. It had happened so quickly after she'd left him and the club. When Raul had told him, Jesse had assumed she'd been on the rebound and in her usual, passionate way, made a quick and rash decision. It hadn't taken him a week here to see that theory had been wrong.

Everything had now changed.

Now Drew was dead. Instead of grieving, if anything Eva seemed to have withdrawn even more deeply. Jesse wanted to help her, but he had no idea how without crossing imaginary lines she'd drawn in the sand over two years ago.

Until Raul—and/or possibly the authorities—got to the bottom of Drew Rowson's murder, all Jesse could do would be to keep her safe. And while doing so, somehow manage to protect his heart.

That night, the Rowson household went from crisis to crisis. The press had camped out in the street in front of the house, despite the gated community. Jesse figured they'd paid off the security guard on duty. When he'd called the sheriff's office to see if they could make the reporters leave, he was told there was nothing that could be done since no one had trespassed. Evidently, once they'd made it past the entry gate, as long as they stayed on the street, their presence was legal.

The landline rang nonstop. Eva finally unplugged the base unit and turned all the others off. Little Liam, sensing something was up, became fussy, then launched into a full-blown tantrum.

The old Eva would have had an epic meltdown. Loud and funny and sweet. The kind that would have gotten even a tired two-year-old's attention. Not now. Eva picked up the screaming toddler and placed him in his booster seat. She leaned in close, nose to nose with her son, and informed him she'd had enough. Her calm yet stern tone somehow worked miracles. Liam's tears dried up and he quietly munched on the snacks she gave him until his dinner was ready. With her silky dark hair in a messy ponytail and faint shadows under her eyes, she still managed to look beautiful.

"I'm impressed," Jesse said, earning a tired smile from Eva.

"Thanks," she replied, sighing. "Motherhood. Definitely one of the skills I'm constantly learning."

He struggled not to frown. Her cell phone rang, interrupting whatever comment he might have been about to make. She pulled it from her pocket, glanced at the screen and sent the call to voice mail.

"More reporters?" Determined to get her to engage, he remained at his post leaning against the doorway, hoping he'd managed to arrange his expression to indicate nonchalance.

Lifting a brow, she glared at him. "No. My mother-in-law."

"I see." He knew better than to respond with any more than that.

After a moment, she turned back to making her own dinner. She glanced back at him over her shoulder. "Are you hungry?" she asked. "I'm making tacos. There'll be more than enough for three."

As if on cue, his stomach growled, loud enough to be heard across the room. He laughed. "I'd love that, thanks. Is there anything I can do to help?"

"Grab us some drinks from the fridge," she said. "Liam has milk in his sippy cup, but I'd like some sparkling water. Help yourself to whatever you'd prefer."

He grabbed them both sparkling water, located the glasses, added ice from the refrigerator and carried them to the table. Once he'd taken a seat, he had to work hard to keep from feeling uncomfortable. He'd been acting as Eva's bodyguard for three weeks now, but so far they'd both kept their distance out of necessity on his part and lack of interest on hers.

Once she had everything ready, she brought it all to the table. She made Liam's plate first, breaking up the taco shell into small pieces and mixing them with his ground meat, lettuce, tomato and cheese.

When she'd finished, she looked up to find Jesse watching her. "Go ahead," she said, her voice completely without inflection. "No need to wait for me."

They each assembled their tacos in silence. A big man, Jesse could easily eat six tacos, which Eva knew, but he restrained himself. This—trying to appear to be someone different from his full nature—was also new.

Eva ate like a mouse, daintily finishing one taco

while helping her son clean his plate. She glanced at Jesse and shook her head. "You don't like my tacos?"

"They're great," he reassured her. "Really delicious."

"Then eat," she ordered, gesturing at the bowl full of ground beef. "You forget I know how much fuel your giant body requires."

At that, he couldn't restrain a grin. Her offhand remark was the closest she'd gotten to the Eva he knew since he'd been here.

He finished the taco meat and shells. Eva talked softly to Liam, smoothing his hair away from his small face. He wondered if she'd try to tell the young boy about his father's passing and if she did, if the toddler would understand.

Because he now felt as if his presence might be intrusive, he got up and carried the plates to the sink. The act of rinsing them and stacking them in the dishwasher helped clear his head. Centered once again, he wiped down the counters and stove before resuming his position in the doorway.

Studiously ignoring him, Eva wiped off Liam's face and helped him out of the booster. "Bath time," she sang. "Let's go get you cleaned up so we have time to read a story after."

The two of them disappeared down the hall. He watched them go, glad Eva didn't simply hand off her son to the nanny and chose instead to mother him herself. That meant the real Eva wasn't gone forever. She was in there somewhere, and maybe one day he'd see her again.

Meanwhile, he hoped law enforcement would find

her husband's killer. He wouldn't feel that she or her son would be safe until they had the shooter in custody.

Raul had wanted him to try to convince her to go home. While part of Jesse could see the logic in this— the Brothers of Sin would die for her—logically, he wasn't sure that would be a good idea either. After all, Drew had probably been killed due to the work he did for the club. Money laundering, mostly. Which Jesse knew about since he'd personally handled numerous transactions during his time undercover working for BOS.

Undercover. Mentally, he pushed the word away, burying it down deep. He couldn't do what he did as effectively if he allowed himself to remember the truth about who and what he was.

The next morning Eva awoke with a pounding headache. The instant she opened her eyes, she remembered today she had to make arrangements for Drew's funeral. His parents had been calling and she knew if she let them, they'd take over all the grim planning, but she felt strongly that, at the very least, she owed Drew this. She'd realized shortly after they'd married that she hadn't loved him, probably at the same time that he'd told her he'd married her for political reasons. A man needed a wife and a family if he wanted to have a prayer of becoming governor. Her father's connections to the large motorcycle club hadn't seemed to bother Drew. In fact, since Raul was well respected, he'd considered this an asset.

They'd slept together exactly once before they were married, just enough for her to be able to make herself believe in the possibility that Liam was Drew's son, rather than Jesse's. Truthfully, Drew hadn't seemed to care; he barely paid the boy any attention. That, more than anything else, broke her heart. Luckily, Liam right now was too young to understand. She'd dreaded trying to explain his father's detachment once Liam had gotten older.

Now she wouldn't have to.

What a mess. She felt horribly guilty. Even though she knew what had happened to Drew wasn't her fault, she'd certainly fantasized enough about what her life would be like without him in it. Even though he'd flatly refused her request for a divorce, telling her in no uncertain terms he'd fight for custody of the son he'd never wanted, they'd both known their short marriage was completely over. Dead, not to be revived.

She'd actually made her peace with it. And even if she'd spent an inordinate amount of time dreaming about what her life could have been like, if Jesse had loved her enough to leave the motorcycle club, she'd been completely unprepared when Drew had announced he'd hired Jesse Wyman to be her bodyguard.

Had Drew known about their prior relationship? She'd suspected he might, but now she knew the arrangement had been suggested by her father. As a lawyer, Drew had done quite a bit of business with the Brothers of Sin and she suspected most of it was illegal and unethical. Par for the course.

Which meant her father was up to his old tricks. When she'd been younger, Eva had bought in to her father's stories about the motorcycle club. Despite their inauspicious name, he'd told her that they'd formed as a symbol of freedom. Their existence, he'd told her, served to help others—those marginalized and overlooked members of society who needed an escape. It had been years before she'd learned the truth. Brothers of Sin worked with the cartels, moving weapons across the border. She suspected drugs also, but her father had been adamantly against that.

Eva had wanted no part of any of that. She'd asked Jesse to leave with her. He'd refused. Clearly, he'd made his choice.

Her father had been disappointed and furious when she'd broken things off with Jesse. She'd suspected Raul had envisioned a future where he could retire and she and Jesse would lead the club together.

Right. Not going to happen. She wanted a better life for her son.

Her phone rang again. Drew's parents. She'd felt horrible that they'd learned about their son's murder on the evening news. She'd been in shock, so much so that it hadn't occurred to her to call anyone. When one of Drew's aides had gently asked if there was anyone she should call, only then had she reluctantly dialed their number. The overwhelming relief she'd felt when she'd gone straight to voice mail had made her feel guilty, on top of everything else.

Despite that, too exhausted to deal with anything else, she let their call go to voice mail. They'd left three messages already. What was one more? She'd phone them back once she'd made all the funeral arrangements. That way, they couldn't take over. She knew if they did, the ceremony would be the antithesis of Drew.

While his parents were super religious, Drew had often claimed he had no use for such "nonsense." And while they'd never actually discussed his wishes regarding a funeral, Eva suspected he'd prefer something elegant and tasteful, as befitted his status as a gubernatorial hopeful. She planned to do her best to give him that. It seemed the least she could do.

She'd finished feeding Liam his breakfast and had put on his favorite Thomas the Tank Engine movie. Though he'd seen it many times, he sat enraptured, giving her precious time to clean up the kitchen and grab something to eat herself. She brewed a quick cup of coffee, hoping the caffeine would give her enough energy to make it through the rest of this day.

After gulping down a bowl of cereal, she headed back to the den and stopped short. Jesse had taken a seat beside Liam on the couch. Together, the two watched the movie, Jesse occasionally pointing out things he liked on the screen and Liam appearing to eat up the attention.

Gazing at them sitting side by side, she couldn't help but notice what had been in front of her face for years. Liam looked so much like Jesse, she realized what she'd always suspected in her heart.

Jesse was Liam's father.

And he had absolutely no idea.

The tears caught her off guard. One moment, she was standing there, hip cocked against the doorway, watching the two of them together. The next, her eyes had filled and she broke down. Covering her face with her hands, she let go and wept. She cried for what might have been, for the terrible loss of Drew's life in such a brutal way. She cried for herself and her son and for Jesse. And most of all, she wept for the way all the beauty she'd once found in life had changed to ashes, dusty and dry and bleak.

Turning away, she tried to cry silently, a skill she'd

perfected in the first months of her marriage. Tears had irritated Drew and made him lash out. Hopefully, the television show would keep Jesse and Liam distracted enough so they wouldn't notice.

She went to the kitchen sink, turning on the water and wetting a paper towel, which she used to blot at her face. When Jesse came up behind her, she froze, hoping if she didn't move, he'd go away.

Instead, he wrapped his arms around her and held her tight, exactly the way he used to. She allowed herself a tiny moment of weakness, so she let him, drawing both comfort and strength from his embrace.

And then, when desire began to stir low in her belly, she took a deep breath and resolutely moved away.

He didn't speak and she didn't want him to. She needed a moment to pull herself together. It alarmed her how quickly the walls she'd so painstakingly built crumbled. Because of him.

Staring straight ahead, she kept her head held high as she went to check on her son. Kara had emerged from her room and sat where Jesse had been.

"I'm going to go out soon," Eva told the nanny. "First I need to shower and get ready."

Kara nodded. "Will you be gone long?"

"Probably. I've got funeral arrangements to make. I have no idea how long something like that takes." She sounded brisk and businesslike, exactly the way she wanted.

Once in her room, she closed the door behind her and locked it. So far, she'd given Jesse clear boundaries and he'd followed them. But now that things had changed, she didn't plan on taking any chances.

After a steaming-hot shower, she blow-dried and

styled her hair. Then she sat at her vanity and expertly applied her makeup, keeping it basic. That done, she chose a simple navy shirtdress and navy flats. After she'd married Drew, he'd overhauled her entire wardrobe, culling everything vivid or bright, telling her those colors made her look cheap.

Today, navy would be perfect. But someday in the future, she planned to get rid of all the navy, black, gray and beige. Or at the least, buy some red and orange, yellow, green and purple clothing. Someday. Not now.

One last quick look in the mirror and she was ready. She'd already made a call to Blackenstock Funeral Home, and Jeremy Blackenstock himself would be meeting with her.

He'd been very solicitous on the phone. Of course, he understood the media attention Drew's funeral would draw. Not to mention all of Drew's business colleagues and politicians who would be in attendance. There would even be a few relatives. In addition to his parents, he had an aunt and an uncle, plus three cousins. As far as she knew, that would be it. Drew didn't have any friends who weren't tied to him due to business, at least that she knew of.

The entire scenario made her exhausted before it even began.

When she emerged from her room, Jesse straightened. He'd taken his usual spot just outside her bedroom door and appeared to have been checking his phone.

"I'll drive," she told him. She knew she needed to be doing something other than being ferried around as a passenger.

"Okay." Jesse nodded, his gaze serious. Of course,

being true to form, Jesse wore his usual faded jeans, a clean T-shirt and his motorcycle boots. He wouldn't wear his gang colors since he wouldn't be on a bike. She kind of missed them. She'd always found him sexy as hell when he wore them. This thought made her blink.

What on earth was wrong with her? What kind of woman even had such thoughts, on the day she was about to plan her husband's funeral?

Resolute, she unlocked her car and slid behind the wheel. A few deep breaths and she had her armor back in place. Jesse got in, taking the passenger seat. She thought about asking him to ride in the back, the way he had before, but then reconsidered. Maybe he felt he could protect her better from the front. Ever since her father had declared that her life was in danger, she'd felt a little paranoid. Only a little, because she suspected part of the reason for such a dramatic declaration was to get her to return home to him and the club. She wouldn't put it past Raul to have totally made the entire thing up.

When they pulled up at the funeral home and parked, Jeremy himself opened the ornate double front doors and ushered them inside. His entire demeanor managed to be both subdued and sympathetic. He took them to a small room paneled in oak and asked them to take a seat at the conference table.

Jesse explained he'd preferred to stand and would wait just outside the doorway. Eyeing him, Eva almost asked him to stay. But realizing the impropriety of such a request, she simply folded her hands on the table and looked down.

The next two hours passed with excruciating slowness. She signed papers, chose the date the funeral would be held and helped Jeremy write the obituary. For this, she'd done some online searching, using a lot of the background her husband's people had provided on his website.

Finally, the time had come to choose the casket. From what she knew of her husband, Drew would prefer something expensive and elegant. When she told Jeremy this, he nodded and took her elbow. Then he walked her past the main showroom, into a smaller and more exclusive one in the back. Here there were only three coffins. They were placed on velvet-covered platforms with strategic lighting designed to showcase their expensive specialness.

They were all different. One very elegant and subdued. Another modern and high-tech, apparently made of stainless steel or some other kind of polished metal. And the third, sitting above all the others, made of polished mahogany that gleamed.

Wearily, Eva pointed to the third one. With its dark wood and pewter finishes, she knew it most closely matched Drew's personality. It would look the best on display for the service.

"Will you have a minister or preacher?" Jeremy asked next. She had to think about that one for a moment. Drew's parents had raised him in a super strict church. As an adult, he'd rebelled and refused to attend any church. Only when he'd begun the process of looking into running for governor had he reluctantly selected a church on the advice of his sponsors. He'd chosen something the polar opposite of the kind of church where he'd been raised. A staid and refined Methodist church on the north side of town. She supposed she'd need to contact that church and see about arranging something.

Once she'd told Jeremy her plans, he nodded. Clearing his throat, he slid an invoice across the table toward her and asked her how she wanted to pay.

The amount seemed staggering, but then she had no idea what a funeral was supposed to cost. Removing Drew's checkbook from her purse, she checked the balance in the ledger and then wrote a check for the entire amount.

"Here you go," she said, handing him the check. Briefly, she closed her eyes, trying to regain her bearings. The numbness had grown stronger since Drew's murder. She felt as if she'd retreated into a thick fog.

A sudden longing to find Jesse and walk into his arms swept through her, shaking her to her core. Where had this come from? Blinking back another threat of sudden tears, she shook her head. Safer, much safer, to retreat back into the soft gray distance where nothing could touch her.

Standing, she realized Jeremy had left the room. He'd left the door open. Smoothing down her skirt, she swallowed and headed toward the exit.

"Mrs. Rowson?" Jeremy appeared, his forehead creased in concern. "There seems to be a problem with the check."

"A problem?" She rubbed the back of her neck. "I don't understand."

"When we went to electronically run the check, your bank declined it."

Stunned, she stared at him. "Why?"

He swallowed. "It appears there are insufficient funds."

"That's not possible." Fumbling in her purse, she pulled out Drew's checkbook and opened it to the ledger. "See?" She pointed. "Here's the balance. There's more than enough to cover that check."

Though Jeremy kept his tone respectful, his firm reply told her he meant business. "Perhaps you'd like to contact your bank and verify?"

"Of course." Hands shaking, she fumbled with her phone, looking up the bank's number and calling it. Once she had an account representative on the line, she identified herself.

"Mrs. Rowson, we're so sorry for your loss," the woman exclaimed. "What can I do to assist you?"

After taking a deep breath, she asked to check the balance in the checking account, since she was also listed as an account holder in addition to Drew.

"Certainly. Just one moment."

Eva gripped the phone, listening while the bank representative typed in the information. "Let me see here," the woman said. "I show a balance of one thousand, six hundred and forty-seven dollars and seventy-eight cents."

"What?" Eva swallowed, again trying to comprehend. "The checkbook ledger shows seventy-two thousand dollars and change."

"That would have been before Mr. Rowson made that withdrawal last Tuesday. Were you not aware of that?"

"Obviously not." Eva didn't bother to keep the bitterness from her voice. "Do you happen to know if he transferred it to another account? Like maybe our savings?"

"No, ma'am. He asked for it in a cashier's check,

which is how it was given to him. Beyond that, I don't know."

Reeling, Eva managed to thank the woman and end the call. She looked up to find Jeremy eyeing her.

"Is everything all right?" he asked.

She wanted to scream her answer, to shout the word *no*. Instead, she looked down at the floor before holding her hand out for the check. Once Jeremy handed it back to her, she got out one of her credit cards. Hoping Drew hadn't done something to it—like maxed it out—she passed it to Jeremy. "There's a mix-up at the bank," she said. "Since I'll need time to get it straightened out, go ahead and put everything on this."

While she waited for Jeremy to run the charges, she couldn't help but wonder what other surprises she'd find as the days passed.

Chapter 3

From his position waiting for Eva in the funeral home hall, Jesse couldn't help but overhear the funeral director inform Eva that her check had bounced. He winced at the shock and dismay in her voice. He listened to her end of the conversation with the bank, as well. Clearly, she'd been completely unaware that her husband had emptied the bank accounts before he'd been killed.

Which brought up an immediate question. Had Drew been trying to pay someone off? Or settle a debt so huge he'd been killed because of it?

These were all questions for law enforcement. He expected them to show up with more questions before the end of the day. By now they would be invested in a murder investigation.

A few minutes later, Eva emerged. She appeared

composed and collected. Only the slight hint of panic in her eyes hinted at her internal emotions.

"Are you ready?" he asked, deliberately keeping his tone light, as if he knew nothing about what had just transpired inside the room.

She nodded. Together they walked outside. Right before they were about to get in her car, she stopped. "Would you mind driving?" she asked, holding out the keys. "I'm not feeling too well and I don't think I should."

"No problem." As he started the car and backed it out of the parking spot, he glanced over at her, aching. She tried so hard to be strong, even though he had to wonder if fate was conspiring against her at every turn.

Once he'd reached the gate, put in the code and entered the subdivision, he wasn't surprised to find two sheriff's department cruisers waiting outside the house.

Seeing them, Eva groaned. "Now what?"

"I'm sure they just want to question you about yesterday," he said. "They've got a murder investigation to work after all."

"I know." Her soft answer made his chest hurt. "I want them to find the killer as quickly as possible. I won't feel safe until they do. And..." She swallowed hard. "Drew didn't deserve that. He had plans, hopes and dreams. I really think he would have made a great governor. He really cares about the people of Texas."

Ignoring the twinge of jealousy, Jesse nodded. "Hopefully the police will have some leads." He considered, then decided to abandon his earlier pretense of not overhearing. "You might want to mention what you just found out from the bank."

She jerked, as if he'd startled her. "Do you think money had something to do with him being killed?"

"There's no way to know. But it could be. Let the police know so they can investigate that aspect of it."

Slowly, she nodded. "Okay. I will."

As they pulled into the driveway, the police vehicles' doors all opened and several officers emerged. In addition to the uniforms, there were also two plain-clothesmen, most likely detectives. Or possibly even Feds, though he'd never known them to ride with local law enforcement like that.

Since this was a high-profile murder, he'd figured the Feds would get involved.

As he'd known they would, all the law enforcement people looked him up and down, not bothering to hide their suspicion. He knew what he looked like, a large, menacing biker with short spiky hair and lots of tattoos. If he'd been in their shoes, he'd have done the exact same thing. He should know, since he'd been on the other side of the table numerous times.

"Mrs. Rowson? We wonder if you might have a moment to talk with us." One of the plain-clothed men stepped forward, his genial expression matching his soft-spoken tone.

Though exhaustion made her wobble, Eva nodded. "Of course. Come on inside."

She led the way through the house, taking them to a formal sitting room that Jesse had never seen anyone use, at least in the three weeks he'd been there. "Have a seat," she said. "I'll just be a moment. In the meantime, Jesse, would you mind seeing if they'd like any refreshments?"

Bemused, Jesse nodded. He watched her until she

disappeared down the hall, no doubt going to check on Liam. Then he turned to the gathering of men and politely asked them if they'd like something to drink.

Most of them declined, but one of the plainclothes guys asked for water. Jesse immediately got him a bottle. After handing it to him, he retreated, heading down the hallway after Eva.

As he'd expected, he found her in Liam's room. The boy sat in the middle of the floor, surrounded by toys and happily playing. Eva sat cross-legged next to him, oblivious to everything else, totally engaged in watching her son. The nanny slouched in a chair in the corner, barely looking up from her phone when he entered.

Jesse stood in the doorway a moment, drinking in the sight of Eva, his heart full of love. She finally glanced at him, the smile that had been hovering on her lips vanishing. "What?" she asked, a trace of annoyance in her tone.

He straightened, careful to keep his expression neutral. "The police are waiting to talk to you."

Immediately, she got to her feet, graceful as always, smoothing down her skirt with the palms of her hands. "Mommy will be right back," she told her son, bending down to kiss his cheek. "Kara, please keep an eye on him for me."

The nanny nodded, still intent on her phone.

"Kara?" A sharp note crept into Eva's tone. "Please put down your phone and do your job."

As soon as Kara had complied, Eva turned and swept past Jesse without saying a word. He followed close behind her, willing his insides to calm. It seemed he'd never be able to keep himself from wanting her. Once this assignment was over, he planned to take himself somewhere far, far away and try to get his life back together. Hopefully, the scenery would involve beaches and umbrella drinks and sun. Lord knows, after putting himself through this particular kind of hell, he'd deserve it.

By the time they got downstairs, Eva the gracious politician's wife was back. She apologized for her delay in a friendly, mellifluous voice and once more offered them refreshments. Again, they declined, except for the one officer who held up his bottle of water. "I'm good."

"We'd like to ask you a few questions," one of the uniforms said.

"Of course." Eva motioned to the couches and chairs. "Why don't you make yourselves comfortable." Choosing an upholstered chair, she sat, crossing her legs demurely at the ankles.

Jesse ignored the curious glances more than one of the officers sent his way. He didn't blame them. If he'd been in their place, he would have been suspicious too.

Once everyone had gotten settled, the questions began. They were mostly routine, exactly the kind of thing anyone would expect. With her posture straight and her gaze clear, Eva answered them all as best she could. No, she hadn't seen anything. The sound of the gunshot hadn't even registered as a danger until Jesse took her down.

"Jesse?" the officer pounced on that. "Who's Jesse?"

"Him." Eva pointed. "He's Jesse. He's my body-guard. My husband hired him a few weeks ago."

"I see." Zeroing in on him, the policeman directed the next question at Jesse. "What company employs you?"

Aware he looked out of place in the tastefully elegant room, Jesse shrugged. Instead of allowing this to make him feel self-conscious, he chose to revel in it. As in, he was a big, bad biker dude. So what?

"Who is your employer?" the officer repeated, pen poised to write the name down.

Though Jesse knew what the other man meant, he pretended not to understand. "I work for Mr. Rowson," he said. "Or did. Now I work for Mrs. Rowson."

"Right. But did you come from a security service? If not, where did Mr. Rowson get your name?"

Eva decided to jump in. "Jesse is a member of my father's motorcycle club, the Brothers of Sin. My father recommended him to my husband."

Since everyone clearly already knew about her connection to BOS, no one bothered to act surprised. Again, several of the police officers eyed him. Since Jesse was used to it, he simply stared right back.

"Okay," the questioner finally said, and then cleared his throat. He pushed his wire-rimmed glasses up on his narrow nose. "What is your last name, Jesse?"

"Wyman," he replied, aware that when they checked, they'd find only the carefully doctored record the Drug Enforcement Administration had put in place. Anyone searching for his background would find a completely false narrative showing a lifetime of crime, even a brief imprisonment. Not too bad, just bad enough to justify him being part of a notorious motorcycle club.

He'd spent nearly four years working undercover. He'd tried to get out a little over two and half years ago, when Eva had asked him to leave the club with her. But he'd worked too hard, gotten in too deep, to blow it all just then. Especially for a woman who would hate him once she realized he was part of the unit that took her father down. Which they would. It was only a matter of time. He'd spent years helping build the case.

Once, all he'd ever wanted out of life was a long and successful career with the ATF. These days, that focus had changed. All he wanted was Eva.

Jesse had grown up surrounded by family in law enforcement. From the time he'd been in elementary school, he'd known what he'd wanted to be. He'd focused on this goal all through high school and college. When he'd been accepted by the ATF, he'd thought he could never be happier.

Until the first time Eva had kissed him. Like a lightning bolt to the heart, he'd been dazed and surprised and then joyful. They were meant to be together.

Except everything she knew about him was based on a lie. And when she'd asked him to leave BOS with her, he couldn't. It wasn't only that he'd taken an oath to do his job. It was because Jesse had to finish his mission, bring the bad guys to justice. He hadn't wanted to let his team down.

Which he guessed meant in the end, his job had been more important. Yet he'd still entertained the idea of revealing all to Eva once the mission had ended, hoping she'd understand.

But she'd left without him. He could understand that. How quickly she'd married Drew was what he didn't get. Heartbroken, he'd told himself it was for the best. Over time, maybe he could manage to forget her. Instead, after so much time apart, he'd become her personal bodyguard.

Simply put, he couldn't win. Not then, not now. All he could do was keep Eva safe and continue to do his job. The ATF sources had informed him that Eva's husband had become an integral part of the Brothers of Sin operation. They'd needed proof Drew Rowson was involved in money laundering. Deep undercover in his role as gang member, Jesse had angled for the assignment to protect Eva because of that, even though he'd known being around her would destroy what was left of his heart.

He would be glad when this assignment wrapped up, even though he might not survive it. One thing for sure, he'd never be the same. Eva was the only mistake he'd made while spending years undercover. He'd fallen head over heels in love with a woman he could never have.

"Any idea why Mr. Rowson found it necessary to hire a bodyguard for you, Mrs. Rowson?"

Jesse spoke up before she could. "I was told Mr. Rowson had received several threats against him once he announced his intention of running for governor. Some of them were against his wife and son. That's why I was brought in."

The detective wrote furiously. "Do you have any proof of those threats?"

"Documentation?" Jesse shrugged. "Not me. I'm just an employee. I'm sure Mr. Rowson had something."

"If he did, he didn't share with me," Eva interjected. "But I can search his office. If I find anything, I'll be happy to send it on to you."

Jesse noticed she didn't offer to let them look. He had to applaud that decision. Who knew what kind of incriminating evidence Drew might have inside his personal desk? In fact, Jesse figured he'd better have a quick look himself, tonight if possible. He'd talk to Eva, once this meeting was over.

"One more thing," Eva continued. And then she told them about Drew emptying the bank account. This got their attention, as Jesse had known it would. They got the bank information and then asked her if she knew of any other bank accounts.

"I don't. But if I find out there are any, I'll be sure to give you a call."

One of the plainclothesmen spoke up. "Would you mind if we did a quick search of his office?"

Jesse tensed up, though he was careful not to show it. The last thing he needed were these local guys getting involved in an ongoing undercover ATF sting. Staring at Eva, he willed her to decline.

"I'm sorry, but this isn't a good time," she replied, smiling to soften the blow. "I really need to be allowed to go through my husband's personal belongings myself first."

Judging by the muscle working in the officer's jaw, her declination didn't sit well with him. But he, like every other law enforcement person in the room, knew there was absolutely nothing they could do about it. They'd have to get a search warrant first.

A few more follow-up questions and the officers stood to take their leave. As they filed past Jesse's position near the doorway, the officer who'd been taking notes stopped in front of him. Pushing his glasses up with one hand, he looked Jesse up and down. "I'd like to see your ID," he declared.

With a sigh, Jesse dug in his back pocket, dug out his wallet and removed his meticulously created driver's license. The ATF had taken great care with it, making sure none of his law enforcement background would show, and Jesse knew it would withstand any kind of scrutiny.

After studying it, the officer snapped a picture of it with his phone and handed it back. "I'd better not find anything suspicious when I run a background check."

Jesse couldn't resist a cocky grin. "You won't. You can rest assured of that."

As soon as the door closed behind the group of officers, Eva turned to eye Jesse. "How bad is your rap sheet?"

He'd always wondered why she'd never asked him about his past convictions during the time they'd been together. He'd figured with her growing up around so much crime, she hadn't wanted to know.

"Nothing major," he assured her. "Mostly misdemeanors, though there might be one felony."

Mouth tight, she nodded. "Any assaults, with or without a deadly weapon?"

"You know, you should have wondered about that when we were dating," he drawled, unable to resist.

"Just answer the question."

Her snappish tone made him smile. "No assaults," he assured her, grateful that they'd decided to leave them off his fake rap sheet. They'd wanted him to appear badass enough to join the gang, but not violent.

"Good," she said. "Because I've decided to allow you to stay. For now. If there was anything violent in your past, I'd have to send you on your way."

By the time the policemen left, Eva had a bad headache. The shocked and hurt look on Jesse's rugged face only made her feel worse. But she'd had to ask, and Jesse knew she was nothing if not blunt.

His answer had reassured her. No matter what else he might have done, she knew he wouldn't lie to her. Head pounding, she walked past him. She rarely liked to take any kind of drugs, even ibuprofen, but right now she needed something. She headed back upstairs to her bathroom, her ever-present shadow, Jesse, a few steps behind her.

Ignoring him, she closed the door and locked it. Then she rummaged in her medicine cabinet until she found the bottle. Though the ibuprofen had expired a month ago, she figured they'd still work well enough. She swallowed them dry and then turned on the faucet, ducking her mouth under until she had enough water to help her.

Wiping her lips on a towel, she eyed herself in the mirror. Other than looking a bit pale, she seemed exactly like the same woman she'd been the day before. When Drew had still been alive. And she had a difficult time grieving, so she tried not to cry.

A widow who couldn't grieve. What did that make her? Some kind of monster? While she'd known she hadn't loved Drew, not the way she'd loved Jesse, maybe not at all, she'd known Drew hadn't loved her either. He'd needed a wife and had courted her. Even though they'd made love, at least in the beginning, the passion had been missing. And after she'd realized she was pregnant, Drew had never touched her again. Almost as if he'd known the baby might not be his. She'd never had the nerve to do a DNA test, afraid of what she might find out.

Thoughts of the past tumbling around in her head,

she sighed. Drew hadn't been a bad husband. Growing up in the club, she'd seen plenty of examples of that. He'd just been an absent, unloving one, showing up only when they both had a public role to play. When he'd stopped making love to her, she'd been too exhausted as a new mother to care. Later, she'd been too proud to try to seduce him. She pretty much figured he'd reject her anyway.

Worse, he'd completely ignored little Liam. That was the one thing she'd never been able to understand. Or forgive.

Now the only man she'd ever loved stood outside her bathroom door. She wished she had the courage to ask him to leave.

After opening the bathroom door, she'd just stepped out into the hall when the doorbell rang. Exchanging a look with Jesse, wondering if the police had forgotten something, she hurried down the stairs.

"Wait," Jesse urged, grabbing her arm just as she reached for the doorknob. "At least look out the peephole."

Because he was right, she did exactly as he asked. Once she saw who stood on her front porch, she groaned. "Drew's parents."

Jesse gave her a puzzled look. "Weren't you expecting them? Their son just died."

Guilt suffused her because once again, he was right. Taking a deep breath, she opened the door.

"Finally," Beth Rowson declared, her sharp voice matching the ice in her gaze. She swept past Eva, her disparaging gaze lighting on Jesse before she marched into the kitchen.

Her husband, Ted, shook his head, his red-rimmed

eyes full of emotion as well as censure. He dragged his hand through his perfectly coiffed head of silver hair, barely dislodging a single strand. He stepped into the foyer, stopping abruptly and eyeing Jesse. "Who are you?" he demanded.

"He's my bodyguard," Eva answered for him. "Drew hired him a few weeks ago."

"Interesting." Ted turned his attention back to Eva. "Why did he feel you needed a bodyguard?"

She answered with the same words Jesse had given the police. "Ever since Drew announced his candidacy, he'd been receiving threats. Some of them included me and Liam. He wanted to make sure I was protected. I've given the police this information and they've promised to investigate."

"Threats. After what happened, it's clear Drew was the one who needed the protection. What I don't understand is why he didn't hire a professional," the elder Mr. Rowson pointed out. "Why a…biker?" The amount of disdain he interjected into that word would have bothered another man. But Jesse had heard it before and was used to it.

Eva, however, had been born a biker. While she wanted no part of that lifestyle, she still had a fierce pride in her heritage. She stiffened, her expression going all regal and frozen. "Do you have some sort of objection to bikers?" she asked softly. "Because I know you haven't forgotten who my father is."

Ted Rowson grimaced. He didn't even have the grace to apologize or even look embarrassed. "You know what I mean," he said. "Maybe my son would be alive today if he'd hired professional bodyguards instead of amateurs."

With that stated, he stamped down the hallway, following his wife to the kitchen.

Eva sighed and shook her head. She squared her shoulders, lifted her chin and followed.

Her mother-in-law had her back to the rest of them, rummaging in the refrigerator with a kind of furious intensity.

"Is there something I can get you?" Eva asked, as politely as she could manage.

Beth barely glanced her way. "Drew always made sure to keep some of my favorite yogurts in here. But I don't see any."

"That's because he only bought them when he knew you were coming to visit," Eva gently pointed out. "I'm sorry."

With an audible gasp, Beth began sobbing. Her husband hurried over to her and gathered her into his arms. They stood that way for a few moments while Beth cried out her sorrow.

Eva's eyes filled too. Drew had been Beth's son, at one time her baby boy, just like Liam was to her now. She couldn't even begin to imagine the grief ripping through the other woman.

After a moment, Beth stirred and moved out of her husband's arms. She grabbed a paper towel off the roll on the counter and blotted at her eyes with it. Ted made his way back to the table, pulled out a chair and dropped heavily into it.

Eva locked eyes with Jesse, not sure what to do. He stared straight ahead, as if he'd mentally vacated the room. She couldn't blame him. She'd been married to Drew for two and a half years and during that time period, she'd seen Drew's parents a grand total of five times. They rarely visited and Drew never went down to Houston to see them. Though she knew he'd planned to once he started canvassing the state for his campaign. Surely, he'd have managed to fit in a visit to his parents on his travels.

Finally, Beth turned around, her face pale but composed. She looked at Eva, her lips pressed tightly together. "Tomorrow, we'll take care of the funeral arrangements," Beth announced, drumming her perfectly manicured scarlet nails on the kitchen counter. "I want to make sure Drew has the best."

"That's not necessary," Eva said, steeling herself. "I've already done all that. The funeral will be at Blackenstock Funeral Home. The arrangements are made. I'll get you the details once they're printed up."

The older woman's perfectly made-up eyes narrowed. "I wish you had waited for me. I really wanted to approve the casket."

Battling the urge to offer to take her to the funeral home in the morning so she could approve of Eva's choice, Eva managed to keep her mouth closed.

When Eva didn't respond, Beth turned to glare at Jesse, who'd parked himself in his usual position leaning against the wall near the kitchen entrance. "Do you have to lurk around like that?" she demanded. "Isn't there something else you could do? This is a discussion among *family*."

Ignoring her, Jesse turned to Eva. "Would you like me to leave?"

"No." Though she couldn't say it out loud, Eva desperately needed an ally. Even though Jesse couldn't involve himself in the discussion, his mere presence gave her strength. And she knew if she wasn't strong, her in-laws would roll over her like a steamroller on freshly laid concrete. Even Drew had been unable to hold his own around his parents.

Abruptly, Beth pushed herself up and walked over to the sink, where she stood staring out the window. Her shoulders began shaking as she silently cried.

In empathy, Eva's own eyes filled again. No matter how overbearing the older woman might be, she'd adored her only son. When Ted made no move to comfort his wife, Eva went to her and wrapped her arms around her. She wasn't sure what to say, so she said nothing.

After a moment, the older woman angrily shoved Eva away. "Tell me, did he suffer?"

"No. They said he was killed instantly." Eva swiped at her streaming eyes, relieved to be crying. "No one saw it coming."

"Not even your *bodyguard*?" Ted Rowson asked snidely.

Eva ignored him. She understood the need to lash out when in pain.

"I want to know who you spoke to with the police," Ted said. "I need to talk to him. I want my son's killer caught as quickly as possible."

"So do I. I won't feel safe until he's caught. I worry about Liam." Eva deliberately brought up her son. Though Drew's parents hadn't seemed keen on the whole role of loving grandparents, she'd never lost hope that if they actually spent some time with Liam, they'd grow to love him.

But even after being reminded of his existence, neither of them asked to see her son. Part of her wanted to march upstairs and fetch him, forcing them to have some kind of interaction.

If her head would quit pounding, she might have. As it was, all she wanted to do was crawl into her bed and try to sleep.

"Do you have anything to feed us?" Beth demanded, using the paper towel to blot the black mascara stains under her eyes. "We've driven a long way. I would have thought your church friends would have brought casseroles and such."

Church friends. She knew now wasn't the time to point out that Drew had rarely attended church unless it had been for a photo op.

"I can make you a sandwich or something," she offered.

The older woman stared at her as if she'd suggested eating raw meat. "Never mind. I'll just send Ted for something."

Eva nodded, the movement sending shards of pain through her head. "I'll make up the guest bedroom for you." Part of her hoped Beth would decline and state that she and Ted would stay in a hotel.

No such luck.

"Don't you have a housekeeper to do that?" Ted asked, looking around curiously. "I thought Drew employed a full household staff."

Though she had no idea where he'd gotten that idea, Eva explained they employed only a nanny to help with Liam.

Again, despite the mention of his name, neither of them asked to see their grandson. Eva wished she could understand why that hurt so badly. She guessed until she stopped being an eternal optimist, she'd be doomed to disappointment where these people were concerned.

Forcing herself to move, she headed back upstairs, first to the linen closet and then to the largest guest bedroom, the one on the opposite side of the house from her room. Jesse occupied the smaller one next to the master bedroom and the nursery. The big room she planned on giving her in-laws.

Of course, Jesse stayed right behind her. When she pulled back the comforter on the queen-size bed, he grabbed the other part of the fitted sheet. "Let me help," he said quietly. "It'll get done faster and maybe you can go lie down."

Hurting too badly to argue, she shot him a thankful look. They made quick work of making up the bed. "Thank you," she told him. "How rude would it be if I left them on their own and went to bed?"

"You're in mourning too," he said, his voice gruff. "No one in their right mind would expect a grieving widow to play hostess. If you'd like, I'd be happy to tell them that you've gone to bed and are done for the night."

To her shock, she actually considered taking him up on his offer. "I've still got to check and make sure Kara has bathed Liam before he goes to bed," she said. "And I always read him a story before he goes to sleep."

"What about them?" he asked, gesturing toward downstairs. "Don't they want to come see their grandson?"

Staring at him, too tired to mask her sadness, she shook her head. "They just don't find him interesting. They never have. I'm not sure why, but it is what it is."

"Would you like me to entertain them while you

do that?" he asked. "Just let me know what I can do to help."

"I'd like that," she said softly. "Take care of them for me. I don't have the energy to deal with them any more tonight."

Though he had no earthly idea what he could talk to them about, Jesse dutifully trudged back downstairs. Drew's parents were discussing Eva, making no effort to lower their voices.

"I'm telling you, she's glad he's dead," Beth Rowson declared. "I knew she never loved our son." With that, she began loudly weeping, repeating over and over that she couldn't believe he was gone.

When Jesse walked into the room, instead of finding Ted comforting his wife, he realized the older man had walked over to the front window and stood staring outside, his back to the room.

Still crying, Beth didn't look up when Jesse entered the room.

"Excuse me." Jesse cleared his throat. "Eva is putting Liam to bed. Would you like me to take you up to see him before he goes to sleep?"

Wiping at her streaming eyes, Beth glared at him. Her husband remained at the window, not even bothering to turn around.

"We'll pass," Ted replied. "We're not all that fond of children."

For the first time ever, Jesse felt pity for what Drew must have endured growing up. "This is your grandson," Jesse continued. "Not just any child. He lost his father, just like you lost your son. I think he—and Eva—could use all the family love and support right now."

At his words, Beth's tears dried up and her expression went from devastated to furious. "Who do you think you are, attempting to lecture us on personal family matters? It's none of your business what we do or don't do."

Since she was right, Jesse shut his mouth and turned to go. Just as he reached the exit, Ted spoke, shocking him.

"Liam is not our grandson. Neither Drew nor we believe he's related by blood. Eva clearly slept with someone else right before she married Drew. All you have to do is look at the boy to see that. There's not a trace of Rowson blood in that child."

Chapter 4

After excusing himself and leaving the two elder Rowsons alone, Jesse kept hearing those words over and over inside his head as he climbed the stairs. *Liam was not Drew's son.* As far as he knew, that left only one other man who might be the father. Blindsided, he wondered why the possibility had never occurred to him.

Probably because he'd known Eva would have told him. He would have sworn she didn't have a dishonest bone in her body.

Now he had to wonder. If she would lie about this, who knew what other truths she might hide. Regardless, it was time for her to come clean. He did the math inside his head, remembering the last time he and Eva had made love. Hell, he'd never been able to forget it, lovesick idiot that he'd been. Now he directed most of his anger at her, though he reserved some for himself, for never questioning the speed at which Eva had conceived with Drew. Little infuriated him more than being treated like a fool.

When he reached the doorway to the bedroom, he stopped short, swallowing back his angry questions. Eva sat with the towheaded toddler in his bed, a large picture book open between them. For the first time, he realized both Eva and Drew had dark hair. Eva's was almost black. When Jesse had been Liam's age, his hair had been the same almost platinum blond. While he knew it was entirely possible for two brunettes to have a blond child, Liam's facial structure told the rest of the story. High cheekbones and a cleft chin. If Jesse were to dig out an old photograph of himself at age two and compare it with a picture of Liam, anyone would be hard-pressed to tell the two apart.

Right then, what was left of his shattered heart crumbled into dust. How could Eva have done such a thing—not only passing off his son as another man's—but denying Jesse the opportunity to know his own child?

Simmering with a quiet fury, he parked himself out in the hallway where he couldn't see them. He wouldn't confront her in front of the boy. The boy who just might be his son. And if that was true, that meant Jesse had been cheated out of the first two years of Liam's life.

By the woman he'd thought he'd loved. Still did, actually. Sadly, he realized he couldn't turn off his emotions so easily. Somehow, even in his angry confusion, he couldn't stop caring about her, wanting her.

Finally, Eva emerged from the nursery, closing the door quietly after her. "He's finally asleep," she said, smiling when she saw Jesse waiting for her. Something of his turmoil must have shown in his expression because her smile faded. "What's wrong?" she asked.

"Where do I begin? Let's see. I found out why the Rowsons don't want to spend much time with Liam," he drawled, careful to keep the bitterness out of his voice.

"You did?" One perfectly arched brow rose. "You asked them?"

"Sort of, yes." Still he waited, giving her the opportunity to open up and tell him the truth.

She shrugged. "I'm surprised they answered you. I can't think of any excuse they might offer that would make sense. What did they say?"

He decided not to sugarcoat it. "They don't believe he's Drew's son."

Her mouth fell open. Rapidly collecting herself, she closed it. "Are you serious?"

"I am." He took a deep breath, trying to unclench his teeth. "And now, after I took a good, long look at him, I don't either. So tell me, Eva. If he's not Drew's, whose son is he?"

Now she wouldn't look at him. Twisting her hands together, she avoided his gaze. "As far as I know, he's Drew's. Of course."

"As far as you know?" The sharp edge in his voice cut through the BS like a knife. "Come on. Is there a possibility that he's mine?"

She swallowed hard. "I don't know." But she wouldn't meet his gaze.

This response had him jamming his hands into his pockets so he didn't punch the wall. "We made love right before you took off for greener pastures. Right before you told me you'd met someone else. You married Drew less than a month later. Refresh my memory, please. When exactly was Liam born?"

"June 7," she whispered. "And yes, if you do the math, it's possible he's yours. But it's also possible he's not."

He saw red. It took several deep breaths before he trusted himself to speak. "I see. Which means what? You were sleeping with both of us at the same time?"

"Of course not." Her head snapped up at that. "Leaving you broke my heart. Drew and I had been talking but not dating. I barely knew him. He took me out to distract me and I had too much to drink."

"Which means what? He took advantage of you?" He shouldn't feel sympathy, not even the slightest twinge, but somehow he did. His love for her made him foolish and weak. Ruthlessly, he pushed it away.

Looking down at the floor, she didn't answer for a moment. When she spoke again, her voice trembled. "About a month later, I realized I was pregnant. That's the entire reason Drew and I got married."

"I want a DNA test." The request came out of nowhere, but the instant he spoke, he knew that was right. "I need to know if he's my son."

Warily, she eyed him. "And then what, Jesse? What do you intend to do?"

The question stopped him dead in his tracks. "I don't know," he answered truthfully. "But I can promise you this. If he is mine, I'm going to want to be part of his life."

She nodded, the pain in her eyes matching his own. "I understand."

"Do you? Somehow, I doubt that."

* * *

Watching Jesse walk away, fury radiating from his very pores, Eva found herself battling the urge to go after him. Because he was right to be angry. The day she'd been dreading had finally arrived. Instead, she found her way to her bedroom, her entire body now aching as bad as her head and heart. *Get some sleep*, she'd thought earlier. As if that would be even a remote possibility now.

Closing the door, she dropped down onto her bed and kicked her shoes off. She kept seeing his face, his handsome, beloved face, and the betrayal blazing from his eyes. She felt like she'd been sucker punched, so she could only imagine how Jesse felt. He'd looked at her like that only once before, as if she'd betrayed him, and that had been when she'd broken up with him and said she'd met someone else. She'd honestly had to use that excuse, knowing if she hadn't, she wouldn't have had the strength to walk away from him.

Even now, she'd wondered how she'd been so strong. And she didn't understand what had possessed her father to send Jesse here after her. Had he somehow known Liam might be Jesse's son?

No. Even she didn't know if that was true. Two dark-haired people could still have a blond child—she'd looked that up.

She heard the Rowsons walking down the hall toward the guest bedroom and shrank inside herself a little more. If they suspected Liam might not be Drew's son, Drew had also considered the possibility. Which explained the great pains he'd taken to have nothing to do with Liam. Just like his parents. Yet Drew had never said a word. Why not? Why the hell not?

It felt like she'd been punched in the gut. Too much, Drew's murder, his parents showing up and now this. No matter what happened, what a DNA test might reveal, Jesse would never look at her the same. She didn't understand why that mattered to her, but it did.

She fell asleep with the lights still on. She woke up several hours later, feeling gritty and groggy and confused.

The clock on the nightstand read 3:18 a.m. The deep of the night, the precursor to dawn. She'd walked the halls at this time often when Liam had been an infant, feeding him, comforting him, trying to keep him quiet so Drew could sleep. She recalled her pregnancy, when she and Drew had shared the king-size bed. He'd never held her then, even during the worst of her pregnancy, when she'd felt huge and ugly and unlovable. When she'd asked him why, he'd said he couldn't sleep when touching another person. Like everything else, she'd accepted his choice. He hadn't seemed loving or devoted or even kind, but she'd kept telling herself that would change once the baby was born, once he became a father in addition to a husband.

But it hadn't. And once again, she'd let herself accept it.

How long ago all that seemed now. Now Drew was dead and she honestly couldn't mourn his loss, though she felt sorrow because he'd lost his life in a senseless act of violence.

Swinging her legs over the side of the bed, she tugged down her long T-shirt and then, just in case, grabbed a pair of running shorts and stepped into them. Slipping on some flip-flops, she padded down the hall toward Liam's nursery. Her precious baby boy slept deeply, the night-light illuminating his impossibly long lashes and unruly golden curls.

Jesse. Pushing the thought of him out of her head, she went downstairs. The absolute silence of the house, broken only by the muted sound of the refrigerator running, soothed her. She got a glass of water from the door in the fridge and carried it outside onto the back patio.

The motion sensor lights flicked on, illuminating the seating area and the motionless figure who sat there. Heart in her throat, she froze. Jesse.

Quickly she stumbled backward, toward the relative safety of the house.

"It's okay," he murmured, his voice weary. "Stay."

Undecided, she didn't move.

"Seriously, Eva. I can leave if you want me to. Clearly, you couldn't sleep either. I wouldn't mind your company. Up to you."

She swallowed and closed the door behind her. It felt incredibly awkward, but she sat, staring straight ahead and sipping her water. She'd come out here hoping to gather her mind, but Jesse had managed to turn her into a mess.

The silence stretched out between them, as wide as the gulf between the kinds of lives they lived.

"I'm sorry," she finally offered. "Honestly, with you out of my life, it didn't seem to matter."

"Did you not think it would matter to me?" The anguish in his voice cut her wide open. Worse, she knew he was right. She'd just never allowed herself to think about even the possibility or the ramifications if anyone learned of the possibility that Drew hadn't been Liam's father.

"Were you ever going to tell me?" he asked. "I've been here for three weeks. You never said a word."

She bowed her head. "I resented my father for sending you, and you for showing up. I didn't need the disruption, the distractions, the temptation, damn it. I wasn't going to bring up something that was—still is—a remote possibility."

Again, that awkward silence. She swore she could hear her heartbeat in her ears. Maybe she should have gone back inside, but they needed to have this conversation, needed to clear the air between them.

"I'm sorry, Jesse," she repeated, letting some of her own exhaustion creep into her voice. "I don't know what else to say. I don't know how to make it right."

She knew what he'd say next, and she couldn't blame him. He'd continue to demand a DNA test so he'd know the truth about Liam. And while he'd be well within his rights, she'd have to ask him to wait until after the funeral and the media circus was over. She might not have truly loved Drew, but she owed him at least that much respect.

Instead, Jesse once again surprised her. He pushed to his feet and moved over to the chair next to her. Cupping his large hand under her chin, he raised her face so she would look at him.

"I should never have let you go," he said roughly. "Worst mistake of my entire life."

She wanted to tell him he was wrong. Choosing the club over her had been his worst mistake. She'd given him a choice and he'd made his. Nothing he could say or do now would undo that.

Despite knowing that, she couldn't make herself look away.

Nothing but trouble. She remembered Drew's dismissive words when he'd figured out she and Jesse had been a couple once. Drew's ego had been large enough that he'd never had a single doubt she could ever prefer another man to him. He'd never tired of telling her how lucky she should consider herself that he'd chosen her as his wife. What went unsaid was that he meant to make her his wife in name only.

She couldn't believe she'd once made herself accept that from him. Drew had never been a full partner; he hadn't even bothered to pretend. And she, she'd allowed her own light to dim. So much so that she wasn't at all certain she could find it again. If not for the fierceness of her love for her son, she thought her light would have been snuffed out a year or so ago.

Now Drew was gone. Though she had absolutely nothing to do with his murder, she couldn't suppress a sliver of guilt. Their marriage had long been over, a union in name only, and she'd spent a fair amount of time daydreaming about what her life would be like without him in it.

Blinking, she pulled herself out of her thoughts and forced herself to focus on right here and right now. The man she'd once loved more than life itself sat next to her, asking for a second chance. At least that's what she thought he meant.

But the Brothers of Sin would always be between them. Jesse hadn't said a single word about quitting the club.

She opened her mouth to respond, and then realized she had no idea what to say. Instead, she shook her head and looked down, her heart hurting almost as much as her head.

"I shouldn't have let you go," he repeated, the intensity of his gaze burning into her.

Trembling now, she backed away, holding his gaze steady with her own. "That wasn't up to you. I made my choice. We both wanted different things, different lifestyles. I grew up a part of BOS. I know what that club entails. I wanted a different kind of life than that. And you... You didn't."

He didn't respond. How could he, when she was right? She knew he had no words, at least not truthful ones, with which to refute her statement. She asked him to choose her or the club. He'd made his choice. Now he'd have to live with it. Regrets or not.

"Now I have a son," she continued. "No way in hell am I introducing Liam to that lifestyle. I want better for him."

"I agree," he replied, surprising her. "But he should also know his grandfather. I know Raul truly loves him."

"Does he?" Privately, she doubted that. Ever since she'd left the club, things had been strained between her and her father. "Is that why he's only seen Liam a couple of times?"

"It's a two-way street," he pointed out. "He's made an effort to try and see you every time he came up here to meet with your husband. But you haven't even once taken Liam to Houston to visit Raul or any of your BOS brothers."

Her eyes narrowed. "Did he put you up to saying that?"

"Not really. I'll admit he's complained more than once about not really knowing his own grandson."

At that, she looked down. But not before she knew

he'd seen the flash of pain across her face. "I love my father," she said softly. "I really do. I just don't love his lifestyle. He's always welcome to visit me and Liam here. I just won't go there. I made that clear to him when I was pregnant. How often he sees his grandson is actually his choice."

The conviction in her voice must have gotten through to him because he finally held up both his hands in defeat. "I get it. It's between the two of you and I'll butt out. But to change the subject, you know Raul has his fingers on the pulse of things. If he says you're in danger, then you are. Both of you."

"I know." She jerked away, hating that she felt bereft without his touch. "And I need to take steps to protect my son. I just don't know what. Maybe I should hire more bodyguards."

"Raul is sending some Brothers. At least three or four. They should be here tomorrow," he said. "And before you say anything, Raul is aware you might not like that, but what's done is done. They'll work just fine as bodyguards." He gave her a look, clearly daring her to disagree.

Though she tightened her mouth, she finally nodded. While she wasn't sure how she felt about her father once again taking control, to the Brothers she was all of their sister. They'd die for her. She loved them, each and every damn one of them, despite not wanting to be associated with the club anymore.

"You know what? They will." Stifling a yawn with her hand, she glanced past him toward the back door. "I think I might be able to sleep now. I'm going to go back to bed."

As she pushed to her feet, she heard a sharp crack,

like a car backfiring. Before she could breathe, Jesse slammed into her, knocking her to the ground.

"Stay down," he muttered. "That's a gunshot."

Before he'd even finished speaking, she heard several more shots in rapid succession. Behind her, the wall of windows in the breakfast room imploded.

Panic clawing at her, all she could think about was Liam.

"Let me go." She pushed at Jesse, trying to move him off her. "I need to get to my son."

"Not yet." He continued to hold her down. "Whoever is shooting is still out there. If you get up, you'll make too easy of a target. You don't want to leave Liam without a mom, do you?"

Put like that… She stopped struggling.

In the distance, she heard a siren. Someone must have called the sheriff's office. She prayed Liam would stay asleep and the Rowsons too.

As the siren drew closer, tires squealed on pavement and a vehicle raced away.

"Now is it safe?" she asked, squirming against Jesse's dead weight on top of her.

"Give it one more minute."

He'd barely finished speaking when the back door opened and Ted Rowson stuck his head out. "What's going on out here?" he demanded. His eyes widened when he caught sight of Jesse and Eva on the pavement.

"Get inside," Jesse ordered. "Now. And turn off the lights. Those were gunshots."

The older man stepped back inside and closed the door.

"Now," Jesse said, easing his weight off Eva. "Stay low and let's go."

Crouched over double, she rushed toward the door and yanked it open. Glass crunched underfoot as she hurried through the kitchen area, heading for the stairs. On the way there, she encountered Beth Rowson, rubbing her eyes and yawning. She wore a fuzzy white bathrobe that must have been overly warm, though she didn't appear uncomfortable.

"What's going on?" Beth asked, her voice heavy with sleep.

"Someone shot up the back of the house," Eva told her as she ran for the stairs. "I'm going to check on Liam."

She took the stairs two at a time. At the top, she forced herself to slow down and try to breathe. If the noise hadn't woken Liam, she didn't want to alarm him with her own panic.

Unbelievably, her son still slept soundly, completely undisturbed. She also peeked into Kara's room. The nanny also hadn't been awakened. Which was sort of a relief. The fewer people she had to deal with right now, the better.

Back downstairs, she found her in-laws huddled together in the kitchen in the dark, still taking care to stay away from any windows.

"Did you call 911?" Ted demanded, his voice shaky.

"Not yet, but—"

"Law enforcement is here," Jesse said, halfway between the kitchen and the front door. "I think you can turn on the lights now. Be careful around the broken glass."

Eva went with him to meet the police. Until now, adrenaline had kept her moving. With that gone, terror had set in and she'd started shaking so hard her teeth chattered. Even worse, she wasn't sure how to stop.

"Deep breaths," Jesse said, taking her arm to steady her. "You'll get through this. Let's make the report and then we'll start cleaning things up."

She nodded, unsure what she might sound like if she spoke. As she headed toward the front, one of the officers rang the bell.

Once she'd opened the door, she invited them in. She led them through the house, realizing for the first time she wore only a T-shirt and shorts, with no bra or underwear. She showed them the broken windows and then she and Jesse reported on what had happened while they were outside on the back patio.

The deputies began snapping photographs, one of them taking notes. They stepped through the room, broken glass cracking underfoot, talking quietly among themselves. When they moved outside, Beth spoke up.

"What were you doing outside at three in the morning?" Beth managed to sound outraged rather than concerned.

"I couldn't sleep," Eva explained, hearing the complete lack of emotion in her own voice and realizing she was beyond caring what anyone thought of her. "I went outside to get some air."

And, of course, both Beth's and Ted's gazes drifted from Eva to Jesse and back again, hers narrow and his appraising.

"Both of you had difficulty sleeping?" Beth finally asked, her suspicion clear in her snide tone.

"Yes." Eva stared at the older woman, practically daring her to speak her thoughts out loud. Right now she felt as if she was walking on the edge of a narrow precipice. Drew was dead, and all the bickering or accusations in the world were not going to change that.

Momentarily, she covered her face with her hands. She still couldn't shake the out-of-body feeling, like none of what was happening could possibly be real. In the space of a few days, her husband had been murdered, she'd learned Drew and her in-laws hadn't believed Liam was his son or their grandson, and now Jesse had come to the same realization. The news vans remained parked in front of her house and they'd been unable to plug in the landline phone due to the high volume of calls.

Now it seemed someone truly wanted to kill her, exactly like her father had said. She just wanted to grab her son and figure out a way to disappear.

Of course, she couldn't, she wouldn't. She'd dig deep and find the strength to deal with all of this and whatever else the universe decided to throw her way.

"You're lucky you had your bodyguard with you," Ted finally said, his voice gruff. "Seems like Drew knew what he was doing, hiring one. You might have been shot."

"Excuse me." The deputies returned from checking out the patio area. "We need to take your statements. Both of you."

Eva went first, keeping her explanation concise and to the point. Standing next to her, the only thing Jesse had to add was the way the shot had seemed to come from high up, like the shooter might have been in a tree or on the roof of another house.

The two officers exchanged glances. "Judging from the angle of some of the bullets, you might just be right. Is there anything else you'd like to add?"

Eva shook her head. Jesse said no and then escorted the policemen out.

When he returned, Eva met his gaze gratefully. An awkward silence had fallen in the kitchen. As she was about to say good-night and flee to her room, Beth's hand shot out and grabbed her arm.

"I think we deserve the truth," the other woman said, her tone hard. "Are you two sleeping together? Eva, have you been cheating on my son with this man?"

Chapter 5

Though Beth Rowson's question appeared to shock Eva, Jesse wasn't surprised to hear her ask it. Ever since their arrival, Drew's parents had been desperate in their grief to assign blame for the loss of their son. Latching on to the possibility that their son might have been cuckolded would be a diversion from what had to be intense heartache.

While he knew she would naturally find this insulting, and he couldn't blame her, he could only hope Eva somehow understood and went easy on them. From Raul Mendoza's fiery-natured daughter, he knew that would be asking a lot.

Straightening her shoulders and lifting her chin, Eva looked from one to the other, her eyes gleaming with what looked like unshed tears. "No, ma'am, I am not sleeping with my bodyguard. I've been with no one but

Drew since the day we got married." She took a deep breath, her tone measured and calm. "To be honest, it's upsetting that you'd even consider something like that. I know you lost your son, but I lost my husband too."

Her husband. Hell's bells, but Jesse actually felt jealous of a dead man. When he'd first learned of her marriage to Drew Rowson, he'd wanted to break something. He'd gone on a two-day bender, despite the danger of losing focus on his real job. Something in him had died that day, even though he'd known she'd eventually marry someone else. A happy ending had never been in the cards for him and Eva. Trite as it sounded, there actually were times when love just wasn't going to be enough. Still, he knew he'd never forget her. Or stop loving her. He wasn't built like that. He'd figured time would eventually blunt the sharp edges of his loss and perhaps that might have happened. Except it hadn't. When Raul had sent him up here to watch over Eva, Jesse had figured the more than two-year time span would have put enough distance between them to give him perspective. He'd been shocked when, instead of finding a happy, glowing Eva doting over her beloved husband, he'd seen two people living remote and separate lives. Not a marriage at all.

No one spoke to break the silence. Finally, Beth nodded, tears beginning to silently stream down her cheeks. Her husband put his arm around her and pulled her close. "I know," she finally said, sniffling. "But since we're being honest… Eva, you really don't seem all that upset that Drew's dead."

Eva gasped. Before she could speak, Ted held up his hand, his lips pressed together so tight they appeared bloodless.

"Beth, that's uncalled for. We all grieve differently. I think Eva is a strong woman. Eva, I apologize for my wife's rudeness."

"Thank you." Tone icy, Eva dipped her head in a gesture of gratitude before turning her gaze to her mother-in-law. "I'm going to overlook the appalling cruelty of your comment," she said. "And I'm not going to dignify it with a response. While I understand how much you miss your son, I don't owe you or anyone else an explanation for anything."

With that, she turned on her heel and exited the room, her back straight and her head held high.

Jesse let her go and didn't follow her. Instead, he eyed Drew's parents and considered whether he should say anything in Eva's defense. Because these people, for whatever reason, had insulted him as well as her. He truly didn't care about their opinion of him, but he couldn't stand when someone disparaged Eva.

In the end, he decided to make a short-and-sweet statement that couldn't be misconstrued in any way. "I think Eva might be in shock," he said. "A lot has happened to her in a short amount of time. Please give her a break."

Ted nodded his agreement but his wife simply looked down at her feet silently, her mouth tight.

Oh well. At least he'd tried. "Good night," Jesse said. "I'll go ahead and see if I can scrounge up something until I can get plywood and nail it up over that window."

Ted frowned. "Drew probably had plywood. Even so, you'll need some help."

Eyeing the shattered window, Jesse considered. Ted was right, damn it. He could have used a couple of his

Brothers from BOS right now. "Let me go check out the garage and see if there's anything in there I could use to block it up temporarily."

"I'll come help you," Ted immediately responded. "Beth, go on up to bed. I'll join you in a little bit."

To Jesse's surprise, Beth nodded and took herself off without arguing.

In the immaculate three-car garage, Jesse looked around. In one area, Drew had set up a workshop. Interesting, as Jesse would never have pegged the other man for the type to work with his hands. Propped up against one wall were several medium-size sheets of plywood, along with several two-by-fours.

"These might work," Jesse said, grabbing them. He handed one to Ted, looking around for a hammer and nails. He located those easily, since it appeared Drew had also been extremely organized, bordering on a neat freak.

Back inside the house, Jesse considered the fastest way to secure the window. Normally, if it hadn't been the middle of the night, he would have taken pains to knock out the remaining shards of glass and sweep them up, but he'd leave that for tomorrow.

With Ted helping, the two men made short work of covering the broken window with plywood. When they'd finished, Jesse returned the hammer and box of nails to the workbench in the garage. Back inside the house, he thanked Ted for his help. "Maybe we can all get some shut-eye now," he said.

"Wait." Ted went into the kitchen and returned holding two cans of beer. "Have a beer with me. I need to decompress a little."

As peace offerings went, this was the kind Jesse

understood. With a brusque nod, he accepted the can and carried it into the den. Ted followed him, taking a seat on the couch opposite Jesse's chair.

"My wife is understandably distraught," the older man said. "As am I. My apologies for the offensive comments earlier."

Not sure how to respond, Jesse settled for nothing. In their short time here, both the Rowsons had disparaged bikers and him and Eva individually. He suspected they had no idea of their son's true character but if they did, he wouldn't be surprised to learn that they'd turned a blind eye.

Truthfully, he really didn't want to know. When the investigation wound down and indictments were handed out, he hoped these two weren't caught up in the frenzy of arrests. His life would go on, but anyone who'd been involved in illegal activities would have a high price to pay.

Ted excused himself and headed off to bed.

Once the other man had gone, Jesse went outside, digging out his burner phone, the one no one knew about. Despite the odd hour, he called his boss, knowing all the guys assigned to this investigation would be in a frenzy after the shooting. And not just because it meant a bad guy had paid the ultimate price to escape justice.

"Sorry to wake you," Jesse began.

"No problem. It's not like I'm sleeping much anyway. I was beginning to wonder when on earth you were going to check in," E.J. Spinkler, assistant special agent in charge, or ASAC, exclaimed. "Everything's going to hell in a handbasket. Do you have a report? Please tell me it will make me feel better."

Since Drew Rowson had been one of the main focuses of their undercover operation, Jesse wasn't sure he could do that. Nonetheless, he filled his boss in on everything that had happened after Drew had been gunned down.

"What about the wife?" E.J. asked. "Do you think she's involved in her husband's business operations?"

"She's not." Drew didn't even have to think about it. "They didn't appear to have a close marriage."

"Keep watching her," E.J. advised. "She might surprise you."

"I will. Raul Mendoza is sending up a few more guys from the motorcycle club to watch over her. I'm not sure what exactly he knows. He hasn't told me, other than to say she and her son are in danger."

"Which makes me believe he might know the identity of the killer."

"Exactly." Jesse actually liked Raul. In his undercover role as biker club member, he'd actually found himself looking up to the older man. Unlike the stereotypical gang leader, Raul handled himself with intelligence and patience. He considered every angle before he acted and while he might be ruthless in his defense of those he loved—he thought of every Brother of Sin as his family— Jesse had seen him act with kindness and compassion too. While Jesse knew the others acted on his direction, to all appearances Raul kept his hands clean.

Initially, Raul had started the Brothers of Sin forty years ago as a simple motorcycle club. He'd been young and wild with only a used Harley to his name. He and three or four like-minded friends would meet up and go for long rides. Based out of Houston, BOS had grown, often in ways Raul hadn't expected.

From what Raul had told Jesse, as the club had expanded, he'd chosen four men to act as his lieutenants under him. Without telling Raul, one of these men had begun selling guns. When Raul learned of this, he'd been okay with it, but he'd drawn the line at getting involved in drugs.

Now, BOS was one of the largest drug dealers in the southern U.S. Some of the weapons had been sold to known terrorist groups, which is why the ATF had sent Jesse in undercover.

The investigation so far would be hard-pressed to directly tie Raul to anything. He had four lieutenants under him who carried out the day-to-day operations. Jesse had tons of stuff on these men, more than enough to arrest and indict them. But the ATF wanted the big guns, the people who provided the weapons and drugs to BOS. Since they were a huge and violent Mexican cartel, Jesse doubted the ATF would be able to do much about them. Twice he'd refused an offer to extend his undercover work into Mexico. He had no intention of going there or dealing with those people. That was on an entirely different level.

He might be prejudiced, but on the whole he'd found the guys in the BOS to be good people, despite the fact that they wore their one-percenter patches proudly. This referred to a comment by the American Motorcycle Association that 99 percent of motorcyclists were law-abiding citizens, leaving only the remaining 1 percent as outlaws.

For the first time in his years with the ATF, he found himself on the verge of losing himself in the role he was playing.

Luckily, he'd managed to pull himself up in time. Eva had had a lot to do with that, with her demand that he choose between her and the club. It hadn't been a choice he'd wanted to make.

"You need to find the info on where Drew stashed the money," E.J. said. "We're not too far from moving in and shutting this thing down."

Though this exact thing was what Jesse had spent years working toward, he felt sick. He wasn't ready to close this chapter of his life, not yet, not while Eva still needed him.

Eva. And his son. For the first time he realized if Liam truly was his son, he'd never be able to close out this part of his life and walk away. He couldn't, wouldn't, abandon his son. Even if maintaining constant contact with the boy's mother meant the gaping wounds on his heart would never heal.

"Earth to Jesse," E.J. said. "Are you still there?"

With difficulty, Jesse forced his thoughts back on track. Eva could always derail him.

"Sorry," he said.

"Be careful," the ASAC said. "If you lose your concentration, you could make mistakes. We're too close to have anyone do anything that might jeopardize the investigation."

Too close. While he knew he wasn't the only undercover operative, he wondered what else the ATF had. He'd been able to provide proof that Drew Rowson laundered money for the club. Lots of money. Which would explain the explosive growth of Drew's real estate investments as they were a useful way to clean dirty money. Lawyering could only take him so far. And Jesse suspected a lot of the funds pushing Drew's gubernatorial campaign came from dirty money. He needed proof. That had been one of the tasks he'd been quietly working on before someone took Drew out.

"Does anyone have any idea why Drew was killed?" he asked. "From what I could tell, the guy didn't have a whole lot of enemies."

E.J. scoffed at that. "Those guys always have enemies. Lot of backstabbing in politics, not to mention when you're also dealing with criminals."

"True," Jesse allowed, even though the code of honor he'd witnessed among the BOS had been steadfast and strong. They truly had each other's backs.

"Anyway, I want you to keep an eye on the wife," E.J. ordered. "Watch her closely. I know the two of you were a thing a couple years ago, so use that to your advantage. We need to know the scope of her involvement."

Though Jesse could have told his boss that would be a waste of time, he knew better. "Will do," he promised. "That won't be difficult at all."

Difficult didn't even begin to describe it.

Liam woke up crying, the baby monitor Eva still used to watch him transmitting his sobs clearly. Though she'd had less than four hours of sleep, Eva scrambled from her bed and staggered down the hall to his room. She gathered him up and held him, rocking him in her arms while murmuring soothing bits of nonsense to him.

"I'm hungwy," he announced, his tears still wet on his baby-soft, chubby cheeks.

She kissed them away. "Then let's go get you something to eat." She settled him on her hip and carried him downstairs.

Alone in the kitchen, she made herself a cup of coffee while Liam sat in his booster, happily munching on Cheerios while she made his favorite oatmeal with milk and raisins. Her stomach felt hollow, so she made enough for her breakfast too.

They ate together, Liam keeping up a running monologue of sounds, some nonsensical, but most of them involving expressing his newfound desire for a puppy. "Doggy, mama!" he said, pounding the top of his high chair for emphasis.

Drew had emphatically said no when she'd asked a week ago. Since he so rarely spent time with his son, he'd expressed disbelief that a two-year-old could string enough words together to be understood.

She hadn't mentioned it again. Maybe she'd revisit the idea once things calmed down. She'd grown up with dogs, large rotties who looked mean but really were sweet and loving. Though now she was thinking of a small dog, maybe a mixed-breed rescue puppy.

After Liam had cleaned his bowl and drunk his juice, she took him back upstairs, hoping she wouldn't have to wake Kara again. Since the nanny's door remained closed, she suspected she would.

With a sigh, she tapped lightly. To her surprise, Kara opened immediately. She'd already showered and dressed and appeared awake and alert, ready to go to work.

"Kawa!" Liam exclaimed, rushing at his nanny and hugging her legs. "Mornin'!"

"Mornin', little bit," Kara replied, ruffling his wheat-colored curls. "Have you been awake long?"

"Not too long. He's been fed," Eva said. "He'll need to be dressed and then I'll have to ask you to keep him in the playroom today. No walks, nothing outside, even in the backyard."

"Why?" Kara asked, confusion furrowing her brows.

Liam zoomed past the nanny, spotting one of his toy trucks in her room. While he played with it, Eva quietly filled Kara in on the overnight events. When she'd finished, Kara's eyes widened. "Are we safe here?" she asked nervously.

"Yes," Eva answered, hoping she spoke the truth. "My father is sending up more bodyguards and I'll make sure at least two are assigned to you and Liam. For now, just keep a close eye on him and stay inside."

Swallowing hard, Kara nodded. Eva kissed Liam on the cheek and hurried to her room to get ready.

After taking her own shower and putting on makeup, Eva dressed in a carefully neutral outfit and went back downstairs. This time Jesse sat alone at the kitchen table drinking coffee. Judging from his damp hair, he'd also recently showered.

Despite herself, her heart skittered a beat when she saw him. "Good morning," she chirped, covering her reaction with a determined upbeat attitude. She'd become a master at that over the past few years.

"Mornin'," he grunted. "You look good. Way better than I feel. But then you were always good at functioning on little sleep."

"I got even better once I had a baby," she said, without really considering the possible impact of her words. "I've been up awhile. I've already fed Liam and had breakfast."

For a second or two, Jesse locked gazes with her

and didn't move. Her stomach swooped but she held his gaze.

"Where is he?" he asked, his voice carefully casual. "Upstairs with the nanny?"

"Yes. Kara will watch over him while I attend to all the final details of the funeral."

He nodded, finally looking away. When he looked back and spoke again, his tone had gentled. "Why do you even have a nanny, Eva? I know you. If there was ever anyone who would be perfect at being a hands-on mother, that would be you."

"Drew hired her," she admitted. "He said he needed to make sure I was available to perform the duties he required of his wife." Even as she spoke, she was aware of how chauvinistic that sounded. She'd thought so at the time too, but figured as long as she could control the situation, she could make it work.

So far, it had. She still spent as much time as possible with her son. Kara had it easy.

Other than narrowing his eyes, Jesse didn't respond to her statement. He didn't have to. She knew exactly what thoughts were going through his mind. After all, they'd been together for over a year. Once, she'd taken pride in considering herself a fierce warrior woman. She'd never, ever been the type to let a man call the shots. Her father had taught her to depend on no one but herself and she'd been damn good at that.

Somehow, without knowing how, she'd obviously changed. She couldn't even pinpoint the exact moment.

Even worse, she felt too numb to be angry enough to do something about changing things. Maybe that would come later. Right now, it would be hard enough to simply make it through the day. She had in-laws to deal with and a funeral to finalize. The media would need a statement, as well.

She got a second cup of coffee and sat down at the table, intent on losing herself in scrolling through her phone. When Ted and Beth Rowson strolled in a few minutes later, already dressed and looking ready to go, that's exactly what she was doing.

With everyone gathered in the kitchen drinking coffee, she knew she should offer to make something for them to eat, but she couldn't bring herself to do that.

Eyeing her, Jesse must have understood. "I'm going to make a doughnut run," he announced. "I'll be right back."

"Get some sausage rolls too," Ted told him.

Jesse nodded as he went out the door. A moment later, the rumbling sound of his motorcycle starting up filled the kitchen.

Eva caught a look of envy on Ted's aristocratic face, though the instant he saw her looking, he looked away.

Fifteen minutes later, Jesse returned with a large box of doughnuts. Everyone grabbed one or two and fell to eating them as if they hadn't eaten for days. Eva stayed back and watched, unable to stomach so much sugar right now. She watched Jesse eat a huge bear claw with obvious enjoyment. There was something sensual in the way he ate, and she had to swallow back the shiver of desire skittering through her.

The doorbell rang at 9:00 a.m. sharp. Everyone fell silent.

"I'll get it," Eva said, sidling away. Jesse detached himself from where he'd been leaning against the counter and went after her.

"Wait." He grabbed her arm. "What if it's the media?"

"Then I'll tell them no comment. I haven't had time to work on a statement to give them."

"Let me handle it," he urged.

"Not this time." Pulling herself free, she marched over to the front door.

When she opened it, Drew's assistant and campaign manager, Lori Pearson, let out a loud cry and fell into Eva's arms.

"I can't believe he's gone," she wailed. Her red-rimmed eyes and disheveled platinum hair testified to her sorrow. "Oh, Eva, honey. I just don't understand how anyone could do something like this."

Leading her inside, Eva closed the door. "Drew's parents are here," she said quietly, taking both the younger woman's hands and willing strength into her. "They're already understandably upset, so please don't make things worse."

Her message appeared to get through. Lori straightened, pulling a tissue from her designer handbag and blotting at her eyes. "Right, right. I'm sorry." She peered at Eva. "How are you holding up?"

"I made most of the funeral arrangements yesterday," Eva replied, circumventing a direct answer. "And last night someone shot out one of my back windows. The police were here at three in the morning and we've already put a call in to a glass place. It's been rough."

Lori's eyes went wide, her false eyelashes giving her an owlish look. "Do you think it might have been Drew's murderer? That's pretty terrifying."

"You don't know the half of it." Eva tilted her head,

considering the younger woman. "What can I do for you, Lori?"

"Do for me?" Echoing Eva's words, Lori's brow wrinkled in confusion. "I came here to see what I might do for you. I know you said you'd already made most of the funeral arrangements, but if you need my help coordinating anything, I'm here for you."

"Thank you." Thinking back to all the decisions Jeremy Blackenstock had said she'd need to make, Eva nodded. "I'm probably going to take you up on that."

"Sounds perfect." Sniffing, Lori wiped at her still-streaming eyes. When she caught sight of Jesse, she looked him up and down slowly. "Well, hello there. You must be the bodyguard."

With a bored expression, Jesse nodded. "I am."

"This is Jesse," Eva said. "Jesse, this is Lori, Drew's assistant and campaign manager."

He dipped his chin in acknowledgment. Lori continued to study him for another moment before turning back to Eva.

"Eva, honey? Do you mind if I say hello to Ted and Beth? It's been a little bit since I've seen them, though I talk to them several times a week."

She did? Keeping that thought to herself, Eva gestured at Lori to follow her as she led the way to the kitchen. Lori patted down her hair, smoothed her pencil skirt and pasted a sympathetic smile on her face.

The instant Beth caught sight of her son's assistant, she leaped to her feet and held out her arms. "Lori."

Hugging, the two women wept, exchanging mostly incoherent phrases about their mutual loss. Eva looked on, a bit shocked. She'd had no idea Lori and Drew's mom had been so close. Judging from Jesse's expression, he felt the same way.

Even Ted's gaze lit up when he spied Lori, though he waited patiently for Beth to finish hugging her before he held out his arms. Lori embraced him too. They clung to each other and Ted cried for the first time since arriving, wiping his streaming eyes almost angrily.

Heaven help her. Eva tried to ignore the twinge of jealous discomfort, but she was only human. Lori had worked for Drew long before he'd met Eva, and of course she'd gotten to know his parents. Clearly, they'd become close. Which might be exactly what they needed, even if it seemed odd that they were closer to Drew's assistant than his wife. She couldn't begrudge them whatever comfort they could get, no matter where they found it.

But Beth's next question made any sympathy Eva might have felt vanish.

"Lori, do you know where Drew kept his will? I'd like to take a look at it."

Even Lori appeared taken aback by the question. "I'm just now starting to go through his papers," she replied. "Once I find the will, I'll be contacting the executor to meet with the attorney and get the probate process started."

Beth nodded, but she wasn't finished. "But you'll let me see it first, right?"

"I'm sorry." Lori seemed to choose her words carefully. "But I have strict instructions and I'm afraid I can't do that."

Though Beth grimaced in disappointment, she didn't challenge the statement. "Can you at least tell me who is the executor?" she asked.

"I'm not sure." A hint of firmness had crept into Lori's voice now. "I haven't actually seen the will yet. I know he revised it after his marriage." She nodded toward Eva. "I'm not privy to the details beyond that."

Neither Ted nor Beth bothered to hide their obvious disappointment. Eva wondered if they somehow honestly thought Drew had left her out of his will. Since she and Drew hadn't gotten around to drawing up a prenup, Texas law was clear on the rights of inheritance. A will could only confirm that and perhaps designate heirship of smaller, sentimental items.

Was there something specific Beth wanted? If so, all she needed to do was ask.

Pushing down the bewildered hurt, Eva reminded herself she'd never truly understood Drew's parents. Drew had often commented that they cared more about their church family than their real one.

After getting Lori a cup of coffee and a doughnut, Eva asked her if she'd mind coming with her to Drew's study. "I hope y'all will excuse us for a few moments," she said to the rest of the room. "I've got some things I'd like to discuss with Lori."

"I'd prefer to be there," Beth announced. Eva stared. She'd thought Drew's mother couldn't shock her any more than she already had. Turned out she'd been wrong.

"I'm sorry," Eva told her firmly. "But this is private. I'm sure you and Ted can enjoy the rest of your breakfast while I take care of this. Or," she tacked on, unable to help herself, "perhaps you'd like to spend time with your grandson. I'm sure Kara has him dressed by now."

With that, she swept from the room, Lori and Jesse trailing behind her.

Chapter 6

Drew's study was a polite word for a man cave, though he'd set up one corner with a huge, L-shaped desk and matching credenza. The large room had dark oak-paneled walls, a seventy-inch flat screen, plush leather chairs, a fully stocked wet bar next to the requisite pool table, with a bunch of fox-hunting prints on the walls.

Following right behind Lori, who managed to walk confidently despite the five-inch stilettos she wore, he entered the room as if he belonged. Even though he wasn't entirely sure Eva would allow him to stay.

Her gaze touched on him briefly before she closed the door. "Jesse, why don't you have a seat." She waited while he settled himself in one of the over-stuffed leather chairs before turning toward the other woman. "Lori, I'm going to need your help getting everything set up with the funeral home. I did some of the initial work yesterday, but there are still a lot of decisions that need to be made."

"I'm ready to help in any way I can," Lori said, nodding.

Taking a seat behind Drew's desk, she gestured toward one of the nearby chairs.

As Eva outlined tasks to the other woman, Lori pulled out an iPad and took notes. Aware he had to be careful not to appear too interested, Jesse crossed his legs as he settled himself into the huge leather chair. He felt relieved Eva hadn't begun talking about Drew's business deals. While he felt on a gut level she hadn't been involved in any of her husband's illegal operations, he'd been wrong before. His emotions were too tangled up with wanting her to think straight. After all, Raul Mendoza was her father and who knows what the shrewd biker kingpin had taught her.

Inwardly, he winced. Even the thought felt disloyal, which was all shades of wrong. There were reasons one shouldn't get involved with a subject while undercover and the absolute failure to be able to remain objective was chief among them. Of course, he'd lost all objectivity the first time he'd gazed into Eva's soft brown eyes.

Eva talked about the funeral arrangements in a hushed tone, clearly going over some sort of checklist the funeral director must have given her. They discussed the burial, what minister Drew would have most likely wanted, even the music and double-checked the obituary. Lori mentioned it would most likely be picked up nationally, so Eva wanted to make sure it was correct.

Once Eva had outlined everything she needed, Lori shut down her iPad and stowed it in her purse. "Thank you for such detailed instructions," she said, smiling. "That makes it a lot easier. I'll get right on this. In fact, I'll stop by the funeral home after I leave here."

"Perfect." Eva stood, smiling. "Oh, and one more favor. Please don't mention any of this to Beth or Ted. I'd prefer just to let them know everything once all the arrangements have been finalized."

Though Lori eyed her curiously, she nodded. "Consider it done."

Though he felt like a cynic, Jesse couldn't help but think she'd realized who'd be signing her paychecks from now on. It certainly wouldn't be Drew's parents.

"I'll touch base with you later today," Lori promised, striding confidently toward the exit. "Let me tell the Rowsons goodbye."

Once she'd gone, Eva let out a huge sigh and began massaging both her temples. "This is a nightmare."

Not sure how to reply, he simply nodded.

"I think I'll ask Lori to help me go through Drew's papers once the funeral is over," she said.

His heart sank. He needed access to those papers. "I can help you," he offered, hoping against hope that she'd take him up on his offer.

"Maybe," she allowed. "We'll deal with that later. Most of Drew's business stuff is in his work office and Lori's already going to have to deal with that. Anything here will be personal."

Or illegal, he thought.

Finally, Eva pushed herself up from behind the desk. "My head is starting to ache so I'm going to try and bypass the Rowsons for now. I need to go cuddle my son for a little while."

Of course, he followed her as she slipped down the

hall, taking a route through the foyer toward the front staircase. As she started up, she turned and glared at him. "You don't have to shadow me all the time."

"But I do," he answered without missing a beat. "That's the thing about being a bodyguard. I can't protect you if I'm not with you."

The doorbell rang. Eva froze. "What now?" she groaned.

"Stay right there," he ordered. Taking the steps two at a time, he opened the front door just in time to see a parcel delivery truck driving away. A medium-size package sat on the front porch. He picked it up, noting it was addressed to Eva Rowson, but there wasn't a return address.

"Did you order something?" he asked, carrying the box inside and setting it on the decorative table in the foyer.

"No." Shaking her head, she waved her hand in dismissal and turned to continue upstairs.

With a shrug, he followed her. They'd just reached the landing at the top when a blast knocked him off his feet. Ears ringing, his first thought—as always—was Eva. He pushed himself up, on his hands and knees, looking for her through the smoke.

She lay on her side a few feet from him, her eyes open and dazed. For one horrible second, he thought she was dead, but then she blinked and sat up. "What..." Licking her lips, she tried to stand.

"The box," he said, finally understanding. "It must have contained a bomb."

When he managed to gain his feet, he went to her, holding out his hand and pulling her up. "We've got to talk about getting you and Liam somewhere safe."

"Agreed." Squinting at him, she seemed to be having difficulty focusing.

"Did you hit your head?" he asked.

"Maybe. I don't know." She brushed off his attempts to feel her head for a bump. "We could have been killed." Her eyes widened. "Liam could have been here," she cried out, apparently suddenly understanding how close they'd come to being killed. She stood stock-still, her entire body violently shaking. Sweeping her with his gaze, he checked for blood or injuries. Other than a black soot mark on her cheek and some tears in her skirt, she seemed unhurt. Physically, at least. Her teeth were chattering now and her wide, unfocused stare told him she'd gone into shock.

"Eva." Unable to keep the tenderness from his voice, he gathered her close, willing his body's warmth and strength to chase away her terror. "You're okay. I'm okay. No one was hurt."

"Not this time," she managed, her voice cracking.

The Rowsons had rushed out from the kitchen and stood in the great room, frozen in place, their faces wearing identical expressions of shock and dismay as they stared up at Jesse and Eva on the landing.

"Call 911," he barked at them, refusing to let go of Eva. "Tell them a bomb went off but no one is hurt."

Ted immediately dug his cell phone from his pocket and made the call.

Still Eva continued to shake. "My son!" She pushed out of Jesse's arms and spun for the hall that led to his room. Her feet tangled and she nearly went down. Only Jesse's quick, instinctive reaction kept her upright.

"Let me go with you," he said. "Please. Let me help."

When her gaze met his, he saw she was on the verge

of tears. Not hysteria though. Not yet. Again, she went for the hall, kicking off her heels and running. Jesse stayed right behind her, leaving the two stunned Rowsons below to survey the damage to the foyer and formal dining room.

Things could be replaced. People were a different story.

The door to Liam's room was closed. Fumbling with the doorknob, Eva pushed it open. Liam and Kara were nowhere in sight.

Eyes wild, Eva spun, searching the room. When she didn't see her son, she staggered. "Liam," she screamed. "Kara, where are you?"

A second later, the closet door creaked open. Kara cautiously poked her head out. "Is it safe to come out?" she asked, her high-pitched voice terrified.

Behind her, Liam popped up. "Mama?" he asked, his blue eyes big as saucers. The instant he saw his mother, he started to cry.

Eva dropped to her knees and held out her arms. "Come here, baby. Oh, thank goodness y'all are okay."

Kara crawled out first, still gripping the toddler's hand. "We heard the explosion and all I could think of to do was hide," she said. Liam broke free and ran to his mother, who gathered him close and began covering his face in kisses.

"Thank you," Eva whispered, looking over her son's head at Kara. "Thank you for protecting him."

Nodding, Kara looked past her to Jesse. "What happened? Is everyone all right?"

"Package bomb," he answered, tearing his gaze away from Eva and Liam long enough to answer the nanny. "The sheriff's office has been called."

All the color drained from Kara's face. "This is the second time in as many days that someone has tried to hurt us. I'm going to have to rethink working here."

Though Eva's jaw tightened, she didn't reply.

"I believe we all might have to consider relocating somewhere else," Jesse put in. "We'll discuss it later."

Kara nodded.

"Eva?" Beth Rowson appeared in the doorway, appearing nervous, as if she'd rather be anywhere else. "The police are on the way." Her gaze drifted past Eva and Liam to Jesse. "Ted and I are going to find somewhere else to stay. It's not safe here."

"That's what I just said," Kara interjected.

Jesse waited for Eva to respond. When she didn't, instead simply staring at her mother-in-law while holding her son, he realized she was waiting for Beth to acknowledge Liam. Instead, Beth turned away.

"We'll get packing," Beth said to no one in particular, as she backed out the door.

Looking toward Eva, Jesse saw Liam peering at him from the safety of his mother's arms. His bright blue eyes, clear and guileless, were framed by impossibly long eyelashes.

"Hey there," Jesse said, offering a tentative smile.

The toddler blinked and then his solemn little face broke into a brilliant smile. He squirmed and broke free from Eva's hold and launched himself at Jesse, wrapping himself around Jesse's legs, holding on tight.

His chest squeezing with an unfamiliar tenderness, Jesse reached down and picked Liam up. He swallowed hard, the back of his throat stinging as he gazed at the boy who probably was his son.

"Higher," Liam demanded, gesturing toward the

ceiling. Jesse understood exactly what he meant. With one smooth move, he settled Liam on his shoulders, keeping a firm grip on Liam's small legs.

Eva watched, her nervous expression letting him know what she thought of that. But to her credit, she didn't say anything, though at any moment Jesse figured she'd demand that he let Liam down.

He'd refuse, he thought. Because this—the very first moment he'd held the boy who might be his son—was something he didn't want to end just yet.

Moving around the room with Liam laughing at his new bird's-eye view, something clicked inside Jesse. This felt right. If he could have made the right choice, the choice Eva had once demanded of him, this—his own family—would have been his reward. Instead, he'd had to honor his commitment to his job, to his unit, to the undercover work he'd spent years perfecting. And in the end, he'd have to live with his choice. He didn't see any way he could possibly have made a different one.

Watching as Jesse bounced Liam around the room on his impossibly broad shoulders, the rush of tenderness almost had her doubling over. She couldn't help but feel slightly nervous that her tiny boy sat up so high, but she knew Jesse wouldn't let anything happen to him. And Liam's delighted, joyous laugh warmed her insides in a sorely needed way.

When Beth had come up, for one heart-stopping moment, Eva had thought she might interact with her grandson, but instead the older woman had turned away. Cold, in an unfathomable way as far as Eva was concerned. At two, Liam was too young to understand or be hurt, but Eva would never be able to forgive the way Drew's parents had treated her boy. Even if they truly believed he wasn't their son's child, they had no way of being certain until Jesse and Liam took a DNA test. And even then, how could anyone blame a two-year-old child?

Finally, Jesse lifted Liam up off his shoulders with a huge swooping movement, delighting the boy but making Eva catch her breath. When he set Liam on the floor, Liam stared up at him with an adoring grin. "I like you," the toddler declared.

Clearly touched, Jesse ruffled the boy's hair. "I like you too, little squirt."

"Not squirt," Liam informed him solemnly. "Liam."

"I know," Jesse replied. "Do you know my name?"

Liam didn't even hesitate. "Jesse."

"Wow. I'm impressed." Jesse bent down so he could look at Liam eye to eye. "How'd you know that?"

"Hmmph," Liam scoffed, sounding way older than his two years. "Mommy says. I hear."

"Good ears."

Grinning at the compliment, Liam ran back to Eva, his excitement palpable.

Eva picked up her son and settled him on her hip. It took her a moment to catch her breath, the surreal feeling of watching Jesse and Liam together still flooring her. Seeing them together, she had to admit she could see several of Jesse's features in Liam's little face. The nose and chin in particular.

Shaking her head, she glanced at Kara, who once again had her phone out, intent on scrolling. "Kara?"

The younger woman looked up and sighed as she closed out her phone app. "Yes?"

"Keep an eye on Liam. I've got a few things I need to work out. He can take his usual nap after lunch."

Kara nodded and shoved her phone in her pocket before taking Liam from her. "Ready to play some more, little buddy?"

Liam nodded. "Trucks?"

"Sure," Kara promised. "Let's go to the playroom."

With Liam on her hip, the nanny pushed past Jesse and left the room. As she reached the door, Liam raised one little hand in a wave. "Bye, Jesse!"

"Bye, little buddy," Jesse responded, his gaze tender, his expression soft and eager. For a moment, Eva thought, he allowed his naked vulnerability to show. But then his mask slammed down, firmly back in place.

Seeing this, Eva battled a sudden urge to weep. She blinked furiously, trying to keep the tears that filled her eyes from spilling. Despite her best efforts, one or two escaped and slipped down her cheeks.

She supposed she ought to turn away so Jesse wouldn't see, but right at that moment she didn't care if he did. She'd done this, kept their boy from him. In trying to do what she'd believed was the right thing for Liam, instead, she'd deprived him of his father, of a family. What they could have been… The thought made her dizzy.

"Eva?" The pain in his voice matched the pain in her heart. Despite the flood of emotion that threatened to overwhelm her, she needed his touch. She hoped he'd reach for her, because she wasn't brave enough to walk the few feet that separated them despite how badly she needed him.

He did. Gently and carefully, he gathered her to him

and held her. As she'd worried it would, his concern caused the dam to break. Again.

She cried, her attempt to weep silently futile despite the palm she held against her mouth. Jesse didn't speak, just continued to be her rock, despite everything, exactly as he'd always been.

Finally, she got herself under control. Wiping at her eyes with the back of her hand, she looked up at him, letting him see her raw emotion and her regret.

Rising up on her toes, she pressed her lips to his, silently imploring him to kiss her, because more than anything she needed to be in his arms, to touch him. Instead, he held utterly still, her name on his lips a warning. "Eva. No."

Embarrassed, aroused and in pain, she stepped away from him.

"This is getting to be a habit," she managed to say finally, trying to make light of her neediness and the way his strong embrace restored a sense of sanity to her world.

For a moment, Jesse only watched her, the raw need in his gaze matching what she felt in her heart.

"We need to talk," Jesse said, his quiet tone serious, his hands fisted at his side.

"Okay."

"I will help you," he told her. "No matter what happens, I won't leave you at the mercy of the wolves."

She frowned. "What wolves?"

"But this—whatever it is—between us," he continued on as if he hadn't heard her. "It's got to stop."

Swallowing hard, she managed a nod. "Agreed." Though she really didn't want to give up the familiar comfort of his arms, pretending nothing had changed would only end up hurting them both. It wouldn't be fair.

"Strictly business," he said, though the intensity still burning in his gaze contradicted his words.

"But we can still be friends, right?"

He hesitated. "Are we, Eva? Friends?"

Unsure how to answer, she slowly nodded. "I think so."

For a moment, he looked away. When he returned his gaze back to her, the remote stranger had returned. "When the other Brothers arrive, we're going to have a meeting and try to hammer out the best way to keep you and Liam safe. We might even teleconference in Raul. I'm thinking you're going to have to stay somewhere else for a little while."

"I'm not going back to Houston." She crossed her arms, hating that she felt it necessary to explain herself to him once more. "And while I'll accept the new bodyguards my father sent, I still want no part of BOS."

"Fine," he replied, to her surprise. "I don't care where we go, as long as no one else knows you're there. That includes Kara. I think it might be time to let her go."

Since she'd been considering this exact possibility, she didn't really want to argue. Except for one point. "Surely you don't think Kara is involved in Drew's murder and the attempt on my life."

"Not at all. But she posts to social media. I'm willing to bet if you pull up her Facebook or Instagram account right now, you'll see something about the bomb."

Frowning, she grabbed her phone and went to Kara's page. To her dismay, he was right. Kara had even taken the time to snap a few photos from the landing at the top of the foyer so she could post them.

"If you don't want to fire her, send her off for a two-week vacation," Jesse continued. "Up to you. Just get rid of her for a little while. Until we know you're safe."

Still stunned, it took her a moment to gather her thoughts and put together an answer. Not only was she shocked and angry, she also felt betrayed. "I can't believe she's sharing details about my life. I'm going to have to talk to her about this."

"Talk away. I doubt she'll listen. If you think you can handle taking care of Liam full-time, send Kara away now. Tell her it's for her own safety. She already said she was going to have to rethink working here."

He had a point. Then and there, she knew Kara had to go.

"I'll terminate her employment this afternoon," she said. "For her own safety, of course." Somehow, she'd scrape together some sort of severance, but with her own financial status uncertain, it wouldn't be as generous as she would have liked. She had the household account that Drew had set up for her. Hopefully, there'd be enough money in there to get them through for a while.

Unless he'd emptied that too. Her heart skipped a beat at the thought.

The doorbell announced the arrival of the police.

Eva and Jesse hurried down to meet them. Odd how quickly she'd, at least mentally, begun to think of them as a couple. Dangerous. She needed to be careful to remember he was only her bodyguard.

When she opened the door, she noticed Ted and Beth must have beaten a quick retreat, as their car was gone.

Once Eva had dealt with law enforcement—and this time, they'd called in the ATF and FBI, so it seemed like a ton of people swarming around in her house—Eva went into the kitchen and grabbed a bottle of sparkling water. "It's too early for wine," she joked, offering one to Jesse.

"True," he replied, accepting the water. "I'm not sure how much we can patch up the front of the house. I can nail more plywood across the door and the blown-out window. It's lucky the blast didn't destroy the stairs. Hopefully, we can get an inspection to make sure it didn't make anything structurally unsound."

"Lucky." She took a swig of water. "This feels like I'm living in another dimension or something. As if none of what's happening could possibly be real."

"That's shock." Grimacing, he slugged back some water too. "I get it."

Wishing she didn't feel such a sense of camaraderie with him, when her cell phone rang, she welcomed the distraction. Caller ID showed Unknown Number, but ignoring her usual policy of letting such calls go directly to voice mail, she answered. "Hello?"

"I know what you did," an unfamiliar voice rasped. "Even better, I have real evidence that you killed your husband."

"Who is this?" she demanded. "And I had nothing to do with my husband's murder." She sucked in air, fury rising in her. "Are you the one who shot out my window? And sent the bomb?"

The caller laughed. "No, but I know who did. I'm thinking I'll take him out next. I need you alive, at least for now. If you're dead, you can't give me the information I need."

"What information?" Gripping her phone, she could barely keep up. None of this made any sense.

"Unless you tell me where Drew stashed my money, I'm going to the police."

"Money?" A headache had begun to pulse behind her temples. "I don't have any money. And if you know who's trying to kill me, you need to tell the police."

"Liar." His flat tone told her that he truly believed it. "You have forty-eight hours. I'll call again. If you don't locate my money, you'll be arrested for murder. Oh, and by the way…cute kid. Love that T-shirt with the trains on it. That nanny is pretty hot too, though her pink shirt is a bit low cut, don't you think?"

Then, while she was still trying to process that, he ended the call.

"What was that?" Jesse asked.

Instead of answering, she pushed down panic and sprinted for the playroom. Sure enough, Kara wore a bright pink V-neck T-shirt. And Liam had on his favorite Thomas the Tank Engine T-shirt. She gasped out loud, swiveling around the room, as if she thought she'd suddenly spy a camera.

Of course she saw nothing like that.

Kara and Liam both looked up when she rushed into the room. They watched her as she pivoted, Kara frowning. "Is everything okay?" Kara asked, worriedly.

"Just fine," Eva managed, pasting what she hoped was a convincing smile on her face as she backed out the door. "Sorry to interrupt you."

She backed right into Jesse in the hallway.

"Eva?" Jesse grabbed her arm. "What's going on?"

Keeping her voice low, she told him everything the

caller had said. "He's watching Liam. He knew what both he and Kara were wearing. I can deal with watching out for myself." Her voice rose. "But I can't let anything happen to my son."

"I understand." He pulled her close. "Listen to me. Go back into the playroom and tell Kara to take Liam down to the kitchen. Or somewhere else in the house. I don't care what reason you give her. But I need them out of there so I can search that room. If there's a camera, I'll find it." He sounded 100 percent certain.

She needed to hear that confidence. Taking a deep breath, she went back into the playroom. Smiling that same fake smile, she hoped the nanny would see the seriousness in her eyes or hear it in her voice. "Kara, why don't you and Liam go down to the kitchen and get snacks."

Kara opened her mouth as if to argue but nodded instead. "Come on, Liam." She held out her hand. Liam took her hand and grinned at his mother as he walked past. When he caught sight of Jesse, his grin widened. "Hi, Jesse!" he bellowed.

"Hey, little man," Jesse replied. He bent down and held out his hand for Liam to high-five.

As soon as they were gone, Jesse headed into the playroom. Eva followed, though she stopped just inside the doorway, taking pains to stay out of his way.

He searched the room like he'd done it before, like a professional. She watched as he methodically went through everything, from the toys and pillows to the ceiling fan and lamp. "Nothing," he muttered. "It's got to be here somewhere."

Finally, he pulled a chair over and eyed the air-conditioning vent in the ceiling. Digging in his pocket, he pulled out a pocketknife and used it to remove the screws. "Got it," he declared. He took out a small camera, examining it with interest. "Pretty damn sophisticated. We need to look for these in the rest of the house."

That said, he got down from the chair, dropped the camera on the floor and crunched it to pieces under his boot.

It turned out there were six more cameras placed in vents all through the house. The one in her bedroom bothered her the worst, though she supposed she should count her blessings that Jesse didn't find one in her bathroom.

He destroyed every single camera. "I wonder how long this SOB has been watching you." His voice simmered with anger.

"I don't know." She caught herself about to chew on her fingernail, a habit she'd broken herself of years ago. "But right now, I need to figure out a place to go. I want out of here."

"Shh." He put his finger against her lips. "We'll come up with something, but don't discuss it in here. Just in case I missed one."

Heart skipping a beat, she fought the urge to lean into his touch. Instead, she collected herself and managed to nod. Part of her—the fierce fighter she'd buried deep inside—refused to let herself be scared away. She'd done nothing wrong. This was her home. "From what the caller said, it sounds as if I have two enemies— or Drew did. The caller who wants some mysterious money, and the other person who is, for whatever reason, apparently trying to kill me."

He nodded. "Eva, Drew had more enemies than you could ever guess at."

Stepping back from him, she cocked her head. "How do you know? As far as I could tell, people seemed to like and respect him."

"Come on. Think about your father. Raul surrounds himself with protection. When you get to a certain level of power, there are always people waiting in the wings to try and take you down."

She knew this. And in addition to his own ventures, Drew did have numerous other business dealings. In addition to those concerns, he'd gone and added politics to the mix. Maybe all of it combined had become a tinderbox waiting to ignite. Still, she couldn't help but wonder if whatever he'd been involved in had been worth the ultimate price—Drew's life.

And, since she knew none of the details about any of these dealings, why had Drew's enemies suddenly become hers?

"I get that, but I don't understand why they're taking it out on me and Liam. Liam's just a baby." Even as she protested, she realized she probably knew the answer already. Men like the caller and the bomber considered a wife and a child collateral damage, nothing more.

Chapter 7

Watching his beautiful Eva continually struggle not to fall apart just about destroyed Jesse. She'd always been one of the strongest women he'd ever met. He'd give just about anything right now if he could help her feel safe again. Hell, he'd settle for the right to pull her close and hold her, letting her draw what comfort she could from his embrace.

Fool's dreams. He'd had over two and a half years to get over her. She'd never know how close to rock bottom he'd come, having to let her actually believe that he'd ever choose the motorcycle club over her. Watching her pack that old Impala with all of her earthly belongings, her lush mouth a grim line as she'd avoided even a single glance his way. His shattered heart had left him a hollow shell of a man, yet still he'd stood there and took his punishment, standing in one of the empty garage bays until her taillights disappeared, taking her from his life forever.

Now it seemed they both had been keeping secrets. She'd most likely been pregnant when she'd left, though she might not have known yet. It should have surprised him that knowing she'd kept this secret from him for over two years in no way diminished his love for her, but it didn't. After all, he had his own secrets. No doubt he'd go to his grave loving Eva.

Sometimes, he suspected Raul knew. During the time he'd been apart from her, Jesse had thought he'd kept his pain buried, hidden deep inside, but sometimes he'd caught Eva's father watching him, a thoughtful sort of sympathy on his craggy face. And when Raul had ordered him to go north to Anniversary and become his daughter's bodyguard, Jesse felt certain Raul had known.

Yet Jesse wasn't sure how he'd survive, being around his Eva and her new husband. He'd always considered himself a strong man, but watching the woman he loved with another man would sorely test the limits of that strength.

He could have turned the assignment down, might even have done so, but his handler at the ATF had been thrilled with the idea. Drew Rowson had been on their radar for a while and they jumped at the opportunity for an "in" with him. Since Jesse had given up everything for his job, he'd had no choice but to go.

Part of him had hoped when he saw Eva again, he'd feel nothing. But, of course, that had been an idiotic supposition. One look at her heart-shaped face and caramel eyes and he'd been lost. Still was, actually. And now they'd created a child together. He felt an ache of loss for the family they might have been, had circumstances been different.

When had his life become a soap opera? He suspected that had been the day he first caught sight of Raul Mendoza's beautiful daughter.

Now he needed to continue to put his feelings aside and concentrate on keeping her safe.

"Come with me." Jesse gestured toward the stairs, letting her precede him. Once they were in the destroyed foyer, he marched her past the ruined front door and outside.

"I don't want to take a chance of being overheard."

Arms crossed, she nodded. "I thought you found all the cameras."

"I tried, but I'm not a professional. I've asked the FBI to send in people to sweep your house. They've agreed to do it this afternoon."

"Thank you." Flipping her silky dark hair over her shoulder, she lifted her chin, her eyes flashing. "I'd really prefer not letting these people—whoever they are—drive me from my own home."

Admiration and dismay warred inside him at her words. "Are you sure that's wise? Maybe you could temporarily go stay somewhere else, where you could be safe."

Her shoulders briefly sagged, her defiant posture gone. "No. I managed to keep a few friends, though Drew drove most of them away. I can't ask anyone to take on the kind of danger I'm apparently in. I won't do that to my friends."

"I can respect that." He took a deep breath. "But you have a child involved. Is there someone you trust who can watch over Liam, just until this is over? Someone who lives somewhere else, who wouldn't be on anyone's radar?"

She thought for a moment and then nodded. "I have a friend in northeast Oklahoma. I haven't seen her in a while, but we're best friends. It never matters how long it's been, when we get together, it's like we've never been apart."

"Has she been here, during your marriage to Drew?"

"No." A shadow crossed her face. "Drew preferred that I didn't associate with any of my old friends."

Jesse bit back a curse. Had the bastard really thought of Eva, beautiful, vivacious Eva, as his possession? He'd known men like that, men so insecure in their masculinity that a need to control their wives or girlfriends drove them.

What bothered Jesse even more was apparently Eva had allowed this. The Eva he knew and loved would never have sat still for this kind of nonsense.

Not his problem, not now, not ever, he reminded himself.

"Call her," he said. He dug out his burner phone, knowing there was no way anyone would be monitoring it. "I'm sure once you explain the situation, she won't mind watching over Liam for a few weeks, or at least until this is over."

Though he knew Eva loved Liam more than herself, she still balked. "A few weeks? Do you really think it's going to take that long?"

He gave a deliberately casual shrug. "Who knows? At least give it a shot. I'd feel a lot better if Liam was out of the line of fire. Wouldn't you?"

His deliberate choice of words got to her, as he'd intended them to. She paled, then pulled out her own phone. "I've got to look up the number," she explained. "I can just use my own phone."

"Please don't," he cautioned. "Just in case someone might be listening in on it, you don't want them to be able to trace the call."

Her eyes widened, but she nodded. Once she had her friend's number, she typed it carefully onto his keypad.

Moving away to give her privacy, he strolled down the sidewalk to the front gate. As luxury properties went, this one was not only beautiful, but also amazingly well protected. A six-foot-tall masonry wall isolated the house from the street, with a wrought-iron lockable gate in the middle. On top of the wall, iron stakes made sure anyone would think twice about trying to scale the thing. This stone-and-brick wall continued all the way around the property. It was almost as if when Drew had the place built, he'd known he was going to need security.

At the end of the sidewalk, he turned and surveyed the yard and what he could see of the neighbors' yards. Since forensics had confirmed that the shooter had shot from an elevated position, it had to have been either from in a tree or from inside one of the nearby homes' second stories or roofs. There wasn't any way someone on the street could have made that shot.

But why? The mysterious caller at least made sense. He felt like Drew had stolen his money and would do whatever he had to in order to get it back. However, Jesse didn't understand what anyone would gain by having Eva killed.

Which meant it most likely had to be personal. A girlfriend or mistress, though again, the logic still felt faulty. Drew was dead and killing his wife wouldn't bring him back.

Then why? He should have felt comforted that some of the best criminal investigators in the Bureau were working on this, but he'd been around long enough to know how many cases each person juggled, and what kind of thing took first priority.

Eva appeared to have finished her call. She walked down the sidewalk toward him and held out his phone. "She's willing to take him for however long I need," she said, her expression sad. "Though I don't know how to get him to her. If I take him, someone might follow."

"You can't take him. All of this depends on no one learning where he's gone. Is there any way your friend might be willing to drive down and pick him up? I could reimburse her for gas."

Eva smiled, though her gaze remained solemn. "If I ask Marie, she'll refuse your offer of money. She's proud that way. Her husband, Mike, is a long-haul truck driver. If he's driving a route anywhere near here, she said she's going to ask him to pick up Liam. If not…" She shrugged. "We'll have to work something else out. I'm to call her back in thirty minutes."

He took a deep breath. "How much did you tell her?"

"Enough. She saw on the news what happened to Drew." She swallowed hard. "She says she tried to call me, but she'd lost my number so she left a message with Drew's assistant. I never got it. I filled her in on the shooter and the bomb, as well as the threatening phone call. She has twin girls the same age as Liam, so he'll have someone to play with. He'll think he's on vacation." The sadness in her tone let him know how much she hated the idea of sending her son away.

"It's for his own safety," he reminded her, again battling the urge to take her into his arms.

"I realize that," she replied. "But that doesn't make it any easier."

His burner phone rang, startling him. Pulling it back out of his pocket, he didn't recognize the number. "Hello?"

"Oh." A feminine voice spoke. "I'm trying to reach Eva."

"Just one moment." He handed the phone to Eva. "I think it's your friend."

Eva spoke for a few minutes, her expression both relieved and nervous. When she finished the call, she gave Jesse back his phone. "Her husband is going to be driving home and will detour through here so he can pick up Liam."

He nodded, not sure what to say.

"Please tell me this is a good idea," she pleaded. "Just the thought of my two-year-old riding in a tractor trailer all the way to northern Oklahoma makes me feel sick."

Again, he had to fight the urge to gather her in his arms. Strictly business, he reminded himself. "Since your friend has children, I'm sure her husband can handle Liam. At least that way you won't have to worry about him getting hurt by that psycho who is trying to hurt you."

His words appeared to calm her. She took a few more deep breaths, then straightened her shoulders and grimaced. "True."

They went back inside the house, silent by apparent mutual agreement. Eva disappeared upstairs, while Jesse remained on the lower floor, puttering around and trying to stay busy until the other Brothers of Sin arrived.

The four bikers Raul had sent roared into town that afternoon. They wore their colors proudly, the rumbling of their powerful motorcycles shaking the house.

The sound brought both Jesse and Eva to the great room.

"My reinforcements are here," Jesse said, thrilling despite himself to the sound of the loud bikes. Before he'd taken this assignment, he'd been a weekend motorcycle rider. He'd come to appreciate the feel of a powerful Harley under him and the camaraderie of his fellow bikers.

Hearing them, Eva grimaced. "I'm glad the Rowsons went to a hotel. I can only imagine their reaction."

Jesse shrugged, curious to see whom Raul had chosen to back him up. Throwing open the front door, he headed down the sidewalk to the gate since they'd pulled up and parked in the front of the house.

When he stepped outside the wall, he took quick stock of the new arrivals. Two of the brothers—Shorty and Patches—he knew well, respected and trusted. The other two he didn't know, which meant they must be either relatively new or had been working somewhere else during Jesse's time in Houston.

"Jesse!" Shorty crowed. "Good to see you, man."

They shook hands, clapped each other on the back. Patches came over, hands jammed in his pockets, and waited his turn. The two men couldn't have been more opposite, Shorty with his beer belly and his bowlegged strut and Patches with his angular, tall frame and hunched shoulders.

They were good people, even if they did occasionally walk on the wrong side of the law.

"Do you know Rusty and Baloo?"

"Nope." Turning, Jesse eyed the other two men. Rusty had a long, red beard and full-sleeve tats on both arms while Baloo looked like he idolized Willie Nelson so much he wanted to look like him. They all shook hands, and then Jesse motioned them close while he filled them in on everything that had been going on.

When he'd finished, Shorty nodded. "So it's even worse than Raul knows."

"Yep." Jesse met their gazes, one by one. "Since Raul sent y'all to guard his daughter, I'm going to assume you're among his most trusted and competent men. We haven't told the police about the caller, though they know about the shooter and the bomb. Based on what the prick on the phone says, Eva has two enemies. Him and whoever is trying to kill her. The caller feels Drew owes him money. We're not sure how much or why."

"But no ideas why someone wants Eva dead?" Patches asked, his raspy voice threaded with anger. Eva had grown up with men like Patches and Shorty watching over her. They considered themselves her big brothers.

"None."

As if saying her name had summoned her, Eva came busting through the metal gate. "Shorty!" she hollered, her entire face lit up with joy. "And Patches."

She hugged one and then the other. "Oh, I can't tell how glad I am to see you guys. I've missed y'all so much."

"You shouldn't have just up and disappeared," Shorty rumbled. "We thought Raul was going to self-combust."

Eva nodded and grimaced. Instead of commenting, she turned to face the other two bikers. "Hello," she said, smiling brightly. "I don't believe we've met."

Patches performed the introductions. Both Rusty and Baloo shook Eva's small hand carefully and politely. "We've heard a lot about you," Rusty said, the admiration in his bright blue eyes making Jesse grit his teeth.

Of course, being Eva, she didn't even appear to notice. Shorty and Patches did, and they both shot Rusty warning looks.

"At least with you four here, we can take the offense," Jesse said. "All I've been doing these past couple of days has been strictly defensive." He glanced at their expensive bikes parked at the curb. "But right now, let's see about moving your rides into the garage."

Having the men her father had sent felt like a homecoming. Eva might not want anything to do with life as part of a motorcycle gang, but Shorty and Patches were like her big brothers. As an only, motherless child, she knew all of Raul's men had considered her their little sister. She'd grown up coddled, pampered and challenged by them. Her life, she reflected, had been good. She'd never wanted for anything and Raul had made sure she understood she could be whatever she wanted. All she'd ever desired had been a family of her own. She'd always thought her husband would be part of the motorcycle club, until she'd grown old enough to realize how many illegal activities the club was involved in. That's why she'd asked Jesse to leave with her, to make their life far away from danger and intrigue. When he'd refused, her heart had been broken, so she'd taken steps to get what she wanted on her own.

But she still loved the Brothers.

As for the other two, she might have met them once or twice, but she didn't really know them. BOS had a large membership and while Houston was their head-quarters, many of the members lived and worked in other cities. Rusty and Baloo were from the Austin chapter.

"Austin, huh?" Jesse mused, eyeing the two men as if he wasn't sure he trusted them.

"We helped Raul avenge Nemo's murder," Baloo said, his tone respectful. "As a matter of fact, Rusty and I were the ones who brought that MFB in."

The MFBs were a large rival motorcycle gang. They were violent and unruly. Capturing an MFB without death or serious injury was a feat to be reckoned with. Eva looked at Baloo and Rusty with new respect. "Wow."

"Yeah," Rusty put in quietly. "We turned him over to Raul for justice."

Eva didn't want to ask what her father had done with him. Things like this—trials without a court, law enforcement based on their own, primitive justice—were among the many reasons she'd wanted out of the BOS. And that didn't even scratch the surface.

But just because she wanted no part of the lifestyle didn't mean she didn't love her BOS family.

"I'm thankful my father sent you," she said, meeting each man's gaze individually. "Each and every one of you. I'm going to guess Jesse filled you in?"

"Yes, ma'am," Baloo responded. "And rest assured, we'll protect you with our lives."

"That hopefully won't be necessary," Eva inter-jected. "Since you're apparently good at catching bad guys, I'm guessing that's why Raul chose you. It would seem I have two enemies—or Drew did. Either way, one of them has called me and threatened me, demanding money. And I have no idea what the other one wants, other than to see me dead."

She'd prepared two other bedrooms—the house had six—for the four men to share, bringing in cots and deciding to let them fight it out over who got the bed. Jesse would continue to have his own room, the one closest to the master bedroom and the nursery.

Then, she left them with Jesse to go over strategy while she packed her son's things in preparation for his trip.

Before she could do that, she had a word with Kara, explaining she was going to be let go—for her own safety. The younger woman appeared both relieved and shocked.

"Will you call me when this is over?" Kara asked, her gaze troubled.

"Of course." Eva hugged her. "Why don't you go get packed, and then we'll talk to Liam together."

Liam, being too young to understand, happily waved bye-bye to his nanny. Kara teared up a little, though her mood improved once Eva handed over her paycheck, plus a nice little severance bonus. Eva had checked the balance online, just in case Drew had decided to empty her household account, as well. Luckily, it had remained untouched.

Once Kara had gone, Eva got busy packing for Liam, pushing down constant panic. Just the thought of sending her son away for a few weeks terrified her. Even though Marie was her best friend and she trusted

Mike implicitly, she'd never spent more than a few hours away from her baby.

After Liam woke up from his afternoon nap, she spent the rest of the day playing with him and cuddling with him. They read stories, made his favorite cookies, which she packed for him to take with him, and discussed his upcoming adventure riding in a big truck. She showed him one of his toy trucks as a point of reference.

The entire time she spent with Liam, Jesse stayed out of the way, though she was conscious of his presence out in the hall. When Mike called on Jesse's cell to say he was nearly there and asking if someone would meet him at the nearby Walmart, Jesse took the call and wrote down the information to show her rather than saying anything out loud.

It's time. Her heart sank when she read the words. Reminding herself that she did only what was necessary to keep her precious baby safe, she carried Liam's bags out to her car. With Jesse standing guard, she buckled Liam into his car seat.

"Do you want to drive?" she asked, gripping the car key fob so tightly her palm hurt.

Gently, he pried her fingers apart and took the keys. "Sure. You'll have to direct me once we get out of the subdivision."

She waited until they were in the car and down the street before asking something else that had been on her mind. "What if they have a bug on the car?"

"Then they'll see we get to Walmart." His reassuring smile didn't touch her frantic worry. Logically, she knew her unsettled panic was about sending her son away, but she couldn't seem to calm herself.

Jesse's big hand squeezed her shoulder. "Hey. It's going to be all right. I'm sure you'll get in lots of Face-Time with him. Stop worrying or he might sense your fear and get upset."

That did the trick. She nodded, forced herself to take several deep, calming breaths.

Mike's big rig was already parked on the outer fringe of the store lot, engine idling, running lights on. Jesse pulled up alongside the truck. He turned to Eva, his expression serious. "You know he's going to be okay, right?"

"I know." Her wry smile tugged at his heart. "Liam will probably consider all of this a big adventure. He'll be just fine. I'm not sure I'm going to be though."

Jesse's other cell phone rang while Eva talked to Mike, a big burly man with a neatly trimmed beard who'd shaken Jesse's hand with a firm yet friendly grip. Seeing Raul's number on caller ID, he stepped away to answer.

"What's going on there?" Raul demanded. "I saw she fired the nanny."

"How the heck do you already know that? We haven't even told the other Brothers yet."

Raul snorted. "Social media. That Kara doesn't even have any privacy settings on her posts. It's a good thing Eva got rid of her."

"I have to agree with that." Wondering how much he should tell Raul, he settled on a partial truth. "But Eva let her go mostly because she's sending Liam to stay with a friend."

"Who?" Clearly outraged, Raul all but shouted the

question. Since he'd always had a volatile personality, Jesse wasn't surprised.

"I can't remember the name," Jesse lied, eyeing the scene as Eva got Liam's car seat out of her vehicle and showed Mike how to fasten it in. Since the only choice appeared to be the passenger seat or the sleeper, Jesse wondered what she'd do. He figured the passenger seat would be best, since most likely the Peterbilt didn't have an airbag.

"Find out," Raul barked. "I need to make sure my grandson is safe."

"Come on, Raul. You know Eva's not going to send Liam anywhere she's not one hundred percent positive he's going to be safe."

Though Raul grumbled and muttered a few choice curse words, he finally admitted Jesse was right. "Is she around?" Raul finally asked. "I'll just ask her myself."

"She's with someone right now," Jesse said. "I can ask her to call you back once she's finished."

Raul grumbled again. "Sounds good. I know my boys arrived. How's it going so far?"

"They just got settled. The sheriff's office, FBI and ATF are investigating the bomb and the shooting. I've been trying to talk Eva into going into hiding, someplace safe, at least until they catch the guy. But you know Eva."

"Let me guess. She refuses to let some scumbag run her out of her own home."

Jesse had to chuckle. "You got that right." He didn't tell the other man that when Eva had reacted that way, it had been the first sign he'd seen that the old Eva still existed. He wasn't sure if Raul knew the extent of how much his daughter had changed.

"Well, keep an eye on her and report back to me if anything changes," Raul said. "When all of this settles down, I've got a big job for you."

Normally, Jesse would have been all over that. Big jobs led to big information he could pass on to his handler. "Thanks, I appreciate that. But right now, I just want to focus on keeping Eva safe."

"And I appreciate that, Jesse. I really do." Raul ended the call just as Eva got out of the big cab and turned around, looking for him. The sheer grief-stricken panic on her beautiful face made his heart constrict.

Shoving the phone into his pocket, he strode over to her. Once again, he disregarded his vow and pulled her into his arms. "It's going to be all right," he promised, tenderly smoothing a wayward strand of hair away from her face. "Smile and make sure Liam understands it's all right. You can fall apart once he's gone."

She nodded, straightening her shoulders and exhaling. With a determined smile on her face, she waved at her son, way up there in the cab. Mike had already climbed into the driver's seat and buckled himself in. "I'll call you when we get home," he said. "It should be in about six hours."

"Call that same number," she said, pulling away from Jesse and stepping up onto the running board and leaning in to give Liam one last kiss on his cheek. Clearly excited, the toddler's blue eyes shone.

Finally, Eva stepped down and closed the door. Liam looked so tiny up there in the huge truck. Eva moved to Jesse's side and slipped her hand into his. Together they watched as the big rig pulled away.

Eva refused to leave until the truck had completely vanished from view. Once it had, she shook her head, her stoic expression chiseled in stone. "Let's go."

He drove them back, all the while bracing himself for her breakdown. But she sat still like a statue, staring straight ahead and not speaking.

Chapter 8

Eva's heart didn't break, though she felt like her entire body had shut down. Liam had been the one bright spot in her life, and she wasn't sure how she was going to function without him. She wanted nothing more than to go home, crawl into her bed and pull the covers over her head.

Escape.

Though she'd worked hard to mostly keep it at bay, the darkness once again threatened to drag her down. She knew this had a name—depression—and she'd been fighting it ever since she'd realized her marriage to Drew was nothing but a sham.

Too ashamed to tell anyone, especially Drew, who wouldn't have cared, or her father, who would have cared too much, she'd been battling this alone, refusing to admit even to herself she needed help. She actually made herself feel better when she forced herself to take some kind of action. So she'd asked Drew for a divorce, honestly believing he'd agree since clearly he wasn't willing to even attempt to work things out.

But she hadn't understood what her value was to him. He needed a spouse, a showpiece on his arm, the picture-perfect family to help him look good politically. It was then he brought up her father and the BOS. She hadn't understood the undercurrents of the world her husband moved in. Apparently, Drew had done Raul a favor to pay off some debt, marrying his daughter. When she'd wanted to end it, Drew had refused and threatened to take her son, even though he barely even acknowledged Liam existed. He'd said he couldn't have Raul as an enemy and she would have to stay. Drew had money, reputation and power. He'd told her she'd lose in any court battle, and she'd believed him. With a few words and a sneer, he'd erased that one tiny spark of hope she'd had left.

The darkness had swirled stronger, the howling winds of pain making her numb. Only Liam had been able to break through. And recently, occasionally, Jesse. Around him, she could remember the woman she'd been, fearless and passionate. She'd begun to ache for his touch, burn with wanting, believing he could bring her back to herself. Only the knowledge that she wasn't the kind of woman to use him like that, to hurt him all over again for her own personal gain, stopped her.

In short, she considered herself a mess. All the craziness—Drew's murder, the attacks on her and Liam and the blackmail threats—only made her want to retreat even further into the safe and comforting numbness.

Once she put the funeral and burial behind her, once the police and federal agencies captured the killer and the blackmailer, she promised herself she'd get professional help. She just had to hang on until then. And if there was one thing Eva had gotten good at, it was hanging on.

Right now, she needed to close her eyes and let everything go.

"Eva?" Jesse's voice. She blinked, realizing they'd pulled into her driveway. "We're home."

It all came crashing back. The worry, the fear, the ever-encroaching grayness that struggled to cover her up. Covering her yawn with her hand, she stretched and then unbuckled her seat belt. She'd learned a long time ago if she acted normal, she did better. Glancing at her house, she jumped as a shadowy figure detached himself from the darkness and came toward them.

"It's just Patches," Jesse told her. "He must have outside front duty tonight."

Heart settling back in a normal beat, she got out of the car.

"Hey there," Patches drawled. "So far, everything has been quiet."

"Good. Have the sheriff's deputies been doing regular patrols, like they promised?"

Patches nodded. "I've seen a marked car pass by here twice so far."

"Perfect."

As Eva went to move past him, Jesse reached out and caught her by the arm. "Not so fast. Let me check it out first."

Surprised, she stared. "Why? If we have two men on the perimeter, and two men inside, what's the risk?"

"Better safe than sorry." Jesse gave her arm a light squeeze. "This will only take a minute. Wait here, and I'll be right back."

"I can do it if you want," Patches offered.

"No, you should stay at your post. Keep an eye on Eva for me."

Eva had heard enough. "I'm right here," she said, the flash of anger surprising her. "Quit talking about me as if I'm a child in need of adult supervision. If you want to check out my house, go ahead. But I'll be right behind you."

Jesse froze, his gaze locking on hers. After a moment, he nodded. "You're right. My apologies. Let's go."

She kept up with him as he strode off, leaving Patches staring after them. She didn't care. The anger felt good, actually. Real and honest emotion, definitely better than the all-encompassing numbness.

He flipped on lights, room by room, as they swept through the house. For the first time since she'd moved in here, she realized how huge and sterile the place felt. Drew had hired a professional interior decorator, so very little of the furniture or artwork had been chosen by either of them. Eva had occasionally added a pillow or a knickknack, trying to add some color to the gray, blue and silver color scheme. Drew had removed them the instant he'd seen them, reminding her that they'd paid good money to make sure everything matched. After a while, she'd stopped trying.

The other two bikers were upstairs in the den, watching television instead of keeping watch, which bothered the hell out of her. Though she really didn't want a lot of company, especially tonight when she had to learn how to function without her son, she did need them to do their jobs and help keep her safe.

Jesse recognized the problem immediately. "Don't you two have something else you should be doing?" he asked, with a pointed glance toward the door. "Aren't you supposed to be keeping watch?"

Exchanging guilty looks with each other, the men jumped to their feet and hurried out of the room. One of them muttered an apology as he went.

Once they were gone, she had no idea what to do with herself. She knew if she got too still, she'd miss Liam way too much.

In fact, she needed a distraction. Maybe tonight would be a good time to start going through Drew's papers.

"Are you okay?" Jesse asked. "You look a little lost."

About to confide the truth, that she was, she shrugged instead. "I need to straighten out my finances," she said. "Finding out Drew cleaned out the joint savings account was a shock. And then there's that man who threatened blackmail unless I pay him what he feels Drew owed him."

Judging from the compassion in Jesse's eyes, he understood anyway, even though he didn't say. "You know, we need to find out why that caller thinks Drew owes him money," Jesse said.

"I agree. But how?"

"Ask him next time he calls. I mean, come on. Does he really expect you to take him at his word? Tell him you need details, proof. Anyone could call and claim a dead man owes them money. You have a right to expect facts."

"You're right. I do." She took a deep breath, before deciding to go ahead and state an ugly possibility. "But what if Drew and he were involved in something illegal?"

For a second, Jesse froze. He blinked and dragged his hand through his hair, making her wonder what he knew. "Do you think that's a possibility?" he asked, his expression seeming to be carefully blank.

"Do you?" she asked, hoping to catch him by surprise.

He recoiled slightly. "Eva, I barely knew Drew. I have no idea what he might have been involved in."

She thought she knew Jesse well enough to know when he was lying, but what he said made sense. Though technically, Jesse had worked for Drew, Raul had sent him when Drew had asked for a bodyguard. Drew had pointedly ignored Jesse and vice versa.

"You knew him the best," Jesse pressed. "Is there any chance your husband might have been involved in something illegal?"

"Though I hate to admit it, you never know. Drew kept a lot of secrets. That's the reason he had his own bank accounts and why I was surprised that he emptied our joint one. Clearly, he needed money for something. But what specifically, I have no idea."

"Even more reason to find out."

Since Jesse might be the only person she could trust right now, with the exception of her father, she decided to ask for his help. "I'd like to go through his papers in his office. Once we're finished doing that here, I'd like to check out his office downtown."

"I think that's a great idea," Jesse replied. "I wouldn't mention this to Lori just yet. It might be better if you surprised her."

Since she hadn't yet reached a decision about whether or not to trust Drew's campaign manager and assistant, she nodded. "Agreed. Do you mind helping me look? You might see something I miss."

"Of course not. When do you want to start?"

"Now. I need something to keep me busy and distract me from worrying about Liam."

A shadow crossed his handsome face, making her wonder. But when he smiled a second later, the kind of smile that made his eyes sparkle and sent a jolt of awareness right through her, she had to wonder if she'd imagined it. Probably so, projecting her own worries onto him.

"Great. Let's get started." After fetching them both a bottled water, she led the way back to Drew's office. Jesse stayed behind her, not too close, but not allowing any great distance either.

"Why are the other two Brothers watching TV upstairs?" she asked, curious. "Why aren't they helping Patches outside?"

"I gave them shifts," he said. "Mostly perimeter guard duty. They're working two on and two off. Patches and Rusty are on tonight. Shorty and Baloo will take over in the morning."

Organized, she thought. Just like her father. Of course, Raul had taken Jesse under his wing and no doubt trained him.

At the end of the hall, she opened the heavy oak door that led to Drew's space. It felt weird to enter the room, since she'd made it a point to stay out of his area.

Jesse whistled as they stepped inside. "This is a hell of a man cave."

Turning slowly, she swept her gaze over the room. "It is," she agreed. "He used it to entertain clients or backers a lot. Only when it was just the men. When their wives accompanied them, we tended to stick to the rest of the house."

He cocked his head, considering. "I'm sensing you didn't come in here often."

She shrugged. "I didn't. Early on in our marriage, Drew let me know of his need for a private space. This was it."

Expression inscrutable, he watched her. "Did you have one too?"

"I didn't need one," she admitted. "When Drew was home, he pretty much kept to himself in here. The rest of the house was mine."

"Sounds lonely."

Despite the sympathy she saw in his gaze, she didn't want to talk about her marriage. Not with him. Especially not with him. "Let's get started with the file cabinets," she said instead of answering. One tall five-drawer cabinet sat on each side of the long mahogany credenza behind the desk. "I'll take the right, you take the left. If you find anything that even remotely seems questionable, please put it on the desk for us to look at later."

"Sounds like a plan," he replied, trying the handle. "Except it's locked."

"He kept them locked, though I'm not sure why. Maybe he thought the cleaning people might get nosy."

Jesse met her gaze. "Or he was worried about you looking at documents he didn't want you to see."

"No, he told me where he kept the key." She swallowed, suddenly feeling worried. "He actually said in case something happened to him. It makes me wonder if he knew something."

"You mean like a premonition?"

"Maybe. Or there might have been earlier threats and he didn't tell me."

She could tell this possibility intrigued Jesse. "Well, hopefully if that's the case, he kept some sort of record of them. That might help narrow down a list of potential suspects."

"He probably did. Drew kept records of everything." She shook her head, remembering. "He even kept a notebook logging what suits and ties he wore to events. He didn't like to repeat himself too often."

Jesse laughed. The rich warmth of the sound felt out of place here, inside the solemnness of Drew's sanctuary. She forced herself to look away, focusing on the oversize desk.

"I actually believe his will is in here, in one of the file cabinets, not at his office like Lori thinks. I could be wrong. I guess we'll find out."

Opening the desk drawer, she located the key. Drew hadn't bothered to hide it because he knew she'd respected his wish for a private space.

Once she'd unlocked the left side, she moved over to the right. They were identical and shared the same key, though it took her several tries to unlock the second one. Once she had, she pulled out the bottom drawer and sat on the floor in front of it. "Let's get to work."

A moment later, Jesse pulled out a drawer and did the same thing.

She'd chosen to work on the right-hand side because

Drew had told her that was where he kept his personal files. The side she'd given to Jesse was for business and political files, at least according to Drew.

They spent an hour sifting through paper in companionable silence. She'd finished with the bottom two drawers and decided to take a break before moving on to the next one.

Standing, she stretched and eyed Jesse. He was so engrossed in reading something that he didn't even notice.

"Did you find something interesting?" she asked, moving closer.

"Maybe." He glanced up at her, frowning. "Did you and Drew sign a prenup?"

"No. We talked about doing one, but never got around to drafting it." She didn't tell him they'd gotten married only when she'd realized she was pregnant. Drew had just put out his political feelers for running for governor and had been informed he needed a wife and family pronto. The timing had been perfect for them both.

Odd how what had seemed perfectly logical at the time now seemed kind of pathetic.

"That's weird," Jesse said. "Because this file contains a prenup, but it's for Drew and someone else."

Jesse handed Eva the document, watching as she read it. She didn't react, at least not in any outward fashion. She simply flipped to the second page and then the third, before starting over and reading the entire thing again.

"It's dated before I married him," she finally said,

as if the date explained everything. "Though I have no idea who Chris might be."

"You don't know a Christine or maybe a Crystal?" he asked, figuring he might as well probe a bit deeper. "Did you know Drew was seriously involved with someone right before your marriage?"

Meeting his gaze, she slowly shook her head. "No. Drew never mentioned anything about a Chris. At all. But then again, he and I never really discussed our previous relationships."

Which meant Drew had no idea Jesse and Eva had been together, unless Raul had told him. He'd wondered about that. "Is it possible Drew and Chris might have been married previously?"

Eva appeared shell-shocked. "It's possible, I guess. Anything is possible at this point." She shook her head.

"I'll need to ask Lori," Eva continued. "She's been with Drew a long time and I'll bet she knew."

Jesse nodded. He thought back to the complete dossier he'd read on Drew Rowson. There had been nothing in there about a previous relationship. Which seemed like a huge oversight. Especially since it had been serious enough to warrant drawing up a prenup.

Eva put the documents aside. "We'll stack anything else unusual here. Let's keep going. We might find more about my husband's past that I didn't know."

Eyeing her, he wondered at the lack of bitterness or rancor in her voice. What the hell had happened between her and Drew? The Eva he knew had been passionate about what she loved. She would never have shrugged off learning her spouse clearly had a past of which she knew nothing.

She turned away, immediately diving back into the

files. He watched her for another heartbeat or two, before doing the same himself.

The pile of questionable documents grew only slightly. There were some papers that seemed to indicate hidden bank accounts in the Caymans that he wished like hell he could figure out a way to photograph without Eva noticing. Since he couldn't, he settled for hoping he could get back to them later.

Finally, after over three hours of sifting and sorting, Eva stretched and announced she'd had enough for one night. He looked up and nodded, saying he wanted to finish going through this one file. He held his breath, hoping she'd leave him alone long enough to snap a few pics of the bank information, but she only dropped back into the desk chair and asked him to please hurry up.

"You don't have to wait," he said, pushing. "I can join you once I'm finished."

Looking down at her hands, which she'd begun twisting in her lap, she didn't move. Finally, she raised her head. The naked emotion in her gaze hit him like a punch to the gut. "I'll wait," she said softly. "Right now, I don't want to be alone."

Swallowing past the ache in his throat, he nodded. "I'll hurry, then."

When he finished, he carefully closed the file cabinet and headed toward the door, waiting while she closed it after him, using a key she pulled from her jeans pocket to lock it. "I don't want anyone else to have access to that room," she said, correctly interpreting his surprise. "I'm still hoping to find the original copy of his will, even though Lori seems to think it's at the office."

"Why?" he asked, deciding to be blunt. "What's

everyone's interest in the will? Texas is a community property state, so there's really not a whole lot he can do to cut you out."

"True. But you saw that other prenup. There could be other women in his past. Who knows if he had other assets or possessions he wants them to have?"

"What aren't you telling me?" he pushed. "Something isn't adding up. I caught that his parents seemed awfully intent on finding the will. What is everyone expecting to find out?"

She sighed. "If you really want to know, I think Drew was involved in a long-term relationship with someone else. For all I know, it might have been with this Chris woman. Clearly, for whatever reason, he couldn't or wouldn't marry her. But that doesn't mean he didn't want her to have something after he was gone."

"If he loved her, why on earth would he have married you?"

His sharp comment made her wince. "I loved you yet I married him," she replied. "You know as well as anyone that sometimes love isn't enough." With a sigh, she brushed her hair away from her face. "All Drew ever wanted was a career in politics. Everything he did—including his job and his friends—was a means toward that end. I might be the daughter of a biker club president, but my father is powerful and has well-connected friends. To all appearances, my dad operates completely above the law. He has the ability to call in favors from a lot of prominent people, including high-ranked politicians. Drew married me for that reason alone. Maybe this Chris, whoever she is, wouldn't have helped his political aspirations. She might even have hindered it."

"That's cold-blooded," he said, before he thought. "Did he actually tell you he married you for that reason?" And if he had, how had Eva, passionate, volatile Eva, been able to accept that? The Eva he knew would never have settled for being second best.

But the Eva he'd known was no longer in existence.

"He did," Eva answered, though she wouldn't meet his gaze.

Back in the main part of the house, Eva went to the kitchen and began reorganizing the pantry. At least this trait of hers remained the same—she'd always liked to keep busy to help distract her. Which relieved him. He'd been worried she'd wander around the empty house like a lost ghost missing her son.

His cell phone rang and she lit up. "It's Mike," she said. Glancing at the caller ID, he saw she was correct, so he handed it to her. She took a deep breath before answering. To his surprise, she put the call on speakerphone so Jesse could hear.

Mike sounded chipper, letting her know they'd stopped for dinner at a hamburger joint east of Tulsa. He put Liam on the line, and Eva carried on an earnest conversation—from the sound of it mostly toddler babble—with the boy. Judging by the jubilant excitement in his high-pitched voice, Liam viewed it all as a great big adventure. His boisterous responses put a smile on Eva's face. But even that was tinged with sadness, because the instant she ended the call, she burst into tears.

Handing him his phone, she turned her back to him, and left the kitchen for the den, shoulders silently shaking while she cried. He stared for one long moment, then muttered a curse and followed her. Vow be damned. He couldn't stand to see Eva hurting so badly.

"Come here," he muttered, walking up behind her and gently turning her to face him. "It's going to be all right."

She made a sound, a low moan like an animal in pain. Her gaze locked with his and held. Her lips parted and then she reached up and cupped both hands alongside his face. She pulled him to her, crushing her mouth to his. Instead of tenderness, she kissed him with raw need, her hunger for him electrifying.

Fire ignited, zinging in his veins, short-circuiting everything but the seductive feel of this woman in his arms. *His* woman, her mouth warm, her tongue mating with his. She pushed herself into him, moving them backward, until he stumbled and fell back into the overstuffed chair, pulling her down, almost on top of him.

This didn't faze her at all. Instead, her eyes gleaming, she straddled him. She gave a soft, sexy laugh, the sound so reminiscent of the Eva he loved that his body responded instantly. She kissed him again, her mouth continuing to move over his in deep, drugging kisses full of passion, full of soul. He slipped his hands up her arms, her skin so silky soft, not sure if he meant to hold her in place or bring her closer. She decided for him, pushing her lush body into his, rubbing up against him, her sensual movements both an unbearable temptation and a demand for more.

He tried to think, to remember his vow and all that separated them, but she moved again, this time in a circle, the heat of her right on top of him, and he lost the capacity for rational thought. Another jolt of arousal had his pulse pounding, his body responding by surging even more in immediate readiness. He wanted her, oh, how he wanted her, needed her, craved her. Because he'd never forgotten the way their bodies fit together, how she'd always cried out with pleasure when he was inside her, and the way they'd somehow instinctively known how to move to bring each other to the peak at the same time.

He had no doubt he'd go to his grave remembering this. He knew he'd never stop wanting her, and the way she could bring him to his knees.

And still, still, even as his body throbbed and he arched into her, he tried his best to resist. "We shouldn't—" he began.

She touched him then, stroking him through his jeans in that way she knew would set him on fire. He swallowed hard, his fingers moving over her skin of his own accord, sliding down one hip, cupping one full breast. He ached to taste her and more.

"Eva…" He tried again, his voice raspy with desire. "Maybe we should slow down. Think about if you really want to do this. You've been through a lot and—"

"Shh." She kissed him again, still moving against him as if she couldn't control her own body. "Make love with me, Jesse. I need you. I need you to make me feel alive again," she whispered, her breath hot against his ear. She moved herself in another circle, her heat caressing his arousal, and he could barely think.

"Alive?" he managed, wondering how she could feel anything but. She arched her back, yanking her T-shirt over her head, and then her bra. Her full breasts spilled free, and even as he leaned forward to suckle one engorged nipple, she pushed up off him. Standing, she shimmied out of her jeans, then her panties, which he couldn't help but notice were black lace and sexy as hell.

When she stood naked in front of him, he forgot all about her underwear, because Eva was every bit as gloriously curvy and as sensual as he remembered.

"Your turn," she ordered, her smoldering gaze making promises he couldn't wait for her to keep. Swallowing hard, he divested himself of his clothes as rapidly as possible. When he also stood naked, his fierce arousal jutting strong and thick, she licked her lips, sending another jolt right to his core.

"The couch?" he asked, reaching for her. But she shook her head and shoved him back into the chair.

"No. Here." Once again she straddled him, shimmying just enough before she slid her body over his. Warm and wet, she sheathed him tightly. Inside her felt so much like going home, he nearly wept.

Instead, he began to move.

They burned, they touched, their dance of desire bringing smoldering ashes to a raging inferno. She destroyed him, and yet remade him, reaching for the pinnacle even as the flames seared his soul.

When she began to shudder, her body clenching, molten honey flowing, he let his tenuous control go and reached for his own climax, finding it with her.

Chapter 9

Eva lay in Jesse's strong arms while their breathing slowed and perspiration dried on their overheated skin. She regretted many things in her life, but this would never be one of them. For the first time in what seemed like forever, she felt alive. Gloriously, sensually alive.

Jesse might not be part of her future, but he was no longer only in her past. She wanted to live in the present, right here, right now, as long as she could.

However, she remained enough of a clearheaded pragmatist to understand that in the end, nothing would have changed between them. Jesse had made his choice. And she'd made hers. If he continued to demand a DNA test to determine Liam's parentage, she'd comply. And if Liam turned out to be Jesse's son, they'd work something out as far as visitation, if

Jesse wanted that. And if he didn't, well, she'd do her best to understand.

She stirred, her body still entangled with Jesse's, and wondered why life had to be complicated.

"We'd better cover up," Jesse said, kissing the hollow at the base of her throat where the pulse still beat erratically. "Pretty soon the guys are going to change shifts and I'm thinking we don't really want them to see us naked."

"The guys." Horrified, she glanced at the windows, relieved to see the blinds were closed. "I can't believe I forgot all about them. We're lucky they didn't walk in on us."

He glanced at the stairs and nodded. "While I'm sure they respect me—and you—enough to turn themselves around and hightail it back up the stairs, maybe next time, we should try this in the bedroom with the door closed."

Next time. Heaven help her, but she couldn't quite bring herself to tell him there wouldn't be a next time. Reluctantly, she rolled away and grabbed for her clothing, fumbling as she got dressed under his watchful gaze.

She'd just tugged the shirt over her head when Jesse stirred and pushed himself up, tugging on his underwear and his jeans with slow, deliberate motions designed to draw her gaze. She couldn't help but watch, her mouth dry and need blooming in her as if she hadn't just slaked it.

"How about a beer?" Jesse asked, once he'd gotten fully dressed. She shrugged and led the way into the kitchen. Opening the fridge, she handed him a cold can before deciding she'd rather have a glass of wine.

Luckily, she had a wine fridge, so she pulled out a bottle, grabbed her electric corkscrew and opened a nice Riesling. After pouring herself a glass, she took a seat across from him at the kitchen table, hoping he didn't try to discuss what had just happened between them.

When the landline phone rang, she jumped, almost welcoming the distraction. "No one uses that number. It's got to be the blackmailer."

"Wait." Jesse jumped up and grabbed some kind of electronic apparatus from the kitchen counter. "It's plugged into the phone line," he said. "Just keep him on the line long enough for me to get a location."

Taking a fortifying gulp of wine, she nodded. "I'll try." And then she took a deep breath and answered the phone.

"Your time is up," the caller said, his voice both gleeful and threatening. The combination sent a shiver down her spine. "Do you have my money?"

"About that," she replied, glancing at Jesse and wondering how she could still find him magnificently sexy in the middle of this. He'd put on headphones and pushed a button on the small machine. Seeing her watching, he gave her a thumbs-up.

"We need to talk about your request for money," she continued, her voice firm enough that she felt it didn't betray her nervousness.

Interrupting her, the man snarled, "You don't have it, do you?"

Instead of shrinking away from the malice in his tone, she kept her voice strong. "First off, how do I even know Drew really owed you anything?"

Pushing back felt pretty liberating, actually. "I mean, anyone could call me up and insist my husband owed them money. How do I even know if that's true? If I took everyone at their word, I'd be handing out money left and right. I'm afraid you're going to need proof."

"Proof?" he repeated, incredulous. "You want proof?"

"Yes. You need to back up your claim. Otherwise, I'm afraid I'll have to consider you just another crackpot trying to benefit from a widow and her horrible loss."

Silence. When he spoke again, his voice had gone low and simmered with fury. "I warned you what would happen if you didn't pay. Don't try to stall me. Do you really want me to go to the media and the police with evidence that you're a murderer?"

"Go ahead," she shot back. "Since I had nothing to do with Drew's death, I'm really interested to see this so-called evidence. Either put up or shut up."

Again, it appeared she'd stunned him into silence. She looked over at Jesse, grinning.

"Keep him on the line," he mouthed.

"Cat got your tongue?" she taunted when the caller still didn't speak. "Come on, it's not that hard. If Drew legitimately owes you money, you should be able to come up with something to document your claim. Otherwise, you need to go away and leave me alone."

One second passed, and then another. "I'll get your proof," he said. "But you won't like it. Goodbye." And he ended the call.

Disappointed, she hung up the phone. "Was that long enough?" she asked.

"No." He made a face. "I just needed a few more

seconds. However, I'm going to let the FBI know he called you again."

She nodded. "Can't they get in touch with my carrier and find out the caller's number?"

"They could. But most likely he either used a burner phone—one that's untraceable—or blocked his number. What showed up on your caller ID?"

"Unknown Caller." She tried not to be too glum. "Which means he blocked his number, right?"

"Probably." Jesse didn't appear too concerned. "Don't worry, we'll figure it out. He's actually not the one I'm concerned with."

"What do you mean?"

"He even admitted he's not the one trying to hurt you, though he claims to know who is. I'm more worried about the guy who took out your window and tried to blow you up."

Put that way... "I agree. Do you have any idea what the police are doing to try and catch him?"

He shook his head. "Unfortunately, I'm not in their inner circle. I know your father has a lot of powerful friends and I'm sure he's pulling strings to make sure they take quick action."

"I know all about my father's friends," she replied, trying to keep the bitterness out of her voice. "Most of them are involved in something shady. I wouldn't trust them as far as I can throw them."

"You don't have to. All I care about right now is catching the murderer and the man who keeps calling you wanting money. I'm beginning to suspect those two might be the same person."

Narrowing her eyes, she took another sip of wine.

"What about the third person who shot out the window and sent a bomb?"

"I really think there aren't a bunch of people out there trying to hurt you," he said, surprising her. "It's likely one and the same guy. He's just trying to mess with your head and make you think you have legions of enemies."

She replayed those words as she lay in her bed alone, hours later, trying to sleep. Oddly enough, they helped. She managed to drift off and didn't wake again until seven.

Her mood was vastly improved—maybe due to the amazing sex, or the idea that she might be dealing only with one psychotic killer. She went through her morning routine humming, a smile on her face. Freshly showered and dressed, makeup and jewelry on, she felt prepared to face whatever the day threw at her.

When she headed for the kitchen, she realized Jesse was already there. Her smile faltered—should she act like nothing had happened? Deciding to take her cue from him, she bid him a cheery good-morning and headed for the coffee maker.

He barely looked up from his phone. While she waited for her cup to brew, she willed her heartbeat to slow. At least he didn't want to have a deep discussion about their relationship before she had her first jolt of caffeine. She didn't either. Actually, she hoped he wouldn't mention it at all. She dreaded telling him nothing had changed. His silence was a good thing. Despite that, her good mood vanished.

At eight, the doorbell chimed. Eva had just taken a sip of her first cup of coffee as Jesse finished his.

"Now what?" she groaned. It could only be either

the Rowsons or Lori. She needed at least another hour before she would even begin to feel ready to face dealing with reality. She hadn't slept well, waking frequently and worrying about her son.

"I'll get it," Jesse told her, setting down his mug on the counter.

Grateful, she nodded and closed her eyes, breathing in the wonderful scent of fresh-brewed coffee. Jesse knew she wasn't much of a morning person and needed time to get going.

A few seconds later Jesse returned with her father at his side. Lori Pearson walked a few steps behind the men, her high heels clicking on the tile floor.

"Come here, baby girl," Raul said, grinning and opening his arms.

Unexpected tears stung the back of her eyes as she jumped up and rushed to her father.

"I got you," Raul said, patting her back. He grinned at Jesse. "Whatever else my daughter might be, she's still a daddy's girl."

Slightly embarrassed, she nodded, wiping at her eyes before stepping back. "What are you doing here?" she asked.

"Do you really have to ask?" he huffed, his expression wounded. "How could you think I'd stay away while someone attacks you? You know better than that."

"And he brought doughnuts," Jesse interjected, grinning as he placed the box in the middle of the table. "Which is perfect. Carbs always help you wake up faster."

Heaven help her, she blushed, which earned both her father's and Lori's interested stares.

"Would you like coffee?" she asked, including Lori in her question. Drew's assistant dragged her gaze away from Raul long enough to nod.

Glad she had something to do, Eva made two cups of coffee. Black for her father, and one cream, one sugar for Lori. As she handed her father his, she couldn't help but notice the way Drew's assistant watched Raul. Hero worship? Or something else?

She told herself it was none of her business and gestured at the table. "Sit. Let's drink some coffee and have a doughnut or two. I didn't sleep well last night, so I need some time to wake up."

"Hmmph." Pulling out a chair, Raul dropped into it. Like everything he did, the gesture seemed large and dramatic. Once, she'd been like that too. "Some things never change, do they, *mija*?"

Helping herself to a doughnut—maple frosting, her favorite—she ignored that. She waited until everyone was seated before biting into it, barely suppressing a small moan of pleasure. Chewing and swallowing, she looked up to find Jesse watching her intently, his gaze hot.

Everyone had a doughnut except Lori, who sipped her coffee and vacillated between shooting worshipful glances at Raul and appraising ones at Jesse. She had a manila folder in front of her and she kept one perfectly manicured hand resting on top of it.

When she realized Eva watched her, Lori pasted on a confident smile. "I got everything handled that you asked me to. Since you chose to have the funeral on Friday afternoon, all the local networks have been notified so they can cover it." She shuffled through some papers. "Oh, and I let the Rowsons know so they can make plans with any other family members."

"What about Chris?" Jesse asked, his casual expression not fooling Eva.

Lori blinked, a fleeting look of panic crossing her face before she vanquished it. "Chris?"

"Yes. Drew's friend Chris."

Lori dropped her eyes, again riffling through papers. When she raised her face again, her expression seemed resolute. "I'm not sure who you mean. If you can give me a last name, I'll see what I can do."

"Never mind." Jesse reached for another doughnut. "I'll take care of it myself."

"What's going on here?" Raul looked from Jesse to Lori before his gaze settled on Eva. "Who's Chris?"

Eva opened her mouth to answer but Jesse forestalled her. "It's not important," he said. "Lori, is there anything else you need? If not, I think you should go. We have important things to discuss."

Her lips tightened. "Since when does a bodyguard give orders around here? I was Drew's campaign manager and personal assistant and one of the few people he trusted implicitly."

"Good for you," Jesse drawled. "I'm sure that's why you won't tell us about Chris."

Lori met his stare with one of her own. "Tell me what you know. I can confirm or deny any misinformation."

Suppressing a flash of anger, Eva set her cup down with a loud thunk. "I've had enough," she said, noting the surprise flash in Lori's eyes. "What's with the secrecy? Drew is dead. Why protect his secrets now?"

"I don't know what you're talking about." Lori drew

herself up. "And I'm offended that you would treat me as if I am hiding something."

Both Jesse and Raul watched the two women with interest. Eva would have said more if her father hadn't been present. For now, she decided to let it go. "Thank you for all your help," she told Lori. "I really appreciate it. This has been a stressful time, and it's possible I've received some misinformation. I'm sorry if I've offended you."

Lori accepted the apology with a dip of her chin. "Here," she said, sliding the folder across the table to Eva. "All the details of both the funeral and burial are in here. If there's not anything else…" She pushed to her feet, stalking toward the exit without waiting for Eva to reply.

About to say she'd be needing access to Drew's business office, Eva decided to wait. If she gave the other woman fair warning, Lori would have time to do a purge of any incriminating documents.

At the kitchen doorway, Lori spun around. "Nice to see you again, Mr. Mendoza. If you need my assistance with any of Drew's final business dealings, you know how to find me."

Raul nodded, his mouth full. He didn't bother to even glance her way.

Jesse got up. "Let me show you out."

"No, thank you." Lifting her brightly painted lip in a sneer, she strode toward the front door. A moment later, she slammed it behind her.

"Lock it," Raul ordered. "I'm glad we got rid of her. Drew might have trusted her, but I've never liked that woman. And we've got some important things to discuss."

* * *

Jesse admired the way Eva rose to the occasion with Drew's snippety assistant. For the first time since he'd been here, he swore he caught a glimpse of the old Eva.

"What's this about threatening phone calls, blackmail and bombs?" Raul asked Eva, his thick brows drawn into a thunderous frown.

"I'm sure Jesse filled you in," she replied, taking another deep drink of her coffee. "Isn't that why you sent Patches, Shorty, Rusty and Baloo?"

"I'm impressed you remember their names."

"You shouldn't be," she shot back. "I might have wanted out of the BOS lifestyle, but the Brothers will always be my family."

Raul nodded his approval. "I would have liked to see my grandson. Maybe next time."

"You should have come earlier." She kept her voice low.

"I would have, but the place was crawling with Feds and cops. You know how uncomfortable that makes me feel." Raul turned his attention to Jesse. "Did you sweep the house for bugs or video recorders?"

"Yes." Jesse told him what he'd found. "I disabled everything, but the FBI has sent an expert to check it out, just in case I missed anything."

Though Raul made a face at the mention of the FBI, he didn't disagree. Instead, he turned toward his daughter, his expression serious. "Eva, I have a pretty good idea of the name of the man who's been calling you asking for his money. Were you aware of Drew's business dealings with the Mexican cartels?"

Eva recoiled, her expression horrified. "The Mexican *drug* cartels? Drew would never do anything like that. He was running for public office."

"I'm guessing he believed he could keep it secret. Drew was heavily involved with them."

"Doing what?" Eva demanded, her gaze furious. "So help me, if you tell me that my husband was dealing drugs, I'm going to break something."

Raul held up a hand, a diamond pinkie ring flashing. "No need for that. He laundered their money."

Eva glanced at Jesse. "Did you know about this?"

How to answer. Since he had known, both from Raul and intel he'd received from his handler, he decided to stick to the truth. "Yes. I knew."

After stewing on this for a moment, Eva shook her head. "Let me guess. While Drew was laundering their money, some of it went missing."

"Bingo," Raul replied. "How did you know?"

"Lucky guess. Especially since the caller kept insisting Drew had stolen his money." She took a deep breath. "Do you know how much money is missing?"

Jesse had heard rumors, but he wanted to hear Raul confirm them.

"Three million dollars," Raul said. "And word on the street is that Drew had an accomplice. That person is the one who probably has the money."

"One thing doesn't make sense," Eva said. "Drew cleaned out all his bank accounts. Why would he do that if he'd stolen that much money?"

"He probably intended to flee. Leave town."

Eva responded exactly as Jesse knew she would. "No. Becoming the governor of Texas was really important to Drew. He'd never run away from that."

Raul shrugged. "He might if someone put a hit out

on him. These cartels are dangerous. Drew should have known better than to try and cheat them."

"Dad, were you the one who set Drew up with them? I know you have a few business dealings of your own with the cartels."

Glancing around the room, Raul gave the tiniest shake of his head. Jesse got it immediately. The older man worried about the possibility that some recording devices remained. He wasn't about to incriminate himself.

"Of course not." Raul's hearty response made Eva start. "You know better than that. I don't have dealings with any drug cartels."

Eva narrowed her eyes but didn't respond. Clearly, she understood why her father would say something so patently false. Since Jesse had been deeply involved with the Brothers of Sin, he understood Raul's remark to be technically true. As leader of the motorcycle club, Raul took great pains to keep his hands clean. Or at least the appearance of that. Since he controlled every aspect of the club's business dealings, including anything to do with the cartels, the ATF and their partners at the FBI considered him accountable. But Jesse had seen with his own eyes the way Raul insisted his men present him with information. He trusted a few of his top lieutenants to take care of things and required reports only when something went wrong. Which rarely happened.

Privately, Jesse thought Raul intended to retire soon. The wind had seemed to go out from under his sails once his daughter had left.

"What about Lori?" Jesse asked, deciding to go with his gut instinct. "Is there any possibility she might be

Drew's accomplice? Maybe she wanted all the money for herself, so she arranged to have him killed."

Both Eva and her father stared at him, Raul with his eyes narrowed in speculation and Eva with open shock and dismay.

"It's possible," Raul allowed.

"No, it's not," Eva countered. "Drew had zero interest in Lori. Believe me, I could tell."

Jesse decided it would be best not to argue that point. Apparently, so did Raul.

"Anyway, what about Chris?" Eva asked, filling her father in on the old prenup agreement they'd found. "Do you have any idea who Chris might be?"

Raul shook his head. "Have you looked through the names of Drew's office and campaign staff? Maybe he had a Chris working for him."

"I checked," she admitted wryly. "No Chris. I'm less worried about that than I am about this person who keeps calling me and demanding a lot of money. Since I don't have it, I just wish he'd go away."

"Do you want me to pay him off?" her father asked. "I have access to that kind of money."

"No." Her response came out a bit too harsh, so she softened her tone. "I do not. To begin with, I have no idea what he's talking about. It could all be some sort of get-rich-off-the-poor-widow scheme."

Raul grunted. "Maybe, but I think it's more likely that Drew decided to keep some of the dough he was laundering. Stuff like that don't fly with the cartel boys."

She thought for a moment. "If that was the case, then why is this person calling me? Wouldn't it be the cartel instead? Or do you think he works for the cartel?"

Her comment had her father grimacing. "Honey, you don't want the cartel after you, believe me. I'll tell you what. I'll personally find out who has been calling you and have some of my guys pay him a visit," he promised. "He will never bother you again."

"No. I don't want any part of murder or illegal intimidation."

Raul looked wounded. "Who said anything like that? I would never…"

Jesse had to admit the man was good. But Eva knew her father well and was having none of his act.

"Dad, I want to let law enforcement deal with that guy. Not only are the local police involved, but the FBI and, thanks to the bomb, the ATF are too."

Making a face, Raul shrugged. "How about while you let them bumble around doing their job, you come visit me. At least there, I know you'll be safe."

Eva looked down. For one moment, Jesse thought she might actually be considering her father's offer. But when she raised her head, he saw the answer written in her stubborn expression.

"I'm not letting anyone chase me out of my own home," she said. "I've done nothing wrong or illegal, and if my husband stole money, I didn't know anything about it."

Raul sighed. "I kind of expected you to say something like that. But, honey, even if you are totally innocent in all this, do you really think that makes a difference to the bad guys? Think of your son. If something happens to you, he'll be an orphan."

Talk about bringing the big guns to bear. Eva's proud expression fell. For a moment, she appeared shattered, devastated by the horrible possibility her father outlined.

Jesse had to suppress a surge of anger at Raul. While he understood—and even respected—the older man's reasoning, he hated seeing Eva hurt. Even for her own good.

"Nothing will happen to me," she declared, her voice steady and strong. "Jesse will make sure of that."

Jesse felt like he'd been punched in the gut. Raul's gaze swung to him before landing back on his daughter. "What if they kill Jesse?" Raul asked, the coldness in his voice giving the words extra impact. "Do you really want to have his blood on your hands?"

"That's enough," Jesse barked. "I'm pretty sure she gets your point. No need to hammer in any gorier details."

To Jesse's surprise, Raul chuckled. "What's the matter, Jesse? Don't like me talking about the possibility of you biting the bullet?"

"I don't," Eva interjected. "Dad, believe me, I well understand the risks. If at any time I feel at risk, I'll leave."

"And come home?" Raul pressed.

"Maybe. Maybe not. I might just go someplace warm and tropical, with a beach and umbrella drinks." Her grin fooled no one. Both men knew Eva well enough to understand she'd never be able to enjoy herself on a vacation with things so unsettled.

"Do you still have your bike?" Raul asked, out of the blue.

"I do," Eva answered, surprising Jesse, who hadn't known. "It's in the garage, covered in a tarp. I've made sure to start it up every couple of weeks."

"Good." Raul pushed to his feet. "Then let's go for a ride. All three of us."

Eva appeared shocked. "I don't know about that. Drew didn't like me riding the Harley, and, of course, I couldn't when I was pregnant. It's been over two years. I'm not sure I remember how."

Jesse felt a pang. She'd always been so sexy, roaring around in her custom maroon-colored Harley. Why on earth would Drew have objected to that?

"No one forgets," Raul insisted. "It's like riding a bicycle."

Watching her prevaricate, Jesse realized he'd give almost anything to see her ride again. "Come on, Eva. Let's do it. It'll be fun."

"Okay. But it'll have to be a short one. I'm seriously out of practice."

Careful to hide his elation, Jesse nodded. "Let's make sure your bike still runs okay. I know you said you've been starting it up every so often, but let's double-check to make sure."

Jesse and Raul followed her out to the garage. She'd parked her bike in one of the bays and covered it with a lightweight tarp. When she pulled the tarp off, she grinned. "She's still pretty. I keep her clean and the chrome polished."

Walking over to the wall, she pressed the button to open the garage door, then climbed on the motorcycle, turned the key and started the engine. The low, melodic rumble sounded as if the motor had recently been tuned up.

"I'm impressed," Raul declared. "You've taken good care of her."

"Of course I have. I learned from the best."

Her compliment made Raul beam. "I parked in the driveway," he said, looking at Jesse. "You game?"

Jesse grinned. "You bet." Maybe, just maybe, the Eva he used to know was on her way back.

Chapter 10

When Jesse uncovered and wheeled out his own black-and-chrome Harley, Eva and Raul waited for him in the driveway. He caught his breath at the sight of Eva astride her powerful maroon Harley, looking so much like the old Eva it made his mouth go dry.

"Come on," she teased, revving her engine. She grabbed her helmet, securing it under her chin before putting on her mirrored aviator sunglasses.

Jesse grinned at her before doing the same. Raul watched them both, his expression inscrutable.

"Where to?" Raul asked. "Eva, you lead the way. I don't know the roads around here."

"I do." Chin up, Eva pulled out. Raul and Jesse followed right behind her.

Jesse rode his bike so much that he rarely even thought about it. Today, though, felt different. Watching the slender woman in front of him confidently maneuver her Harley gave him a thrill that reminded him of how he used to feel when he got his first bike. The entire world had looked different, the colors brighter and more vibrant, viewed up close and personal from his motorcycle.

For right now, he allowed himself to pretend the old Eva had come back.

After they left Eva's gated neighborhood, they roared through downtown, drawing more than a few stares. Once they reached the residential area on the other side of town, Eva turned left, heading east. The winding road took them into the sparsely populated wooded countryside. Jesse had taken a few rides here by himself, marveling at the leafy isolation. Having lived most of his life in crowded, busy Houston, he'd never taken the time to visit east Texas. In the time he'd been here, sometimes he thought how much it felt like visiting another state.

Now, with his Harley rumbling under him and the most gorgeous woman in the world leading the way, he thought he'd never been anywhere more beautiful.

Finally, Eva pulled into a driveway and turned around, heading back toward town. Jesse and Raul exchanged glances but they followed her.

This time when they roared through town, they attracted a lot of attention. Jesse wondered why, but since most of the people were outside on the sidewalks, strolling to either one of the downtown restaurants or shops, he figured the noise of the bikes caught their attention.

As they pulled up to Eva's neighborhood and stopped at the gates so she could enter the code, he couldn't help but wonder what her neighbors thought of the big bikes. For the first time, he understood Drew's dislike of all the attention they tended to draw. Especially in a well-heeled part of town like this.

As for himself, to hell with what the neighbors thought. Jesse was just glad to see Eva back, for however long it might last.

As they pulled up into her driveway, she punched her remote and motioned to them to pull into her garage. Once she'd killed her engine, she removed her helmet and shook her hair free. Her eyes sparkled as she grinned at Jesse and her father. "That was fun!"

Raul grinned back. As for Jesse, he stared at her and could barely catch his breath. His chest ached.

Eva's eyes narrowed. "What's wrong with you?" she demanded. "You look like you just ran over a squirrel or something."

Dragging his hands through his hair, Jesse turned away. He didn't want her to see the need in his face. "Nothing's wrong," he said, his voice gruff. "It was just good to see you ride again."

"Thanks." She tossed her head and looked away.

"That was fun," Raul said. When Jesse looked up, he realized the older man watched him closely. "Come on," he said, clapping Jesse on the back. "Let's go inside. You look like you could use a beer."

Eva's cell rang. She grimaced as she glanced at the caller ID. "It's Lori. Hello?"

She listened a moment, all the color leaching from her face. "Thank you for letting me know. My DVR is set to record the midday news, so I'll check it out."

Once she ended the call, she grabbed the remote

and turned on the television. "Lori says we're on the noon news."

"We?" Raul asked, frowning. He hated publicity, and preferred to stay in the shadowy background as much as possible.

"Yes." Expression grim, she pulled up the news and clicked it on.

A banner flashed across the top of the screen, announcing the upcoming stories. "Cold front to bring rain," read one. And another, "Grass fire threatens ranch." Finally, "Local politician's wife returns to her biker roots."

Eva cursed. "One time. I ride my bike one time and this is what they have to say?"

"What's the big deal?" Raul looked from her to Jesse. "Who cares if you return to your biker roots? Drew's gone and as far as I know, you're not running for political office. What difference does it make?" Raul's dark eyes flashed. "Don't tell me you're ashamed of where you come from."

"I'm not," she shot back. "But right there is the reason Drew didn't want me riding my Harley around. We haven't even buried him yet. I can only imagine what people will think."

"The Eva I knew never cared what people think," Jesse put in, even though he knew he should keep his mouth shut.

Eva glared at him. "Well, maybe I've changed."

"Then change back," Raul suggested, his dark gaze snapping.

Instead of responding, she aimed the remote at the TV.

Fast-forwarding until she got to the story, she clicked Play. They all watched the cell phone video of the three of them rumbling down Main Street, their bikes gleaming in the sun. The female newscaster read the story with a faint thread of amusement in her voice.

Jesse waited until it was over before saying his piece. Though she'd bared her body to him, allowing passion to claim her, she'd held back her inner essence. "I agree with Raul. Haven't you hidden your true self long enough?"

Both men waited while Eva digested both the story and their words. When she finally lifted her chin and nodded, a shiver snaked up Jesse's spine. Her dark eyes, so like her father's, flashed. "You know what? You're right. I've missed riding my Harley and I had fun today. Thank you both for talking me into going."

Raul grabbed his daughter and crushed her in a bear hug. "That's my girl," he said, his voice full of approval.

More than anything, Jesse wished he had the right to hug her too. Instead, he jammed his hands in his pockets and walked toward the back door. "I'm going to go check on the guys," he said, and escaped.

"I'll join you," Raul said, hurrying after him.

Once Raul and Jesse had gone outside to visit with the other Brothers, Eva kicked off her boots and leaned back in her recliner. She'd spoken the truth—riding today had felt good, as if she'd managed to escape to another time when she'd been an entirely different person.

The landline rang, effectively destroying her moment of peaceful enjoyment. Only one person routinely called that number. For a moment, she considered not answering—after all, Jesse wasn't here with his tracer gadget. But then, she was done hiding from reality. She'd face this head-on.

"I saw you on the news," the caller said. "Rejoining the Brothers of Sin isn't going to help you. I want my money."

"I want my proof," she replied. "It seems like you might be having trouble coming up with that."

"Ask Drew's assistant for the ledger. The *other* ledger, the one he keeps locked in the safe behind his desk. That's where you'll find your proof."

She took a deep breath. "Was Lori in on this with him?"

"She knew. Whether or not she received a cut, I have no idea. But it's probably likely she did, as money to keep her mouth shut. If she knows where the three million is, I would be surprised if she doesn't take it and try to run."

Wincing, Eva shook her head. It was bad enough to learn that the man she'd thought was an upstanding— if remote and cold—citizen had been involved in so many illegal activities. But then to find out Lori, the woman she'd trusted implicitly, had participated too?

"Did you kill Drew?" she asked, her heart skipping a beat or two. "Or have him shot?"

"No." The answer came swiftly and certain.

"Did Lori?"

This time, the question made the caller chuckle. "No. Actually, I'm ninety-nine percent sure that the cartel had him killed for trying to cheat them. Now, since I was Drew's partner, they're going to come after me next. I need that money to pay them, to show them good faith, understand? This isn't about me being greedy. This is about me not wanting to die."

Stunned, she wasn't sure what to say. In the end, she settled for the truth. "I don't know where the money is. Drew emptied out our joint savings account before he was killed."

"Then find out," he demanded, effectively destroying what little sympathy she'd begun to feel for him. "Or I'll make sure you suffer right along with me. You and that little brat of yours. I'll give you until after Drew's funeral."

Which meant he knew when the service had been scheduled.

"Who are you?" she pressed, refusing to allow him to intimidate her. But he'd apparently already ended the call, as she heard only silence.

About to go tell Jesse, she decided to wait. She wanted to call Lori and arrange to ask the other woman to her face.

Lori answered on the second ring.

"Do you have time to grab lunch with me?" Eva asked, her tone friendly. "There are a couple of things I'd like to discuss." She named a popular café in the heart of downtown Anniversary.

"Are you riding your motorcycle there?" Lori's tone sounded a bit disdainful. "Because I really don't want to draw a lot of attention."

Squelching her annoyance, Eva said she'd be driving her car. Lori agreed to meet her in thirty minutes.

Wondering whether to ask Jesse to accompany her, she looked out the kitchen window and spied her father, Jesse, Shorty, Patches, Rusty and Baloo all sitting on the patio shooting the breeze. Why wasn't anyone on guard duty? Had Jesse somehow decided the risk was gone, or had Raul distracted him and the other

Brothers? Though disappointed, right now the situation suited her. She preferred not to have to explain her plan.

Because she didn't want anyone to worry, she dashed off a quick note saying she was meeting Lori for lunch and left it propped up on the kitchen counter, facing the hallway.

Since her car sat parked in front of the house, she slipped out the front door, hurried to her vehicle, started the engine and backed out of the driveway. No one ran after her.

Driving always calmed her nerves. She waited until she was out of the subdivision gate before cranking up her radio on the classic rock station. Singing along to Bob Seger, she pulled into the parking lot of The Catfish Hut and found a spot close to the door.

Lori had already arrived and waited just inside. She'd changed from the morning and now wore a business suit and pumps, making Eva wonder if she considered this a business meeting.

"There you are," Lori exclaimed, hugging Eva and doing the air-kiss thing on both cheeks. "I'm so happy to see you came without your bodyguards."

Her words sent a shiver up Eva's spine. Had she made a bad decision, sneaking out of the house without Jesse? But then she looked around at the crowded restaurant and relaxed.

"I've got a few things I'd like to discuss with you," Eva replied. "In fact, I need to request one of the back booths. I'd prefer to have privacy."

"Already done." Had Lori always been so smug? She lifted up her tote bag. "I've got several documents I wanted to go over with you too."

The hostess led them to the back room of the restaurant, to the more secluded area where people went to discuss business. She showed them into a corner booth tucked into an out-of-the-way area. "Will this work?"

"Perfect." Lori smiled. "Thank you so much."

As they took their seats, Eva eyed Drew's assistant, wondering why the other woman acted as if she were the one who'd called this meeting.

Lori kept up a steady stream of chatter until the waitress arrived to take their drink orders. They both asked for sweet tea, and went ahead and requested the catfish platter.

Once the teas arrived, Lori pulled several manila file folders from her tote and placed them on the table. "I'm not sure if you're aware, but Drew owns several other properties, most of them in Texas. The largest one is a cattle ranch up in the panhandle." She slid one folder across the table. "I've compiled a comprehensive list of them and what they might be worth on the real estate market should you decide to sell."

"Thank you." Eva looked the other woman directly in the eye. "Do you think any of them are worth three million dollars?"

Lori blinked. "That's a mighty specific amount. I'm not sure. But if you consult a Realtor, I'm certain they could tell you."

"Lori, I'm done playing games. What do you know about the missing three million?"

Lori swallowed, the only sign that revealed her unease. "What are you talking about?"

Pitching her voice low, Eva relayed everything the caller had said. When she finished, Lori had recoiled and was staring at her as if she thought Eva had lost her mind.

"Drug cartels? Money laundering?" Lori shook her head, her voice full of simmering anger. "How could you possibly believe Drew was capable of such awful, illegal things? He was an upstanding business leader with political aspirations. He would never have done anything that might jeopardize his chance of becoming governor of Texas! He believed in what he was doing and wanted to make a difference."

Eva couldn't tell if the other woman truly believed her words or had become a damn fine actress.

"Whether you like it or not, it would appear Drew was involved in all this," Eva began. Their catfish arrived just then, and she had to wait until the waitress left before continuing. "I have someone making threats and demanding this missing money. Drew cleaned out our joint bank account before he was killed. Someone sent a bomb to my house and shot out my back window. So don't sit there and try to make me believe you're completely in the dark. You were Drew's assistant and campaign manager." She took a deep breath, noting Lori's shocked expression.

"Why don't you think about it while you eat," she said, stabbing the perfectly cooked catfish fillet with her fork. "But know this. I'm going to find out the truth whether you tell me or not."

Lori pushed her plate away. "I just lost my appetite."

"Suit yourself." Eva shrugged, putting her first delectable catfish bite into her mouth and chewing slowly. "But you'll be missing a dang good meal."

Eyeing her, Lori finally reclaimed her plate and started slowly eating, though she continued to watch Eva the way a trapped mouse might a hungry cat.

Finally, after eating about half her fillet, Lori put

down her fork. "I didn't know what to do," she whispered. "Drew and your father were really tight. I think you should ask Raul about all of this."

"I already have. He told me everything he knew." Eva leaned forward. "Has it ever occurred to you that you might be in danger from the cartel too? Especially if you knew about the missing money?"

Lori's eyes widened. "But I wasn't involved in any of that. Yes, I overheard bits and pieces of conversation— enough to put two and two together—but Drew never asked me to do any of the legwork for that part of his business."

"Knowing makes you complicit. I wonder what the FBI would think about that."

Face flushing, Lori stood. "Are you threatening me?" Her strident tone caused several other diners to glance their way.

"Of course not," Eva said. "Sit down. Please. I have a lot more I'd like to discuss with you."

Though Lori sat, she didn't look happy about it. "Discuss or question?" she asked, her voice as tight as her mouth.

"Both." Eva sighed. "I'm not your enemy, you know. And if Drew was having an affair with a woman named Chris, what difference does it make if I find out now? Drew's gone."

"I don't know anything about that," Lori replied quickly. Too quickly. "I tried to stay out of Drew's personal life as much as possible."

"I'm sure you did," Eva said, even though she was anything but. "Except you worked for Drew for a long time. You know stuff."

Lori started, jumping slightly when the waitress appeared, asking if they wanted dessert. Both women declined and asked for separate checks.

Eva tried to think of something to say, anything that might get Lori to open up. "I'd like to stop by Drew's office after this," she said, slightly gratified by Lori's horrified expression.

"Why?"

"Because I can." Eva sighed. "And judging by your reaction, you *do* have something you want to hide."

"I promised Drew…"

"Promised him what?"

Lori bit her lip. Instead of responding, she shook her head.

"Okay, then." Eva stood and grabbed her check. "I can follow you to Drew's office, if you're going that way. If not, I'll just let myself in and poke around a little."

"You can follow me." Lori jumped up so quickly she knocked her fork onto the floor. She hurried toward the cashier, paid and waited for Eva, tapping one high heel impatiently.

"What are you driving?" Eva asked her once they got outside.

"That white Volvo." Lori pointed. "I'll meet you there."

Which Eva took to mean Lori hoped to have enough time to hide a few things. Once again, Eva didn't understand why.

"Sounds good." Hopping into her vehicle, Eva waved as she backed out of her spot, pulling out into the road before Lori even reached her car.

Drew's office wasn't but a few blocks away, so Eva had already made it to the lobby before she spotted the white Volvo pull up. Briefly, she debated rushing upstairs. Instead she waited at the elevator for Lori to appear.

The other woman hurried inside, slightly out of breath. "There you are!" she said brightly. "Is there anything in particular you're looking for that I could help you find?"

Eva gave her a sharp look. "Stop. I'm just trying to get some answers. Apparently, there is a lot about my husband that I didn't know. A *lot*. I intend to get answers whether you help me or not."

Lori opened her mouth and then closed it.

They rode the elevator up in silence, standing side by side. Once they reached the third floor, they exited. Eva waited while Lori unlocked the door to Drew's suite of offices.

Stepping inside, Eva stood, taking it all in. She'd been here only a few times over the course of her marriage and not recently. Drew had hired the same interior designer here that he'd used to decorate the house, so the reception area as well as his and Lori's offices reminded her of his office at home. Elegant and masculine. It struck her as she stood there that Drew would never again come striding through that door. She felt it like a punch in the gut. She might not have loved the man, but he'd been part of her life for the last few years.

Lori must have seen something on her face. "I'm sorry, Eva," she said quietly. "I know it must be difficult."

"It definitely would be a lot easier if he hadn't been involved in illegal money laundering and who knows what else," Eva replied, her voice brisk. "And if as a result of him stealing money from criminals, I didn't have someone calling me demanding I repay them. Or shooting up my house and trying to blow me up."

"Yikes." Lori raised her hands up in the classic gesture of defeat. "You win. I'll show you where he kept all his private, top-secret files. I know where he kept the key."

Finally, they were getting somewhere. Lori led the way into Drew's office, opening his middle desk drawer and retrieving a full key ring. "It's one of these," she said, turning to the back wall and removing a large, framed picture that concealed a safe. Instead of a keypad, it had an inset lock.

Lori began trying keys. Her fourth attempt turned out to be the right one. "Here we are," she said, opening it. Once she had, she stepped back, allowing Eva to see the inside.

Instead of stacks of cash, there were several large envelopes and folders, stuffed with papers. Eva moved forward, half-afraid of what she'd find.

"I'll leave you to it," Lori told her, backing out and closing the door behind her.

Eva transferred everything from the safe to the desktop, then she pulled up a chair.

As she'd suspected, the first folder was full of financial records. Clearly, Drew maintained several bank accounts in the Cayman Islands. The recorded balance of them made her stomach churn. No way he could have amassed this much money so quickly. There was more than enough to pay back the missing three million dollars—assuming she could gain access to the accounts. From what she vaguely remembered reading about such things, doing so would be difficult, if not impossible if Drew hadn't put her name on them.

Judging by these records, he had not. She would have to go through the long, tedious court process before she could touch any of that money. There wasn't enough time for that.

Replacing the bank records in the envelope, she moved on to the next folder. When she slid it toward her, she realized an old-fashioned photo album was underneath.

Intrigued, she decided to check that out first. It had to be old, since people rarely printed out photos these days, preferring to store them in the cloud or on CDs. As far as she knew, Drew hadn't been any different. With the exception of their wedding pictures, which they kept in a glossy white album similar to this one. Maybe Drew had printed extras, though why he'd keep them in a safe, she couldn't fathom.

Slowly, she opened the album. An enlarged photograph of Drew decorated the first page. But instead of her, Drew had his arm around some man's shoulders. Both of them beamed at the camera, eternally young and clearly, blissfully happy. Drew appeared to be in his late twenties or early thirties at the time it was taken, which made it around ten years old.

Studying the picture, she wondered. She thought she knew most of Drew's friends, even the ones he'd known since childhood. And she was familiar with his business associates. This man in the photo was none of these. She didn't recognize him. That didn't mean much—he could have been an old friend who'd dropped out of Drew's life long before she entered it.

Carefully, she removed the photo, hoping she might see names and a date written on the back. But the back was completely blank.

Once she'd replaced the picture under the clear plastic, she turned the page. More photos of Drew and his friend, arm in arm, gazing into each other's eyes, and finally, embracing. Love and adoration showed in both men's expressions. Some of the pics were reminiscent of staged wedding photographs. It dawned on her that maybe, just maybe, this man wasn't merely Drew's platonic friend. Clearly, they were much, much more to each other.

She got up, carrying the photo album, and walked to the door and out into the hall, making a beeline for Lori's office, where Lori sat working on something at her desk. Eva slid the photo album across the desk. "Who is this?"

Lori paled. "I'm not sure," she hedged, swallowing hard.

"Come on, Lori. Tell me."

Looking away, Lori appeared to be considering. When she finally met Eva's gaze, resignation mingled with pity in her expression.

"That's Chris," Lori said. "The man Drew truly loved."

Chapter 11

Enjoying the familiar sense of camaraderie he felt hanging out with Raul and the other Brothers of Sin, Jesse squelched the occasional twinge of guilt. He liked this life, too much sometimes, and while he knew identifying too closely with the bad guys had long been a danger of a long-term, deep undercover assignment, it had actually gotten to the point where Raul and the other Brothers no longer felt like bad guys. That alone meant it was time to get out.

But he also knew Raul's men were working toward something huge with the drug cartels, and though that information hadn't yet been shared with him, it was only a matter of time. That bust, that huge freaking bust, would not only leave a large hole in the cartel's delivery network, but might also net a few of the top players in the game. It would be the culmination of years of undercover work. If he could just hang in there.

Pushing away his heavy thoughts, he left the other men and went inside to grab them all a beer. The house felt strangely silent and empty. He called for Eva, looking around the entire downstairs before deciding to check out the second floor. He noted no signs of forced entry and nothing to indicate a disturbance.

Taking the stairs two at a time, he pushed back the awful sense of foreboding prickling at the back of his neck. "Eva?" he called. "Where are you?"

Nothing but silence answered him.

Damn it.

Not finding her in any of the rooms, he ran downstairs and started to rush outside to get Raul. A folded slip of paper on the kitchen counter caught his eye. He snatched it up and read it, cursing under his breath. She'd gone to meet Lori for lunch. Alone.

He stood still for a moment, trying to gather his thoughts and calm his racing heart. As far as he could tell, while Lori might be annoying, she wasn't dangerous. But the fact that Eva had blithely gone into town, unprotected and exposed, worried the hell out of him.

No way he could tell Raul though. The last thing Eva would want—or need—would be her father and her bodyguard roaring into town on their bikes. But he knew if anything happened to her while she was out there, it would be on him.

He had to find her. Since she'd taken her car, and his bike was out, that left one possibility. Drew's sleek and sporty Porsche still occupied one stall of the oversize, three-car garage. All he needed was to find a key.

Rummaging around in the garage, he nearly jumped

when his phone rang. Seeing Eva's name on the caller ID brought an interesting combination of relief and rage.

"Where are you?" he demanded when he answered, not even bothering to say hello.

"I'm at Drew's office downtown, with Lori," she replied, her voice vibrating with barely suppressed excitement. "I found out who Chris is."

"Chris?" For a moment, he didn't make the connection. "You mean the Chris that was on the prenup we found?"

"Exactly!"

Intrigued, he waited for her to explain. When she didn't, he prodded her. "Well? Are you going to tell me who she is?"

"That's just it. Chris isn't a 'she.' Chris is a man. And judging by the photo album I found, he and Drew were deeply in love."

It took a moment for her words to sink in. "Drew was gay?"

"Apparently. Which explains a lot." She didn't elaborate, but he got the idea. "His parents are super religious, so I'm guessing that's why he felt he had to keep it a secret."

"I get that," he mused. "Plus, with his political aspirations…"

They both fell silent. When Eva spoke again, a tinge of sadness colored her voice. "I had no idea he wasn't living an authentic life. He always seemed so confident, so self-assured, as if he knew exactly what he wanted, where he was going, and how to get there. I wish he had told me the truth."

"Would knowing have made any difference in how

you felt about him?" he asked, not sure he really wanted to know.

"Yes, it would." She took a deep breath. "I'm not sure if you realized this, but Drew and I were never close. I would have understood his complete and utter rejection of me much better if I'd known he was in love with someone else."

His heart squeezed. He hated to think of Eva being rejected, especially by the man she'd married.

"Anyway," she continued, her voice brisk, "I've got tons of paperwork to look through. I'm thinking I'll just bring it home."

"When are you leaving?" The thought of her driving alone made him extremely nervous. "I'll head up there and accompany you back."

"No need," she answered quickly. "I'm about to bag all this stuff up and head home."

"I don't like it. For all we know, that crazy guy could have you under surveillance."

"I'll be fine," she responded. "I'll text you when I leave. Seriously, no need for you to come downtown."

Reluctantly, he agreed.

Raul wandered in just as Jesse ended the call. "What's up?" he asked. "You look like somebody died."

Rubbing his temple, Jesse grimaced. "I just got off the phone with Eva."

Raul glared. "Eva isn't here? You're her bodyguard. Why aren't you with her?"

"Because she left when we were all out on the patio talking. I had no idea until I found this note." Jesse held out the slip of paper, waiting while Raul read it.

"You should have gone after her."

"I thought about it," Jesse conceded. "But since I had no idea where she went…"

Raul glared at him. "You are supposed to be protecting her."

Something inside Jesse snapped. "Like you did when you encouraged her to marry Drew? Did you ever think about how hard it must have been for Eva to be in a loveless marriage? Especially when—" He stopped, choking on what he'd almost said.

"Especially when what?" Raul demanded. "Finish what you were about to say."

Closing his eyes for a moment, Jesse bowed his head. "Especially when she knew how much I loved her."

"Loved?" Raul's tone softened. "Past tense? Or do you still care about my daughter?"

Undercover ATF agent Jesse warred with real-life Jesse. In the end, he went with the truth. "I love Eva. Always have, always will."

"Does she feel the same way?"

Again, Jesse replied honestly. "I don't know. I'd like to believe so. She did once."

"Then what are you waiting for? Where is she now? Is she still at lunch?"

"No. She called me from Drew's office downtown. Lori's there with her. Eva's going through Drew's things." Jesse waited, expecting Raul to demand he hop on his bike and head down there.

Instead, Raul nodded. "Did she find anything interesting?"

Though Jesse knew the older man meant about the missing money, he nodded. "She did. She found evidence that leads her to believe Drew might have been in love with someone else."

Raul crossed his arms, his multiple tattoos moving as his muscles did. "In love with who? That Chris person you two mentioned earlier?"

"Exactly. Eva found a photo album of Drew and Chris. It meant so much to Drew that he kept it locked in his personal safe."

Judging by Raul's deep frown, hearing this did not make him happy. "If he was in love with someone else, then why did he marry my daughter? He's the one who asked me to set her up with him after seeing a photo of her. Was this other woman married or something?"

Jesse took a deep breath. "That's the thing. Chris isn't a woman. Chris is a guy."

For the space of several heartbeats, Raul stared at him as if he thought Jesse might be joking.

"I'm serious," Jesse finally said.

"Damn it." He dragged his hands through his shaggy, gray hair. "But why? Why would he hide that? Why pretend to be something you're not?"

Hearing that, Jesse felt a pang. Though Raul didn't know, Jesse was also doing exactly that, pretending to be a biker and a bodyguard, when he actually was undercover ATF.

Jesse shrugged. "I don't know."

"Hmmph." Raul scratched his chin. "Are you going to fix things up between you and Eva?"

"I'm damn sure going to try," Jesse replied.

Pinning him with his gaze, Raul narrowed his eyes. "I want my daughter happy, you understand?"

"I do too." Jesse meant it, with every fiber of his soul. "She belongs with me."

For the space of a heartbeat, Raul simply watched him. Finally, he nodded. "Then make it happen, man." Raul's phone rang. "I need to take this," he said, frowning. "Excuse me." And he wandered off, heading upstairs toward his temporary room.

Jesse's phone pinged, indicating a text. Eva, letting him know she was on her way home. His stomach clenched, aware he should be with her, keeping her safe. He'd have to make sure she understood the extent of the danger she'd opened herself up to by taking off alone like that.

Outside, the other guys continued to talk, though it was getting close to time for two of them to begin their security shift.

More than a little antsy, Jesse decided to keep busy until Eva got back. He'd always found cooking to be a great way to relieve stress, so he headed toward the kitchen to see what he could maybe rustle up for dinner.

In the refrigerator he found Eva had thawed a large package of pork chops. Perfect. Whistling, he got busy prepping everything he'd need to make a delicious meal. He'd just finished getting everything ready when he heard the front door opening.

Relieved, he let out a breath he hadn't even realized he'd been holding. Safe. She was safe.

"Hey there," Eva said, walking into the kitchen and eyeing him and the food. "That looks amazing."

He let his gaze roam over her, unable to keep from wanting her as much as he wanted to breathe. He thought back to earlier, when he'd realized she wasn't in the house and the awful, paralyzing fear he'd felt.

"We need to talk," he said, jamming his hands down into his pockets to keep from touching her.

Raising her head, she eyed him. Absentmindedly, she tucked a silky strand of her hair behind one ear. "About what?"

"You taking off like that. It's not safe. I know you're aware."

Slowly, she nodded. "I just needed some space."

Though she likely hadn't intended them to, her words wounded him. "Don't do that again." He kept his tone curt. "If you don't want to be with me, then grab one of the others."

Eyes wide, she stared. "What's wrong with you?"

He almost abandoned the idea then and there. After all, with the undercover assignment still hanging over him, he couldn't come out and declare his undying love right now. There were so many intricate layers and he knew it could all come crashing down around him at any moment. "I'm not going to pretend Liam isn't mine."

"You don't know that for sure," she replied, but her protest sounded weak.

"I still want a DNA test. As soon as possible. I have to know."

"That's fine." She swallowed. "But please, for the sake of decorum, can we wait to even discuss this until after the funeral tomorrow? I really don't want to hit Drew's parents with this just yet, even though they clearly already figured out Liam isn't Drew's." Her small smile faltered, though she tried. "Actually, I hate to prove them right."

He thought of the way the Rowsons had treated her and Liam. "I have to agree with you on that."

"Good." She went back to shuffling through paperwork. When he didn't move or leave, she glanced up at him, brow raised. "What?"

"I still want to talk about us," he said, refusing to feel awkward. "We made love, Eva."

"I know." Again the fleeting ghost of a smile. "I was there."

"That changes things."

Her eyes flashed. "Does it? I'm sorry, but I don't see how."

Again, the pain, like a knife to his heart.

About to respond, he made himself consider. Because, in a way, she was right. She'd asked him to leave the motorcycle club and he'd refused. Because he couldn't. Not only that, but his entire presence in her life had been one giant falsehood. And he was utterly and completely tired of living that lie.

He wanted her. He needed her as badly as he needed air to breathe. But he'd taken an oath as an ATF officer and he had to see this thing through. Hopefully by the time that had been accomplished, there'd still be something left to save. There had to be. Because he didn't know how he could go on without her.

"You're right," he finally conceded. "I'm guessing we just need to make sure it doesn't happen again."

Part of him hoped she'd deny that, say something along the lines of why couldn't they continue to have a physical relationship at least. Though he knew that would be wrong, he'd take whatever part of her that she was willing to give.

"I guess so," she replied, squelching that hope. "Now if you'll excuse me, I need to go get cleaned up. It's going to be a long day tomorrow, with the funeral and everything. Would you mind letting me know when that amazing-looking dinner is ready?"

He could only nod. There seemed to be nothing else he could say.

The day of the funeral dawned appropriately overcast with a threat of rain coming in from the south. Almost if even now, Drew Rowson made sure to direct the weather to what he found appropriate.

Shaking off a particularly strong bit of melancholy, Eva continued getting dressed. In a way, this funeral wasn't only to memorialize the death of her husband, but also the end of her marriage and all the hopes and dreams she'd once had. Though they'd died a slow, painful death over the last few years, today would be the day they were finally laid to rest along with Drew.

Smoothing down her black dress, Eva chose a pair of low-heeled pumps. She eyed herself in the mirror. With her diamond studs and subdued necklace, she looked nothing like the wild biker chick the local news station had been showing. After the third time they'd run the story, she'd had to turn the TV off. She could only imagine what Drew's parents must have thought if they'd seen it. Since she hadn't heard from them at all, she suspected they had.

Hearing a knock on her bedroom door, she opened it to Jesse and tried not to stare. Jesse in faded jeans and a tight T-shirt was one thing. Jesse in a dark blue suit that looked as if it had been tailor-made for him was something else entirely.

"You look nice," she managed, her mouth dry. How this man could, even now on the day of her husband's funeral, affect her so strongly, she'd never understand.

Her comment made him smile that slow, sexy smile that sent heat straight to her belly. "So do you. We clean up well, don't we?"

Before she could answer, her father appeared. Like Jesse, he also wore a dark suit, though his was charcoal with pinstripes. He'd even made an attempt to slick back his unruly gray hair. "Ready to go?" he boomed, clapping Jesse on the back and peering at his daughter with a trace of worried concern.

"I am," she answered, summoning up a weary sort of smile. "But before we do, I just want to say thank you. Having you here with me and supporting me means the world."

Raul kissed her cheek, clearly pleased. Jesse simply dipped his chin in acknowledgment of her words. She forced herself not to let her gaze linger on him, choosing instead to rummage in her purse for her car keys.

"Will you drive?" she asked him, holding up the keys. He nodded, taking them from her without another word.

They rode in silence to downtown Anniversary, turning right on Ninth Street. When they reached the funeral home, the sight of the black hearse and limos made her breath catch in her chest.

"It's going to be okay, sweetheart." Raul patted her hand. "I'm right here."

She nodded. There were already a few other cars in the parking lot, even though the memorial service wasn't for another hour. She and Drew's parents had been asked to come early.

Once Jesse parked, the three of them walked into the somber but elegant lobby of the funeral home. A tall, gaunt man wearing a suit that clung to his bones greeted them and directed them to the proper area.

Eva's heart sank when she saw that Ted and Beth Rowson had already arrived. They were deep in conversation with Jeremy Blackenstock, who hurried over the instant he caught sight of her. She could have sworn he appeared relieved to see her.

"There you are," he said, his dulcet tones conveying the right mix of sympathy and comfort. "How are you holding up?"

Dragging her gaze away from her in-laws, who were both shooting hostile glares toward her, she focused on Jeremy. "I'm doing okay."

"Glad to hear it." He cleared his throat, clearly uncomfortable. "Drew's parents are requesting changes to the service. Even though I've told them we couldn't accommodate their requests at this late hour, I'm afraid they are very insistent."

Her jaw had begun to ache from clenching it so tightly. "I'm sorry. Please ignore them. They have no business trying to change things. I've already informed them that everything has been handled."

If anything, Jeremy's discomfort seemed to increase. He shifted his weight from one foot to the other and tugged on his collar. "They brought a preacher," he said. "He apparently believes he's going to—"

"No." Tamping down irritation mixed with anger, Eva shook her head. "Where is he? I'll have a word with him."

"He's in the other room, going over his notes." Jeremy glanced back at the Rowsons, who continued to glare. "I've never had this happen before."

"I'm so sorry." Drama of any kind was the last thing

she needed or wanted. Especially now, on today of all days. She knew the press would be covering the service, and she doubted Ted and Beth would welcome any unfavorable coverage. "I'll speak to them, as well."

Relief flashed across Jeremy's normally composed face. "Thank you." He moved away, heading toward the front entrance where his staff member greeted arrivals.

Jesse leaned close, a big, handsome man wearing a well-fitting suit. "If having a preacher gives his parents some peace, what does it matter? Drew's gone, but I'm thinking he was close to his mother and father. Surely he'd want you to do whatever brought them comfort."

Stunned, she stared at him. Because he was right. She'd just have to figure out a way to mesh what she'd planned with their vision.

"Thank you," she told Jesse softly, wishing she had the right to kiss him, right then and right there. "I'll speak to the preacher and have him coordinate his talk with the ones I have planned."

Once she'd gotten Preacher Miller with Lori—who, armed with her clipboard, was in charge of coordinating everything—and brought Jeremy up to speed, she made her way over to talk to Ted and Beth.

Beth eyed her, appearing slightly apprehensive, while Ted seemed only weary. Grief lay heavily on both their shoulders.

"I've asked Preacher Miller to coordinate with the other speakers," Eva said. "I'm so glad you were able to have your own preacher come to help with the service."

Ted nodded. "He's a good man."

Eva nodded, searching for something else she could say. When Beth reached out and touched her arm, she started.

"Thank you," Beth said, her eyes filling with tears. "Having Preacher Miller speak words of comfort means a lot to us."

Eva pulled the older woman in for a quick hug. "Let's go get set up. People will begin arriving soon and we'll need to be ready to greet them."

She turned and walked back into the other room, sure Drew's parents were right behind her.

The service went off beautifully. The news reporters were respectful and quiet and stayed near the back of the room. The packed room contained not only politicians, but other attorneys and judges who'd worked with Drew over the years, as well as many people who'd made the long drive from Drew's hometown. Eva kept her head down, the closed casket making it easier. She might not have loved him, but she still couldn't believe his life had been taken so violently and so soon.

After, she and her father and Jesse rode with Ted and Beth in the first two limos to the cemetery. All the other mourners followed behind. Once they were all gathered under the green tent, the preacher said a few more words and they each placed a white rose on the casket before it was lowered into the earth.

Drained and numb, Eva sat in a folding chair and watched. Glad of her dark sunglasses, she watched Beth sob in Ted's arms and hoped the other woman didn't wonder why Eva hadn't cried.

The ride back to the funeral home felt endless. Sitting next to Jesse, hip to hip, knee to knee, she would have given much to have had the right to turn to him for comfort. Of course, she couldn't, so she sat staring straight ahead.

Finally, with Jesse driving and Raul in the back seat, she returned home. Raul immediately disappeared to his room, saying he needed to change.

Jesse, clearly sensing her mood, stayed out of her way, though he remained with her.

She took to prowling from room to room, not sure what she hoped to find. The sharp staccato sound of her heels echoing in the big empty house matched the emptiness inside her. Engaged in a silent struggle, she ached to turn to Jesse for comfort but knew that wouldn't be fair to him.

More than anything, she missed her son. Liam's joyful little laugh and fierce hugs would have gone a long way toward making her feel alive again. Instead, the gray cloud of doom had settled around her, leaching all the brightness and light from the world.

If she knew a magic spell that would help disperse it, she'd say it.

Now, she felt as if she stepped in quicksand and was sinking. It would be only a matter of time before she disappeared completely. If the men searching for the missing three million dollars didn't kill her first. She couldn't let that happen, because Liam needed her.

Shaking her head, she tried telling herself to snap out of it. While that hadn't helped in the past and most likely wouldn't now, she hated this perceived weakness inside herself.

A plan of action. That's what she needed. Except she had no idea what Drew might have done with the money. If she couldn't find it, she would be screwed.

She decided to act as if the police or the FBI would catch the caller or find the money or whatever. Once they'd taken care of the threat, she could go on with figuring out a way to regain her life.

When all this was behind her, the first thing she would do would be to sell this house. The place was too big and pretentious and had never truly felt like home. She'd move somewhere smaller, maybe down in the Hill Country west of Austin. That way she'd be closer to her father, but away from Anniversary with all its small-town ways and memories.

She'd start over in her new life as a single mom and maybe finally figure out who she was meant to be. If Jesse crept into her thoughts here, she firmly pushed him away. As long as he chose the BOS over her, she and he had no future together. If he wanted to be a part of Liam's life, it would have to be on her terms.

Of course, she wouldn't deny him. Liam would need a father figure.

"Are you okay?" Jesse's deep voice startled her out of her reverie.

Too tired to lie, she shook her head. "No. I'm not."

"Is there anything I can do to help?"

Make love to me. The desire sprang up, irrational and strong, blazing like a fire through her sluggish blood. She almost said the words out loud. Almost. Instead, she swallowed them back, stuffing them down into the deepest part of herself, hoping they would stay there.

"Thank you for asking." She summoned up a polite, impersonal smile that she knew matched the emptiness in her eyes.

Jesse had removed his jacket. He studied her quietly, his broad shoulders filling out his crisp white shirt.

"Come here," he said, his voice gruff as he held out his arms.

Heaven help her, but she walked right into them as if there'd been an invisible rope between them and he'd given it a tug.

As he held her, she felt the warmth begin to flow back into her limbs. She could smell the faint, familiar scent of his cologne, the same mint and musk that he'd always worn. He didn't speak, didn't try to ask her questions or attempt to fix whatever her problem might turn out to be. Instead, he simply offered the comfort of his touch.

Blinking back tears, she wondered how his embrace could still mean so much to her, especially since she no longer had the faintest idea who she really was.

Chapter 12

When Eva stepped back from his embrace, letting her go felt a hundred times more difficult than it should have been. Jesse turned away, hoping he could manage to tamp down his arousal before she noticed. Hell of a thing, wanting to make love to the widow the day of her husband's funeral. Only the fact that it had never been a real marriage kept him from feeling like a total tool.

"Hey, you two." Raul sauntered into the kitchen. He'd already changed out of his suit into his usual jeans, T-shirt and motorcycle boots. "How about we go for a ride? Might help clear some of the melancholy."

"Great idea," Jesse replied. "I need a minute to change."

Eva didn't move. "You two go on without me. The last thing I need is the media reporting on the biker woman rumbling around town after her husband's burial."

Though disappointment clouded his face, Raul shrugged. "Suit yourself. Jesse, I'll meet you out front. I'll talk to one of the guys and have them keep an extra close eye on things while you're gone."

Jesse nodded and hurried upstairs to change. He didn't dare look at Eva. He knew if he did, he'd feel compelled to try to talk her into going. He knew as well as she did how much a ride in the fresh air and the country could improve one's mood.

After he changed and headed out to the garage, Eva was nowhere in sight. Both Shorty and Patches had joined Raul in the driveway, their bikes gleaming.

"Rusty and Baloo will keep an eye on things," Raul said, raising his voice to be heard over the rumble of his motor.

Jesse nodded, wheeling his own Harley out of the garage. As he did, he couldn't keep from eyeing Eva's bike, parked in the garage.

"It's a damn shame," Raul commented, noting where Jesse looked. "I didn't raise her to be ashamed of who she is."

"I'm not sure she's ashamed." Why he felt compelled to defend her, he wasn't sure. "I think it's more that she doesn't want to draw any unwarranted attention."

Lowering his sunglasses, Raul stared at him. "Whatever," he finally said. "Ready to rumble?"

The other two revved their engines in answer. Jesse climbed on board, started his bike and followed them.

As usual, people noticed when they roared down Main Street. Jesse had to wonder why people acted as if they'd never seen a motorcycle before. They all stared and some of them even shielded their children, as if they feared they'd be attacked. Since he knew the Brothers of Sin were involved in illegal activity, Jesse guessed they were probably used to it. As for him, it still stung.

They hit the back roads outside town and continued north. The farther they traveled, the more uneasy Jesse felt. While he trusted Rusty and Baloo, he didn't feel comfortable without his eyes on Eva.

Finally, Raul pulled over on the edge of a country road. "What do y'all think? Should we keep riding or head back?"

Of course, Shorty and Patches voted to continue on.

"I'm going to go on back to the house," Jesse said. "If the rest of you want to enjoy the day out here in nature, I'll leave you to it."

Raul frowned. He checked his watch. "It is getting late. You're probably right. We shouldn't leave Eva alone for so long, especially on the day of Drew's burial."

Though Shorty and Patches grimaced, they didn't argue with their leader.

With Raul in the lead, they turned their bikes around and headed back the way they'd come.

It seemed to take forever to get back to Eva's subdivision. When they finally made it through the gate and pulled up in her driveway, Jesse fought the urge to hop off and run for the house to make sure she was okay.

Instead, he made himself go slowly. Once inside, he headed to Eva's room. Her door was closed, so he tapped lightly on it. "Eva? Are you okay?"

When she didn't immediately answer, he tried again.

"I'm fine," she finally said, her voice shaky. "I need some space. I'll be down soon."

Jesse backed away. More than anything, he wanted to bust through that door and gather her in his arms. Since she clearly didn't need that, he'd do as she requested and leave her alone.

Back downstairs, he walked outside where Raul stood talking quietly to the others. Now that he knew that Eva was safe, he wasn't sure what to do with himself.

Evidently, Raul had the same problem. Eyeing Jesse, he waited until Shorty and Patches had parked and gone inside to speak. "Is she okay?"

Jesse managed a nonchalant shrug. "I think so. She's holed up in her room. Says she wants to be left alone."

"That makes sense." Raul sighed. "Has Eva had any luck finding the missing money?"

"No."

"Then I'm going to cover it," Raul said. "I can liquidate some assets and take care of the debt."

Battling his inner ATF agent, Jesse kept himself from answering any questions. "I'm thinking you might want to discuss that with Eva," he said.

"Maybe so." Raul jammed his hands in his pockets. "There are a lot of things I need to talk to her about. Do you mind if I tell you something in confidence?"

Dread coiling in his gut, Jesse nodded. He'd been undercover too long. He thought of this man as a friend. He really didn't want to know something he might be obligated to report. "Go ahead."

"I'm thinking of retiring."

Whatever he'd been expecting Raul to say, it wasn't this.

"Retiring? From the club?"

"Yeah." Raul grimaced. "I'm tired of the grind. The cartels want more and more and there's too much in-fighting. I've got some money stashed away and I'm thinking I'd like to take off to a tropical island. The only thing keeping me from doing that is Eva and Liam. When this is over, I'm going to see if I can talk her into going with me."

Jesse froze. He swallowed hard, struggling not to reveal the depths of loss he felt at the idea of Eva disappearing forever, along with his son. He'd worked hard on getting over her in the time they'd been apart. Her marriage to Drew had made that somewhat easier. Then Raul had sent him here around her and his traitorous heart had started back up where it had left off.

In love.

And now he had Liam to get to know.

Blinking, he forced himself to focus. "You're talking complete identity change, aren't you?"

"Of course." Raul chuckled. "I don't want there to be any chance that someone could tie me back with my former life of crime." He squeezed Jesse's shoulder, his expression growing serious. "I've been lucky, you know. There've been several times when I could have ended up either dead or in jail."

Not sure what to say, Jesse nodded. "I can imagine."

"You can go with us," Raul offered. "I know how you feel about my daughter, and now you have a son to think about."

Stunned, Jesse stared. "You know?"

Raul nodded. "I suspected."

"I've asked for a DNA test," Jesse admitted.

"I think that's a good idea. Either way, let's all take off together."

The idea carried more appeal than it should. "I think you need to run it by Eva and see what she says. But yeah, I really wouldn't be happy if she disappeared with my boy. I haven't even had a chance to know him."

"True." Releasing him, Raul walked toward the door that led into the house. "Let's go find Eva and see how she's doing."

The instant they stepped into the kitchen, Jesse could tell something was wrong. Eva stood at the kitchen counter, an open bottle of wine in front of her, a half-full wineglass in her hand. Her dark eyes seemed huge in her pale face.

"What's going on?" Raul asked. "You look like you've seen a ghost."

"The early news just ended," Eva said, her voice wavering. "They said the FBI is investigating Drew for campaign violations. Lori Pearson is, according to the news story, cooperating fully. I tried to call her and she wouldn't take my call."

Jesse cursed. This was the first he'd heard of that. Usually, his handler stayed on top of things and kept him fully briefed.

Though Raul didn't speak, judging from his steely glare, he was furious. "You know she was fully involved. She's selling out her dead boss to try and save her own skin. Though I can't really blame her, I'm guessing she doesn't care what an investigation like that will do to you."

"Obviously not." Eva took a long drink of wine. "I'm dreading when his parents find out." Looking from Jesse to her father, she sighed. "They also showed footage of you two on your bikes. They're speculating about the Brothers of Sin's involvement in all this."

Raul didn't appear worried. He shrugged. "They can check into it all they want. We weren't involved.

Drew did some work for the cartel, not us. We might have introduced them, but that's where our involvement ended. And I'm pretty damn sure none of that involved his campaign funds."

"Well, the press is having a field day." Eva took another sip of wine. The vulnerability in her eyes tugged at Jesse's heart.

"Just don't answer your phone," Jesse advised. "It's bad enough you've got some guy demanding money and making threats against you, but now this. I'm imagining you'll be getting calls from all sorts of news outlets."

"I already have." She pointed toward her cell. "I had to turn it off. They were blowing up my phone. Someone published the number."

Muttering under his breath, Raul excused himself and took off for the stairs. Jesse and Eva silently watched him go.

"He's probably going to make some calls and try for damage control," Eva said wearily. "Though I think it's too late for that."

The doorbell chimed, interrupting whatever else she'd been about to say. Eva stiffened. "Surely those reporters aren't going to start pounding on my door."

"I'll go see who it is," Jesse offered. "Wait right here."

He checked the peephole first. When he saw Ted and Beth Rowson standing on the doorstep, he winced. For a few seconds, he debated not answering and pretending no one was home, but he caught sight of Baloo standing to one side of the older couple and figured he had no choice but to answer.

He'd no sooner opened the door when Beth Rowson

pushed past him, demanding to see Eva. Ted reached for her, no doubt intending to try to calm her, but she shoved him away hard.

"Where is she?" Beth strode past him on her way toward the kitchen.

Before Jesse could answer, Eva stepped out into the hall. "Beth?"

Beth stopped short, as quickly as if she'd been jerked on a chain. She glared daggers at Eva, her complexion mottled with fury. "How could you?" she demanded. "Why on earth are you so intent on ruining my son's reputation? What did he ever do to you to make you so hateful?"

"Are you talking about the news story?" Eva stared right back, clearly undaunted. "Because I don't honestly know how you could possibly think I had anything to do with that. It was all Lori Pearson."

"Right," Ted scoffed. "We know Lori. She was completely loyal to Drew. She'd never turn on him like this."

Looking from one to the other, Jesse had to wonder how much Drew's parents knew. Had they possibly been aware that their son had been misusing campaign funds? If so, it seemed likely Lori would implicate them too.

"Perhaps you should rewatch the news coverage," Eva pointed out gently. "They said Lori was cooperating with authorities. Of course, I didn't believe that for one second. But when I called her, she wouldn't take my call."

Ted and Beth exchanged glances. Jesse could tell by the shell-shocked expressions on their faces that the possibility had never occurred to them until they'd seen it on the news. Had they just now realized Lori might have betrayed them?

He saw the moment Eva came to the same realization. "You knew," she said, the disbelief in her voice matching the shock in her face. "All along, you knew full well what Drew was doing. Were you in on it with him and Lori?"

Beth slapped her. Hard enough to send Eva reeling. "How dare you," Beth began.

"Lady, you'd better get a hold of yourself right now," Jesse ordered, trying to tamp back the fury. "That was uncalled for."

"Don't even think about moving one inch closer to her." Raul appeared in the doorway, his furious expression and clenched fists a warning. "Touch her again and I won't be responsible for what happens to you."

"Threats," Ted muttered. "Just great. Now we've got a biker threatening us. Maybe my hunch was right. Did your motorcycle gang have something you were holding over my son's head? Something you used to get him involved in illegal activities?"

Jesse could hardly believe his ears. He didn't dare look at Raul, because he knew exactly what the other man would be thinking.

One hand to her cheek, Eva finally spoke up. "You need to leave," she said, her voice flat. "I want both of you out of my house right this instant."

No one moved. Jesse wondered if Drew's parents would attempt to ignore Eva's order. Not on his watch. "I'll escort you to the door," he said, taking Beth's arm and turning her forcibly around. "Let's go."

"Get your filthy hands off me!" she screamed, slinging herself backward toward her husband. She flailed about, still trying to get to Eva. "You cheated on my son and tried to pass off another man's child as his. I'll never forgive you for that."

Ted caught her and held her with one arm, both keeping her close and stopping her from any further hysteria. "Let's go," he said, edging them both backward toward the front door. Both Raul and Jesse advanced toward them, which served to hurry them along.

"You're not welcome here again," Raul snarled. "And if you ever lay a hand on my daughter again, you'll have me to answer to."

Ted hustled his wife out the door without another word. Jesse slammed it behind them, turning the lock on the dead bolt.

When he and Raul returned to the kitchen, they found Eva holding up a bag of frozen peas to her cheek. It took every ounce of self-control Jesse possessed not to go to her.

"Are you okay?" he asked, managing to keep his distance.

She nodded but didn't speak. He could tell by the wobbly set of her mouth that she was trying not to cry.

Raul went to her and roughly pulled her in for a hug. "They're awful people," he murmured, smoothing her hair away from her face. "Don't let them get to you."

"All of this is getting to me," she said. "I miss my son. Whenever I try to follow up with the police, they act as if they have no idea who I am or what I want. There's three million dollars missing and I have no idea where it might be. Oh, and someone not only calls and threatens me, but they shoot out my window and try to blow me up. I honestly don't know how much more I can take."

"About that," Raul said, steering her toward the table. "I need to talk to you about a plan of mine. I'm thinking you might find it interesting, especially after everything that's happened to you."

Jesse edged out of the room. He didn't want to hear any more. If Eva jumped on the idea of taking their son and disappearing to some remote tropical island, he would have to speak up. And right now wouldn't be the best time to do that.

Unless… He could go with them. The idea sorely tempted him. If not for the fact that both Eva and her father knew a man who'd been living a lie, he might seriously consider asking if he could join them.

Eva watched Jesse withdraw into himself and fought back tears. She could take the Rowsons' enmity and rancor, she could take the whole world thinking that her former husband had been a cheat and a con man, but she didn't know if she could accept Jesse distancing himself from her.

She'd been wrong. Making love with him *had* changed things. She just hadn't wanted to face it. Yet while she had to acknowledge that, she also knew some things remained unchanged. Jesse's commitment to the motorcycle club and the fact that he apparently would always choose that over her. Even knowing they'd had a son together clearly wasn't enough to pull him away from the BOS.

That stung. Hell, more than stung. It freaking hurt.

And even then, even knowing the painful truth, somehow her foolish heart still wanted him.

Long after darkness had fallen, Eva tossed and turned in her huge bed. Tired of trying to rationalize her physical desire with her shattered heart, she got up and went to her window. Outside, the full moon illuminated her yard and the brick wall surrounding it. She caught sight of one of the biker guards leaning against the massive live oak tree, one end of his cigarette glowing red in the shadows.

Home. And yet, not really. Though she'd lived in this house for over two years, it had never felt like hers. Not only had she not been part of choosing to buy it, but even the decorating had been done by a designer. When she sold it, she thought she'd offer it fully furnished.

Movement outside caught her eye, making her tense up. A pinpoint of light swept the ground below, the low buzzing sound unlike anything she'd ever heard.

The man below her caught sight of it finally, as it neared her window. "Get down," he shouted. "It's a drone."

She'd seen enough movies to know what drones could do. Jumping aside, she dropped to the floor and crawled toward the door, glad of her dark room. If the thing was armed, she wanted to make herself the smallest target possible. Luckily, her window was closed. She figured if it crashed into the glass, the drone would come apart.

By the time she reached her closed bedroom door, the thing hovered right outside her window, its bright light illuminating most of her room. She dived for the door just as the drone tapped against the glass, lightly and precisely enough to tell her whoever controlled it was very good at the job.

She'd just turned the knob when the drone exploded, blowing out her window and sending shards of glass like deadly weapons into her room.

"Eva!" Jesse's voice, yelling out her name. She focused on that, despite the stabbing pain in her leg. Somehow, she managed to pull the door open and half fell into the hallway, one hand against her leg.

Heart pounding, she scrambled away from her doorway, dimly registering the trail of blood she left in her wake.

"Are you all right?" Reaching her, Jesse scooped her up in his muscular arms and hauled her farther down the hall. Outside, she could hear men yelling. One of the voices sounded like her father's.

"Is everyone else okay?" she asked, concerned.

"As far as I know," Jesse answered. "Though I haven't been outside yet to assess the situation. What happened?"

"It was a drone rigged with explosives." Briefly she closed her eyes. When she reopened them, she found his face mere inches from hers. "Someone aimed it right at my window."

Fury warred with concern in his dark eyes. He focused intently on her. "There's a lot of blood. Where are you hurt?"

Hurt. Odd how being with him made everything else fade into insignificance. In his arms, she finally felt safe. Glancing down at her bare leg, she saw a large piece of glass sticking out of her thigh. "There." She pointed. "It went in kind of deep, but I'm going to pull it out. Can you grab a towel or find something I can use to stop the bleeding?"

Instead, he took a look himself. "Luckily, that thing lodged in the fleshy part of your leg, rather than near an artery or something. Do you have any more wounds that you know of?"

"I don't think so." She took a deep breath, assessing. "Nothing else hurts."

"Good." Though his tone seemed light, the grim set of his rugged jaw told a different story. Releasing her, he got up and disappeared into the guest bathroom, returning with a large bath towel. "This ought to work," he said, handing it to her. "How about I yank it out and you apply the towel? Then, you can tell me where I can find bandages and antiseptic so we can get you fixed up."

Instantly, she nodded. "Thank you," she managed. "I can be all brave in theory, but if I really think about it…"

"I got you," he said, his voice gentle. "Are you ready?"

"I think so." Just in case, she looked away. "Go for it."

"One, two, three… It's out." He took the towel from her and pressed it against her leg.

Surprised, she shook her head. "Seriously? I didn't even feel that."

"Good. You lucked out. It could have gone in a lot deeper."

"Has anyone called the police?" she asked.

"I don't know. Let me check with Raul and the guys. If not, I'll make sure it gets done."

The front door slammed open. Someone rushed inside, taking the steps two or three at a time. Breathing hard, Raul stopped short when he saw her, still on the carpet near the landing.

"What happened?" he demanded. "Eva, are you hurt?"

"I'm fine," Eva answered. "I got cut by a piece of glass, but Jesse got it out."

Though Raul nodded, he paled when he saw the blood. "Are you sure you got it all? I saw what that explosion did to your window."

"I was just about to double-check," Jesse said. "Hold still, sweetheart. Let me look."

Though she knew better, that *sweetheart* got her. He used to call her that, right in the middle of lovemaking, the sexy rasp in his voice sending her over the edge every single time. She blinked, her face heating as she realized where her thoughts had gone.

Luckily, neither Jesse nor her father appeared to notice. "So far so good," Jesse announced. "Once we get that cut cleaned and bandaged, you should be good to go."

After letting Jesse do exactly that, she swallowed a couple of ibuprofen and gingerly stretched. For the first time she realized she wore only pajamas, nothing underneath. Luckily, the baggy, oversize T-shirt wasn't revealing.

"You got blood on your pj's," Raul pointed out. "You'd better go change." He glanced at his watch. "It's late, but if there's any plywood around, I can get it nailed up over that window so you can sleep."

Though privately she knew there was no way she could make herself go back into that room tonight, she nodded. "There's some left in the garage from when we had to board up the other window. Jesse can show you where it is."

Raul held up his hand. "No need. I can find it. You go change. Jesse, you stay with Eva. It'll just take me a few minutes to get this done so we all can go back to sleep." He took off, heading for the garage.

Looking down at her bloody pajama pants, she glanced toward her bedroom door. While she didn't consider herself a coward by any stretch of the imagination, she couldn't seem to force her feet to move in the right direction.

"I can get them for you," Jesse murmured. "Just tell me what you want and where to find them."

His compassion ignited a spark to warm her inner chill. "The third drawer down in my main dresser has my pajama bottoms. Any pair will do."

He nodded. "Wait right here."

As if she intended on going anywhere. Wrapping her arms around her middle, she watched as he disappeared into her room. Though the idea of his hands on her personal things made her feel slightly unsettled, she appreciated his offer of help.

"Here you go." Returning, he handed her a pair of black-and-red-plaid flannel bottoms.

Since she didn't have the heart to tell him those were for winter, she thanked him and took them into the bathroom to change. Once she had, she wadded up the bloody pair and placed them in the trash.

After washing her hands, she stepped back into the hall. The sound of hammering told her Raul was already hard at work boarding up her window. The knowledge should have made her feel safe, but didn't. If she let herself, she knew she'd keep seeing the bright light of the drone approaching her window, crawling away and almost making it just before the thing exploded.

No thank you. Her bedroom would be off-limits for

tonight, maybe longer. Since all the guest rooms were occupied except for Liam's room, she could either sleep on her son's twin bed or take one of the couches. She'd figure that out in a bit.

"The police are on their way," Jesse said, as soon as she approached him. "Do you want me to get you a bathrobe or something?"

She needed a bra. Swallowing back her pride, she asked Jesse to get one for her. Instead of asking any questions, he hurried back into her room and brought her one back. Though she felt her face heat when she took it from him, she avoided his gaze, murmured thank you and once again went into the bathroom and put it on.

When she emerged, she thanked him.

"All done," Raul announced, emerging from her room holding a hammer. "It's not pretty, but it will work until you can get a window guy out here to re- place it."

"The police are on the way now," Jesse informed him.

"Great." Raul made a face. "I'll just skip that entire scene. If anyone needs me, I'll be in my room, sound asleep."

He took off, carrying the hammer with him.

Eva shook her head. "Some things never change."

"I guess not." Jesse gestured toward the stairs. "Are you ready to go down?"

With him right behind her, she went to the first floor and took a seat in the den to wait. The neighbors were not going to appreciate more police cars, but they had to have heard the explosion. Between gunshots and two bombs, she was pretty sure they were wishing she'd move. She couldn't blame them. But, since none of this was her fault, she refused to allow herself to worry too much what her neighbors thought.

The police arrived, asked their usual questions and took a look around both the backyard and her bedroom. When they'd gone, Eva sighed. "Why do I feel like that was just a huge waste of time?"

Jesse shrugged. "I'm sure they're working on it."

"Are you? I don't get the feeling. And since the FBI and ATF are supposedly involved, why haven't they been out here?"

"They've got a lot on their plate. Since no one has been harmed, they're probably focusing more on Drew's murder than these attacks."

"Seriously? Are you saying someone needs to get killed before the big guys take notice?" Without waiting for him to answer, she grimaced. "No wonder my father dislikes law enforcement so much. I'm beginning to see his point."

Chapter 13

Jesse tried like hell to keep his expression neutral, but Eva's casually cruel words felt like a knife to the heart. While he understood her reasoning on one level, on the other, law enforcement was what he did. Not only that, but his job made up every component of his life, from working undercover for the last several years, to all the work and dedication he'd put into earning his place in the ATF.

"I'll make some calls in the morning," he promised. "Surely someone, somewhere has made progress on this case." And he would. He'd not only call his handler at the ATF, but pull some favors from a friend or two at the FBI. This was beginning to get ridiculous. On other cases, he knew the various agencies would have been working nonstop to not only locate Drew Rowson's killer, but to learn the identity of the man who'd been threatening Eva. He had to wonder if anyone had even been able to track this Chris person down.

"Thank you. We need some answers and we need them now." Eva's words echoed Jesse's thoughts. "I think it's ridiculous that they can announce on TV that they're investigating a dead man for possible campaign violations, but say nothing about finding his killer."

"True, but there might be a lot going on in the background that we're not aware of," he cautioned. This was also a fact. The DEA, working in conjunction with the FBI and ATF, had spent years tightening the net around the Brothers of Sin. Drew's involvement created a difficult balance. They had to move with extreme caution or risk blowing a huge case wide open.

When the time came, the entire motorcycle club would be going down. He had to wonder how Eva would look at him once she realized he was part of the operation that sent her father, and numerous others she regarded as family, to prison.

Shaking it off, as he had ever since becoming involved with her, he gestured toward the stairs. "How about you try and get some sleep?"

She didn't move. "My room is full of glass."

Good point. "We can clean that up in the morning. You can have my bed. I'll make a pallet on the floor or take the couch."

Eyeing him, she considered. "I can always sleep in Liam's little bed."

"There you go." He covered his mouth to mask a yawn.

Without saying another word, she turned and made her way up the staircase. He followed her, intending to see her safely to bed before trying to grab some shut-eye himself.

At the doorway to Liam's room, she stopped. After looking into the empty room, she turned to face him. The stricken look on her lovely face and the vulnerability in her eyes had him taking a step toward her.

"I can't," she said simply. "I just can't. I miss him way too much. Being in his room will do nothing but make it worse."

"Then you can have my bed," he offered immediately. "I don't mind."

Instead of arguing, she nodded. "Okay."

Once they'd reached his room, she stood on the balls of her feet between the doorway and the bed, almost as if she were poised to run. He thought he understood her uncertainty. "I'll sleep downstairs. You won't need to worry about anything, I promise."

"Thanks, but I might have to be the one on the couch." She gestured toward the window. "Every time I look at a window, all I can see is that drone flying close, its bright light trained on me, right before it exploded."

He thought about pointing out that there were windows in the downstairs den too, but decided against it. She'd realize that soon enough. "Wherever you feel most comfortable," he said instead, expecting her to push past him and make her way back to the first floor.

Instead, she cocked her head and considered him. "Come here." The low thrum of desire in her voice ignited an answering spark deep within him.

Battling himself, he didn't move. "Why?"

"I need you to distract me."

His mouth went dry. "Distract you how?" he managed, even though he knew.

Instead of answering, she crossed the distance between them. Reaching up, she cupped his face with her hands and pulled him down to her lips and kissed him.

As always, every single resolve he'd struggled to hold on to went up in a blaze of lust.

"I don't think…" He made one last valiant effort.

"Then don't," she said, right before she removed her sleep shirt, bra and flannel pajama bottoms. Gloriously, breathtakingly naked, she took his hand and placed it on her bare breast. And he was lost.

Shedding his clothes so quickly they tangled at his feet, he pulled her close and kissed her.

Of course they ended up in bed. How could they not, when he'd always been unable to resist her? Eva was both his Waterloo and his nirvana, and his last thought before he gave in to the inferno raging between them was that—no matter what happened—she would forever be his love.

After, Eva lay dozing in his arms, sated and happier than she should have been. Whatever else he might be, Jesse had the power to make her body come alive. Smiling, she refused to allow herself to think about her problems or the future, choosing instead to revel in this moment, in the pleasant way her body ached yet her inner turmoil felt calm and at peace.

Jesse, Jesse, Jesse. How could he not understand what he meant to her? How could he choose the BOS over her? Until the day she died, she would never understand his choice.

Again, she rejected her own thoughts. They brought

too much pain, and she wanted to allow herself to bask in her happiness, however temporary.

Her phone buzzed, the insistent sound reminding her she'd left the ringer on vibrate like she always did when she went to bed. "Who could that be?" she asked, loathe to leave his arms.

"It's three in the morning," Jesse commented. "Only bad news comes at this hour of the night. You'd better answer it."

Though she'd much rather just let the call go to voice mail, she reluctantly pushed up from the bed and crossed to the dresser. Jesse's room, though much smaller than the master bedroom, somehow felt cozier and more welcoming. Of course, a lot of that probably had to do with the fact that Jesse occupied it.

When she snatched up her phone, the Unknown Caller on the display made her groan. "If this is a wrong number…" she muttered, before answering with a muted hello.

"Did you like my drone?" a familiar voice taunted. "I wanted to attach a note, but couldn't figure out how to do that since the entire thing was going to explode."

"You called my cell," she countered, shocked. "How'd you get this number? It's private."

"I was tired of your boyfriend trying to trace my call on your landline. Last chance. Everything—the gunshots, the bomb, the drone—they've only been warnings. I'm done playing around. Do you have my money or not? If not, I'm afraid I'm going to actually have to kill you."

"But you said—"

He cut her off. "It will be awful to leave Liam without a mother."

Though that sentence felt like a punch to the gut, something he'd no doubt intended, she refused to reveal her reaction. One thing she'd learned at her father's knee was to never give the bullies what they wanted.

"Why are you doing this?" she asked, letting at least the internal weariness she felt creep into her voice. Jesse sat up in the bed, instantly alert. She nodded, pointing to her phone and shaking her head.

"I need my money. Now. I'm done playing around. If you don't pay up, your life is over, along with that pretty-boy bodyguard of yours. Do you follow?"

"I do." She took a deep breath and then decided what the hell. "Once again, I don't have the money. I have no possible way of even getting a tenth of that sum. You weren't the only one Drew stole from. He emptied all my bank accounts."

After a few seconds of silence, the caller cursed. "I don't believe you."

"I don't care. And for your information, killing me still won't get you your money. I'll be dead and you'll be out of luck. I'm sorry, I don't know what to tell you."

More curses, some of them virulent enough that, despite growing up around bikers, they were new to her ears.

As he wound down, she decided to go ahead and give voice to a suspicion that had been growing steadily in her thoughts. "Maybe you should let it go. By the way, *Chris*—if this is you—I know all about your relationship with my husband."

"He *told* you?" the caller gasped out, apparently before he thought better of it. "I find that impossible to believe."

Though she'd known the truth deep inside, learning her gut instinct had been right shook her. "No. I found a photo album of the two of you that he kept in a safe in his office. Also some documents. At one point, he must have contemplated marriage. He had a prenup drawn up."

Silence. "Hello?" she pressed. "Are you still there?" Again, no answer. Pressing the end call button, she faced Jesse, grimacing. "He hung up."

"Did he admit to being Chris?"

"Pretty much, though he didn't come out and confess it in so many words. He's now threatening to kill me if I don't come up with three million."

"He's an amateur," Jesse said.

"How can you tell?"

"First off, his attempts have been pretty ineffective so far. And they've all been the kind of thing someone who has no idea what they're doing would try."

Intrigued, she eyed him. She loved the way he caressed her naked body with his gaze, making her wonder if he wanted to go another round.

Focus, she reminded herself. "If shooting my window out, mailing me a bomb and then sending an explosive drone at me makes him an amateur, what would a professional do?"

Jesse grimaced. "Are you sure you really want to know?"

Maybe she didn't, but there was no way she'd be admitting that now. "Yes."

"He would have sent a small group of men to grab you. You'd have been blindfolded, maybe drugged, and taken to some remote and secure location where they would hold you prisoner and torture you. They'd make a demand for ransom from your father, he'd pay, and maybe they might let you go free. Most likely not though. Guys like that prefer to tie up any loose ends."

His comments, delivered in a dry tone, made her shudder. "Then I guess I ought to be glad he's not a professional."

"Yes, definitely. But that's what the cartel will do to him, if they suspect him of having something to do with the money disappearing. And there's a strong possibility he knows it."

"But why does he think I would have any idea where Drew might have stashed the money?" She swallowed hard as a horrible thought suddenly occurred to her. "What if the cartel thinks that too?"

"To answer your first question, in law enforcement, when a husband steals large amounts of money, the wife usually is in on it."

"In law enforcement? How would you know?" she asked, genuinely interested.

"I watch a lot of TV," he countered, shrugging. "And as to the second, if the cartel truly suspected you of anything, they'd go to your father. Three million dollars isn't enough to jeopardize a profitable business relationship like they have with him."

"It's not? To me, three million dollars is a lot of money." Dragging her hands through her hair, she prowled the confines of the small room. "I just want this to stop. All of it. Drew's been buried, I've contacted an attorney and made an appointment to start the probate process, and I want my life back. I don't understand why the police are not getting anywhere on locating this guy. Seriously."

Jesse nodded. "I agree. Like I said, I'll make some

phone calls in the morning. Come back to bed." The sexy rasp in his voice made her go weak inside.

Still, she hesitated. If she spent the night wrapped in his arms, would that turn this into more than what it actually was? She hadn't really thought past needing him as a distraction. She'd certainly gotten that. They'd enjoyed each other in a physical way. Cuddling or curling up beside each other to sleep would not only be foolish, but painful. The fact that she'd allowed herself to drift off after lovemaking should have galled her to no end.

Despite that, she wanted to march herself right back over there and crawl back into his arms.

"I'll pass." She smiled to show him she meant no harm.

Something in his gaze told her he knew her thoughts. "It's three in the morning," he pointed out. "We've already discussed this, so where will you go?"

Relief flooded her, though she refused to acknowledge it. She hated that she felt she needed some sort of justification for wanting to be with him.

"You're right," she said, shutting her mind down to all rational thoughts as she crossed the room and slid under the covers and next to the warmth of his very sexy, muscular body.

He wrapped his arms around her, and she was still there the next morning when she woke.

Savoring the moment, she allowed herself the luxury of studying his sleeping face. His rugged and chiseled features were softer in slumber.

Moving slowly, she eased out from under his arm and slipped from the bed. Though she tried her best to be quiet, he opened his eyes and sat up. "What's going on?"

"I've got an appointment with a probate attorney this morning," she told him, pulling on her pajamas and hoping her dad was still asleep. "I also want to follow up with the police."

"I told you I would do that." He dragged his hand through his already tousled hair. "And I'll definitely be going with you to the lawyer."

Of course. Because he was her bodyguard, after all.

The meeting with the attorney went exactly as she'd expected. She'd filled out forms and brought a copy of the will, the bank statements and papers from the brokerage detailing all their investment holdings.

During the meeting, which lasted a little more than an hour, Jesse remained in the waiting room, cooling his heels.

When she finally emerged, the sight of his rugged, familiar face made her want to smile.

"All finished?" he asked.

"For now." The attorney, a tall thin man with a goatee and wire-rimmed glasses, studied Jesse curiously. "And you are?"

"Jesse is my bodyguard," Eva replied, before Jesse could answer. "Drew hired him a couple of weeks before he was murdered. He wanted to make sure I was safe."

The lawyer appeared suitably impressed. "I'll give you a call once all of this is logged in at the courthouse. Once the judge sets a hearing date, you'll have to make an appearance."

"Thank you." Gripping her purse, she straightened her shoulders and tried to appear confident.

Jesse stayed a few steps behind as she exited the office. They waited for the elevator in silence. Once the doors opened, they stepped inside. With any other man, she might have felt awkward. Instead, she found herself entertaining fantasies of stopping the elevator between floors and seducing him. The thought made her entire body heat. She glanced at him sideways, wondering if he might be thinking the same thing.

When the elevator arrived at the lobby, she impulsively took Jesse's arm, earning a surprised look. She simply smiled as they headed toward the entrance.

Pushing through the front doors, they stepped outside. Flashbulbs exploded. A small crowd had gathered, all talking at once. Shouting out her name, asking questions, each trying to be heard over the others. "What the…" Eva dug in her heels, turning to face Jesse, not bothering to hide her panic. They were surrounded on three sides by cameras and video recorders and reporters. No less than five news vans—two of them national—were parked in the street directly across from the building. She'd have to get past them to reach the parking lot and her car.

"Jesse." She gripped his arm. "What do we do?"

"Keep your head down and stay close," Jesse ordered. He immediately began hustling her past the crowd of reporters, all shouting out questions.

Grateful for him, she held on tight. A few of the reporters were brazen enough to follow, still shouting out questions.

Jesse took her around to the passenger side and helped her in before he took the driver's seat. The silence once the car doors were closed was welcome.

She waited until Jesse started the engine, backed out

of the spot and turned onto the street before exhaling. "What was that all about?"

"I don't know." The grim set of his jaw told her how he felt about what had just happened. "I'm going to venture a guess that there's been another revelation of some sort about Drew."

Immediately, she began scanning the radio stations. "Maybe we'll hear something." But though she continually searched, she found nothing mentioning Drew Rowson. "This is crazy," she said. "Have you had a chance to contact the authorities for a progress report?"

Jesse shook his head. "Not yet. I'll check in with them in a little bit."

"You'd think the police would have notified me if they'd learned something important."

"I'm sure we'll find out soon enough," he said. "And someone would have called you if they'd made a major breakthrough in the case."

Though she nodded, she wasn't entirely convinced. She didn't like the way the police had handled this entire investigation. It was almost like there were multiple other things going on at the same time. She couldn't help but wonder what.

When they reached the house, as soon as he parked in front of the garage, Eva bolted. Shaking his head, he followed, but she was moving so fast he barely caught sight of her as she barreled up the stairs.

In the kitchen, he found Raul, sitting at the table drinking black coffee and eating a sandwich. "What's up?" he asked, eyeing Jesse. "You look kind of frazzled."

"Maybe," Jesse conceded, dropping into a chair.

"Eva and I just left her attorney's office. When we walked outside, we were mobbed by reporters."

Raul finished chewing and swallowed. "Why? What's happened now?"

"No idea. We tried every station on the radio, but couldn't find anything."

Finishing the last of his sandwich in two huge bites, Raul pushed to his feet and carried his plate to the sink. "Let me know when you find out," he said, before ambling off.

Jesse's burner phone rang. Glancing at the caller ID, he nearly groaned out loud. It was his handler, E.J., and Jesse had a pretty good idea why he was calling.

"The entire office saw your pretty mug on TV this afternoon," E.J. drawled. "What the hell were you thinking?"

"I had no idea those reporters would be there," Jesse protested. "And I still have no idea why."

E.J. snorted. "Drew Rowson again. Man, that guy had more secrets than even we knew about."

"What now?"

"Someone leaked to the media a story that Rowson had a secret lover. A *male* lover." E.J. paused, apparently to let that sink in.

"It had to be Chris," Jesse mused out loud. "That was Drew's boyfriend, and we're ninety-nine percent sure he's the one who's been threatening Eva. You heard about the exploding drone?"

"I did." E.J. went silent for a moment. "You mean you *knew* about Drew being gay?"

Jesse explained about the photo album and the prenup they had found. "She even challenged the caller the last time he phoned her. Told him she knew about him and Drew. He hung up."

"Interesting. Any idea on the status of locating him and bringing him in?"

Frustrated, Jesse dragged his hand through his hair. "I was about to ask you the same question. I promised Eva that I'd look into that. I assumed the big guns had been brought in on this."

"Sorry, no. We've got bigger things to focus on, you know that. We left that up to the local uniforms. I think they might be working with the FBI. Check with them."

As usual, the various agencies apparently weren't communicating. Or, if they were, it was to coordinate making sure no one screwed up taking down all the major players in the upcoming drug bust. The very one Raul had mentioned.

"I'll do that," Jesse said. "Sorry about the unwanted exposure. But it wasn't like I had a choice."

"Just be more careful," E.J. cautioned. "We can't have anything jeopardize the takedown. We've been working too hard on this."

"I'm well aware." Jesse hoped his dry tone wasn't lost on his supervisor. "I've been right here in the thick of it for nearly four years."

"Well, keep after it. Once we're done, you can take a long, well-deserved vacation." With that, the assistant special agent in charge hung up.

Stomach churning, Jesse shoved his phone into his pocket and went to find whichever Brother was on duty and ask him to keep an eye on Eva. Since he couldn't clue Eva in on what he'd learned without revealing his source, he'd have to keep this one to himself. For now, he needed a break. A fast-and-furious ride on his Harley might go a long way toward helping him clear his head.

He found Patches on the back patio, feet up on the brick fireplace, smoking a cigarette. The other man grinned when Jesse put in his request. "Damn straight, I'll keep an eye on her. That little lady is one hot tamale." Patches whistled, blowing out smoke at the same time. "I wouldn't mind getting some of that, let me tell you."

Jesse wasn't sure when or how he moved, but he had the other man by the shirt collar and shoved him back against the wall before he realized what he was doing.

"Hey, man," Patches protested. "What gives?"

"Don't you even think about touching her, you hear me? She's *mine*." With that, he let Patches go, shoving him away.

"Got it." Patches stumbled backward, his expression conciliatory. Only the quick flash of fury in his eyes revealed how he really felt.

Jesse didn't care if he made an enemy of the man. "You know what? Clearly you can't handle being a temporary bodyguard. I'll find one of the other guys. You go back to doing whatever you're doing." He stalked off without giving Patches a chance to answer.

Raul met him on the stairs. "What the hell just happened?" he demanded. "I thought you were going to deck him."

Refusing to allow himself to feel foolish, Jesse told Eva's father what Patches had said.

Raul's expression darkened. "I'll have a word with him."

"Good." Still trying to tamp back his fury, Jesse swallowed hard. "Would you mind keeping an eye on Eva while I take my bike for a spin? I need to get some air."

"No problem." Raul waved him away. "Go. Get it out of your system. I'll see you when you get back."

Relieved, Jesse turned around and headed for the garage.

As soon as he left the gated neighborhood, he finally allowed himself to relax. His bike purred beneath him, the quiet rumble soothing. He rode the local streets, wishing he could avoid downtown Anniversary, but there was no way to reach the interstate without going straight down Main Street.

Once he'd left the town behind him, he gradually opened the Harley up, pushing everything from his mind but the wind and the bike and the pavement under his tires.

He rode until the frustration coiled up inside him had loosened its claws. But no matter how far he went, he couldn't shake the image of Eva's eyes, gazing at him with desire and love, her lush mouth open to receive his kiss.

Damned, that was what he was. He saw no way this could end well for anyone, especially for him. For the first time in his long and distinguished career, he'd begun to actually consider getting out. He wanted a life with Eva, even though that might be an impossible dream once she learned the truth about him.

Fool that he was, he couldn't help but hope. He'd always heard love could find a way. Maybe the time had come to find out if that was actually true.

Turning around, he made his way back toward town and Eva.

He wasn't entirely certain what he intended to do, but for the first time in years, he actually felt a glimmer of hope.

Chapter 14

Eva stood one hip cocked against the kitchen counter, clearly just finishing up a call when Jesse walked into the kitchen. Judging from her shell-shocked expression, it hadn't been a good one. He figured it had either been Ted or Beth Rowson or Lori, though possibly the anonymous caller might have decided to make another futile attempt.

When she dropped her phone on the counter, she momentarily covered her face with both hands. For one heart-stopping moment, he thought she might burst into tears, a prospect that terrified him.

Swallowing hard, he waited, resisting the urge to go to her and wrap her up tight in his arms.

Finally, she raised her head, her expression resolute, and met his gaze.

"What's going on?" he asked.

"That was the FBI," she replied. "They've located Chris—Drew's Chris—and brought him in for questioning. They said he won't answer anything. Now he has an attorney and is trying to make some sort of deal." She took a deep breath. "He also is demanding to meet with me face-to-face."

Instantly alert, Jesse resisted the urge to swear. "Are they going to allow you to do that? The guy has been trying to kill you, after all. I'll be honest, I'm not sure how I feel about that idea."

"They assured me I'll be safe." She looked down at her phone as if she expected it to have the answer. When she lifted her chin again, he saw determination in her gaze. "I want to talk to him. He must be pretty desperate to have been threatening me like that."

"And attempting to kill you," he growled. "If this Chris guy is involved with the cartel and they're looking to him for that three million dollars, then yeah, he's right to be scared. But he's not right to take his fear out on an innocent woman."

"I agree." The faraway look in her eyes had him concerned.

"Then why are you even considering meeting him?"

"Because I've got questions that only he has the answers to." The determined lift of her chin told him she'd already made her decision.

"Then I'm going with you," he stated.

"Why?" she shot back. "Since he's in police custody, I'm not in danger anymore. So I'm thinking you might be done with your bodyguard duties."

"Not hardly. I'm not going anywhere until this entire thing is wrapped up." But the instant the drug bust went down, he'd disappear. That's what undercover operatives always did. One minute they were there, the next, vanished in a puff of smoke.

Only this time, he'd be leaving his heart behind.

Enjoying Jesse's companionship over coffee felt like the first time Eva had relaxed in forever. She'd never met another man like Jesse, one who not only could be her best friend and supporter, but who could turn her on with a smile or a touch. Sadly, she suspected someone like that came around only once in a lifetime.

When Eva's cell rang and caller ID showed the Rowsons' number, Eva scowled and immediately sent the call to voice mail. Dealing with any more of Drew's parents' nonsense was the last thing she felt like dealing with.

"Drew's parents," she explained. "No way am I taking that call."

"I don't blame you." His warm smile caused an answering warmth to bloom inside her.

A moment later, her phone chirped to let her know she had a voice mail. Good. She'd play it back later. Maybe. Or maybe not.

"Have you two seen the paper?" Raul brought the newspaper into the kitchen, his expression dark. "This is unreal," he growled, dropping it onto the kitchen table in front of Eva. "Talk about trying to make something from nothing."

Sliding the paper in front of her, she saw the front-page photo first, tucked into an article at the bottom. The picture was an old one of her and Jesse, cuddling up in a restaurant booth. It had been right before Christmas, long before she'd ever met Drew. Expression full of joy and love, she had a Santa hat perched jauntily on her head. Jesse had just kissed her and their gazes were locked on each other with that particular kind of intensity only lovers understood.

Now, that felt like a lifetime ago. She felt a twinge of envy for the people they'd been back then.

One of the bikers' girlfriends had taken that picture. How and why the newspaper had obtained it, Eva had no idea.

Jesse came over and stood behind her, his breath tickling her cheek. He pointed and cursed. The large headline teased innuendo. "Gay Politician's Wife Secretly Involved with Biker Bodyguard." She gasped out loud. Who the hell was feeding this nonsense to the press?

"Oh, it gets even worse," Raul said. "Now they're speculating that Jesse might be behind Drew's murder. Even more reason the two of you ought to consider disappearing with me. I can get you both new identities made in a couple of days."

Eva shook her head, still reading the article.

"I don't think so," Jesse responded, reading over her shoulder. "Eva, I wouldn't be surprised if Lori was the one who fed this story to the paper. She's the only person who could have come up with enough factual-type evidence they'd find necessary to run it."

"No wonder Drew's parents just called," Eva groaned. "I'm guessing they're going to find a way to blame me for this."

"Probably." Jesse eyed her over his coffee cup.

Groaning, Eva pushed the paper away. "I'm tired of dealing with stuff like this. I miss my son and I want my life back."

"That can be fixed," her father said. "We can go

pick up Liam right now. Since Chris is in custody, I'm guessing the danger has passed."

Stunned, she stared. "You know what? I'm not sure. I don't think it's safe yet to bring my baby home." Glancing at Jesse, she half expected him to disagree. Instead, he nodded.

"Then once you have Liam, you all can join me on my journey to paradise," Raul continued, as if she hadn't spoken.

"I don't know about that," Eva demurred.

"This is your only shot, you know. You need to make up your mind soon," Raul continued. "I'm going to be taking off in the next day or so."

"What?" Both Eva and Jesse raised their heads, staring at the older man in shock. "Are you serious?"

"Yes. Things are getting too hot. The Feds are breathing down my neck. And some of the guys I had working for me evidently got BOS involved in bad stuff. Drugs, mostly. But really bad stuff. The kind of thing I always swore to stay away from. By the time I found out, we were in too deep. They knew I wanted no part of it, but they went ahead and did it anyways. I'm done. I want to wash my hands of the entire thing."

He took a deep breath, glancing around the room as if he wanted to make certain he wasn't overheard. "They just notified me a big exchange is going down. I told them to cancel it but they refused. It's out of my hands now. I'm not going to go to prison for something I had absolutely no part in."

"Oh, Dad," Eva cried. "If you take off, then Liam will grow up without ever knowing his grandfather."

"Not if you go with me," Raul replied. "Think sun and sand and turquoise water. I've got plenty of money stashed away—earned honestly, I assure you. Neither of you will ever want for anything."

Eva glanced from her father to Jesse, seriously considering the prospect and wondering what he thought. Being Jesse, of course, he knew better than to open his mouth, so he pretended a sudden interest in rereading the newspaper article. This made her want to shake him.

"Jesse?" she finally asked. "What do you think?"

Talk about laying her heart bare. This was as close as she'd ever get to asking him one more time to give it all up and go with her. Choose her. Choose love.

The moment he raised his head, her heart sank. Expression carefully blank, he shrugged. "That's up to you," he said. "I can't make that choice for you."

Though she nodded, she had to turn away. She needed a moment to gather herself, regain her composure. Her father's watchful gaze missed little, so she had no doubt he saw full well the extent of her heartache. As for Jesse, she had no idea what he knew or whether he cared. In his nonanswer, he'd given one. Unfortunately, he was right. She had to decide what was best for her and Liam alone. And in her heart, she already knew the answer. With or without Jesse, she and her son belonged in Texas.

"I can't," she finally said. "I want Liam to be raised here, in Texas. I don't want to spend my life on the run and in hiding. I've done nothing to warrant living like that. Neither has Liam."

Raul nodded, though his crestfallen expression revealed he'd hoped for a different answer. "I understand."

"Isn't there any alternative?" Eva asked. "Surely there's something else you can do?"

"Not really." Raul's attempt at appearing unconcerned fell flat. "But don't worry about me. I'll be fine. And I can always reach out to you periodically, in case you change your mind."

"Thanks." Looking at the two men she loved the most, Eva turned abruptly and left the room.

It took every ounce of self-control Jesse possessed not to go after her. He actually pushed to his feet before realizing she wouldn't welcome his presence. Not right now. Maybe not ever. Damn, he hoped he was wrong.

He swore he could feel her pain. A moment later, they heard the sound of her climbing the stairs.

"You know, all she ever wanted was a normal life," Jesse said. "Instead, she's been through hell and back. Eva deserves better than that."

"Damn right she does." Raul grimaced and shook his head. "That's why I hoped she'd go with me. She'd want for nothing. And sun, sand and ocean would go a long way toward healing her."

"I don't disagree," Jesse replied.

Raising his eyebrows in surprise, Raul studied him. "Would you have gone if she'd decided to go with me?"

Though the answer to that question should have taken a lot of contemplation, Jesse answered immediately. "Yes, I would."

"You'd leave everything behind, just like that?"

Slightly shocked at his own response, this time Jesse made himself consider the question. Once, his career with the ATF had been his entire life. It simply was never enough. Now, he realized his existence could be

so much more than just a job. He wanted his family—
Eva and Liam, even if the DNA test revealed the boy
wasn't his by blood. "I would," he replied, his voice
certain.

Expression pleased, Raul nodded. "That makes me
feel like I'll be leaving her in good hands. Promise me
you'll look after her."

"Of course." More than anything, Jesse wanted to
offer the other man some sort of plea deal, let him know
he didn't have to disappear. But he didn't have the authority and it would take a little time for him to run the
idea through the proper channels. Of course, he had no
idea whether Raul would even consider such a thing,
but maybe it wouldn't hurt to put it out there once he
had it approved. The tricky part would be to make sure
no one knew about Raul's plan to disappear. It might
be wrong, and even go against everything he'd ever
stood for, but Jesse had no intention of giving up Eva's
father. Not even if his failure to do so cost him his job.

The next morning, Eva rose early, full of a curious combination of anticipation and dread. Today she
would finally meet Drew's Chris, the person her husband had apparently loved. Also, possibly the person
who'd invested a great deal of effort in threatening
and trying to kill her, all in a quest for three million
missing dollars.

After breakfast, Jesse drove her downtown to the
Anniversary sheriff's department. Eva hadn't been
sure how to dress—after all, what did one wear to meet
one's husband's lover? In the end, she settled for a pair
of fashionably torn jeans tucked into boots, a cute tunic
top and chunky gold jewelry. Torn between wearing

her hair up or not, she'd settled on down, wanting a more casual look.

"You look beautiful," Jesse told her, almost as if he somehow knew she needed reassurance.

"Thanks," she replied, fidgeting with her bracelets. "I'm not sure how this is going to go."

"It'll be fine. They'll have him in restraints. There's no way he's going to be able to hurt you."

"Except with words," she reminded him with a wry smile. "That's always a distinct possibility."

When they arrived at the police department and parked, she found herself sitting frozen in her seat, wondering if she could make herself get out of the car.

Instead of rushing her, Jesse simply sat with her, waiting until she felt ready.

Finally, she felt foolish doing nothing. "Let's go," she said. "I might as well get this over with."

Inside, the receptionist greeted her by name, clearly recognizing her. "Let me tell the sheriff you're here," she said, picking up the phone.

A moment later, a uniformed officer appeared. "The suspect is being held in a cell in our holding area in the back," he announced. "The sheriff has asked me to bring you to the interrogation room. He'll meet us there with the suspect."

Eva nodded. Her heart had begun pounding and her mouth went dry. Briefly, she felt dizzy and wondered if she might faint. But then, as she caught Jesse's worried gaze, she remembered her resolve to reclaim her innate strength. Straightening her shoulders, she lifted her chin and marched after the police officer with purpose in her step.

They were shown to a nondescript room—gray

walls and floor, black plastic chairs and a long metallic table that looked as if it might have been intended originally for the autopsy department.

Jesse pulled out a chair for her and Eva sat. For a moment, she thought Jesse intended to stand right behind her, but he took the chair next to her instead.

The door opened and Sheriff Brown entered, his large stomach preceding him. Two armed officers brought in a tall, slender man with his wrists and ankles shackled. When his bright blue gaze met hers, Eva almost gasped out loud.

Because Chris Jay, with his patrician, chiseled features and thick blond hair, was as breathtakingly, stunningly beautiful as any man could be.

While they studied each other, the sheriff ruffled paperwork. Finally, he cleared his throat and motioned to the two guards that Chris should be seated. He chose a chair directly across from Eva.

"Hello." The flash of his warm smile was another surprise. "It's about time we finally met."

Beside her, she felt Jesse tense up.

"I guess so," she responded. "Since clearly you didn't succeed in killing me."

"I told you that wasn't me. You clearly have another enemy."

She snorted, unable to help herself. "I know you claimed that early on, but later you forgot you'd said that. I don't think that's going to help you now."

Chris's amazing eyes narrowed, but he didn't dispute her statement. "Are you planning to press charges?" he asked, his tone as banal as if they were merely discussing the weather.

"Of course. I'll have nightmares for years about that drone."

He nodded. "I loved him, you know. Drew and I had something special. Did you ever care for him?"

"That's none of your business," she replied, keeping her tone as even as his. "Why did you think he stole your money?"

"It wasn't mine," he replied. "It was ours. We were planning to use it to start a new life together."

"Only it didn't belong to you," Sheriff Brown interjected, checking his notes. "According to this, that money belonged to a drug cartel out of Mexico. Drew was laundering it for them and stole it."

"So say you." Chris gave an elegant shrug. "Drew felt that he had earned it for going over and beyond his duties."

Looking from one man to the other, Eva wasn't sure what to say. She believed laundering money might be a federal crime though, so she figured the FBI would be arriving soon.

The sheriff confirmed her thoughts a second later. "We're only holding him for the Feds," he said, his expression pained. "He's facing a multitude of charges, from racketeering and money laundering to attempted murder."

Jesse spoke up for the first time. "If that's the case, then why is Eva here?"

"Good question." The sheriff nodded his approval. "I asked Mrs. Rowson here for two reasons. One, because Mr. Jay here assured me that he wanted to apologize." He shot Chris a hard look of reproach. "And second, I'm guessing the FBI will need to ask you a few questions."

"Not without her attorney present," Jesse quickly responded.

"And you are?" Brown pinned Jesse with his gaze.

"He's my bodyguard," Eva said. "And it's possible he's right. While Drew never involved me in his business dealings, now that I've been made aware he committed several crimes, it's probably best that I obtain legal counsel."

Chris burst into laughter, surprising them. He began an insulting slow clap, eyeing her with what appeared to be begrudging approval. "Look at you," he chortled. "Pretending to be all innocent. Everyone knows about your connection with the Brothers of Sin. Hell, I'd venture a guess that's why Drew even married you in the first place. Your father pulled a lot of strings to help Drew get the high-paying jobs."

She stared at him as if he'd spoken another language. "My involvement with the Brothers of Sin is minimal at best."

"Right. I'm sure you funneled that stolen three mil right into their hands, didn't you?"

Jesse pushed to his feet so quickly, he knocked his chair to the floor with a clatter. "You're a fool. You haven't got the faintest idea what you're talking about. When was the last time you saw Drew?"

"You're not FBI, are you?" Chris sneered. "I think I'll wait for their questions, thank you very much."

Shaking his head, Jesse turned to the sheriff. "In addition to all the other charges, he needs to be investigated in Drew's murder."

Chris gasped out loud. "I would never!" he exclaimed, his tone indignant. "I adored Drew. I would never harm a hair on that man's head. Why would you even think I would kill him?"

"I can think of three million reasons," Jesse drawled.

"It wasn't me, I can assure you." Drew cocked his head and thought for a moment, his expression darkening. "I'll bet it was that bitch. Drew was going to cut her out and she didn't like it."

Eva glanced at Jesse, who shrugged.

"I'm talking about Lori Pearson, you fools." Chris pointed at the sheriff. "I wouldn't be surprised if she's halfway to Mexico right now. When was the last time anyone checked on her?"

"Why should we believe anything you have to say?" the sheriff drawled.

But as a chill raced up Eva's spine, she *knew*. What Chris said made sense. Another look at Jesse and she realized he'd reached a similar conclusion.

"Sheriff, would you mind sending a couple of guys to round up Lori Pearson? There's definitely merit to what Chris here has to say."

Arms folded, Sheriff Brown stared. "On what merit? I haven't seen a single reason why we would suspect Ms. Pearson of anything."

"Can't you just bring her in for questioning?" Eva asked. "I definitely think it's worth checking out."

"We've already talked to her once." Clearly hesitant, Sheriff Brown frowned. "But I guess it wouldn't hurt to try again."

"If you can find her," Chris interjected. "I'm pretty sure she's in the wind by now."

Stomach churning, Eva wondered if he was right. She remembered Lori's weirdly fluctuating attitude, her reluctance to let Eva in Drew's office and her

strange comments regarding Drew's will. Add to that
the salacious details that had been anonymously leaked
to the press…

As soon as they got back to the house, Jesse excused
himself and started making phone calls. He left a voice
mail for E.J., seriously annoyed that his handler wasn't
immediately reachable. Next, he called the Dallas FBI
office, asking for the special agent in charge. When the
receptionist tried to put him off and take a message,
he dug up a name from memory, which got him put
through to Mary Pena. Luckily, she remembered him.
Once they got the obligatory chitchat out of the way,
he got down to business with his questions. While she
wasn't actively involved in this particular operation,
she was able to point him in the right direction.

However, since he couldn't come out and identify
himself as an undercover ATF agent, he ended up getting the runaround.

Frustrated, he called E.J. once more. Again, his call
went to voice mail. He left yet another message and
debated making the trip to Dallas himself. Since it was
still early afternoon, if he was lucky, he might make it
to the FBI offices shortly before closing time.

In the end, he decided to exercise some patience.
Sure enough, the sheriff called Eva a couple of hours
later with bad news.

Lori had disappeared. When the sheriff's deputies
had gone by to round her up, they'd found an empty
apartment and no trace she'd ever worked in Drew's
downtown office.

After relaying the news to Jesse, Eva withdrew, saying she needed time to think. He nodded, keeping his

distance, but staying close just in case. She seemed beside herself. Pacing the hallway from the front door to the kitchen, she kept shaking her head and muttering that she should have seen this coming.

Finally, Jesse stopped her. "Even if you'd known, what could you have done?"

"I don't know." But she finally stopped moving. "It's just that she was in my house and I shared meals with her. To think she might have done something like this…"

He risked touching her shoulder, a quick, gentle squeeze. "They'll find her. My understanding is that there are multiple agencies involved now. Not only the Anniversary PD, but the FBI too."

"I sure hope so."

"Come on." Taking her arm, he steered her toward the kitchen. "Let me get you something to drink and we can sit down and brainstorm."

She slowly nodded. "I'd like that."

Once she'd taken a seat at the table, he poured them both a cup of coffee and fixed hers the way she liked it—one cream and two sugars. "I just can't believe Drew trusted her. I did too. Heck, even his parents did. If what Chris said is true and she actually did this, it will be a betrayal of the worst kind."

"Agreed." Pulling out the chair across from her, he took a sip of his coffee. He allowed himself to feel a moment of contentment before focusing back on the reality of his situation. "However, we don't have any proof. Only his word. To be honest, I don't really trust him."

"True." She made a face. "After his numerous attempts to kill me, he's now trying the equivalent of saying *just kidding*."

"Maybe we need to take another look in Drew's office. Though she's probably scrubbed it clean of anything that would even remotely implicate her, there's always the possibility that she might have missed something."

Eva brightened. "Good idea. Though I'm thinking Sheriff Brown or the FBI would have gotten a search warrant by now."

"I'll double-check." Privately, he thought if they hadn't, then no one was doing their job.

"I'm glad I caught you both together," Raul announced, strolling into the kitchen. "I'm going to give you one last chance."

Both Jesse and Eva looked up.

"Last chance for what?" Eva asked.

Jesse thought he already knew. The huge drug deal. Jesse's only orders were to watch Eva in case their intel turned out to be wrong and she ended up being involved. Though Jesse could have told E.J. that he knew with 100 percent certainty that she wasn't, he kept his mouth shut. After all, he still hadn't decided how he planned to handle all that would certainly occur after the bust went down.

"Last chance to join me in paradise." Though Raul smiled, the tension in his gaze told of his inner turmoil. "I'm leaving tomorrow morning. I think it's best to get the hell out of the country before this crazy drug exchange goes down."

Though Eva nodded, her crestfallen expression revealed her shock and dismay. "So soon?"

Raul went to her and squeezed her shoulder. "Please come. We can go collect Liam and be on our way. I've got a private jet fueled and waiting."

Chapter 15

Clenching his jaw, Jesse watched as myriad conflicting emotions chased across Eva's beautiful face. "I can't, Dad. I wish you would consider some other alternative."

"What, jail?" Raul laughed, a sound totally without humor. "I got this, baby girl. And believe it or not, I understand. This is for you." He pulled a thumb drive from his pocket. "There's information on Drew and also Lori on that. Take a look at it, but wait to give it to the Feds until I'm gone. Ask for immunity. This will clear you and should make sure you're free from prosecution, but make sure."

Accepting the thumb drive, she nodded. "I promise."

Raul kissed her cheek before turning to face Jesse. "I want you to drive me to the airport. I'll have Shorty keep an eagle eye out for trouble here. Oh, by the way,

I'm giving you my bike, unless the Feds confiscate it for auction."

Touched, Jesse agreed. "When do you want to go?"

"I think now." Raul's answer surprised him. "One thing I've learned is it's best to not stick to a schedule. I've got my pilot on standby. I'll call when we're five minutes out and have him meet us there."

"Why so soon?" Eva protested. "Can't you wait until the morning?"

Raul told her he couldn't. Jesse understood. Now that the older man had made sure his daughter wouldn't change her mind, he'd decided to cut his losses and take off. Too much could go wrong in a short time, so why take a chance?

Eva folded her arms. "Has it ever occurred to you that I might want to see you off too?"

Smiling sadly, Raul kissed her cheek. "I think it's best if you stay here. I still have a lot of enemies and I don't want to take a chance of putting you in a dangerous situation."

Her mouth tightened. "But if I was going with you, I'd be with you. What's the difference?"

"I'd have taken additional precautions," he said. "And if you're trying to tell me you've changed your mind, I will set them up immediately."

Eva shook her head. "I haven't changed my mind. But if this is going to be so dangerous, why take Jesse?"

"Because he can handle himself." Ruffling her hair, Raul moved away, signaling to Jesse that he was ready to go.

Raul had packed two medium-size bags. Jesse loaded them into the car, staying back a respectful distance as Eva hugged her father and they said their goodbyes.

Once they'd finished, Jesse waited to see if Raul planned to say goodbye to his guys. They weren't assembled to see him off, which seemed a bit odd.

"I didn't tell them," Raul replied when Jesse asked. "Honestly, I have no idea who I can trust anymore. With the exception of you, that is." He clapped Jesse on the back.

Swallowing back his guilt, Jesse nodded and got in the car.

Raul kept up a steady stream of chatter, directing Jesse toward the smaller regional airport. "Normally, I would have had to pay off some local officials to get permission to land and take off from there," Raul said smugly. "But this jet is registered to a fictional eccentric billionaire and I let leak that Anniversary was on the short list for his fake company headquarters, so everyone was really amenable. I've had my pilot file a completely false flight plan, but even if the Feds eventually figure out it was me, it won't matter."

Jesse nodded, not sure how to respond. He could only hope that Raul didn't decide to go all buddy-buddy and actually mention his true destination. If he did, Jesse planned to interrupt and stop him. He truly didn't want to know.

Though Jesse had decided against mentioning anything about a plea deal to E.J., in case even the mere suggestion raised alarm flags, he wanted to see if Raul would like to give it a shot. At the very least, he could offer Eva's father another choice instead of disappearing.

"Have you ever thought about maybe going to the authorities and telling them you weren't involved?"

Jesse asked, just as they turned down the back road onto the private airstrip.

"Like they'd believe me," Raul snorted. "Plus, I might be a lot of things, but I'm not a snitch."

"I know," Jesse replied. "But since these guys went against your wishes and got involved with a rival cartel..."

"How did you know that?"

Perplexed, Jesse shrugged. "You told us. Both me and Eva, remember?"

"No, I told you what they'd done, but I never mentioned anything about the cartel."

Stomach clenching, Jesse tried to play it off. "I guess I just assumed." Damn, he'd blown it. He knew better, but he'd managed to mess up. Every instinct screamed an alert. But this was more than being caught in a lie. He'd also betrayed the man he'd come to love like a father. He took zero comfort in knowing at least he hadn't jeopardized the entire assignment.

They pulled up in front of a gleaming silver Gulfstream and parked. Instead of climbing out, Raul gave Jesse a long look.

"You're a Fed, aren't you?" His flat tone matched the disappointment in his eyes.

Jesse thought for a moment and then decided what the hell. "I am. I've been undercover this entire time."

"I could shoot you, you know."

"I know." Jesse nodded. "But you won't. You're too decent for that."

This made Raul laugh. "Maybe so. What are you going to do? Arrest me?"

"No." Jesse took a deep breath. "I'm going to let you go and pretend I never saw you leave."

Raul considered him, as if trying to determine if

Jesse spoke truth. "You know you might lose your job over this."

"I'm going to quit as soon as all this is over," Jesse replied. "I can't do this kind of work anymore. I've gotten too involved."

Expression too wise, Raul nodded. "You love her, don't you?"

"Yes. I always have and I always will."

"Are you going to tell her?" Raul asked, his expression both curious and compassionate.

"I am. I don't really have a choice. If she and I are ever going to have a life together, we can't begin it with lies."

The pilot stepped outside the jet door, signaling a crew member who came and collected Raul's bags. Once again, Jesse knew Eva's father could snap his fingers, give a simple order and have his people take Jesse down.

"Best of luck, Jesse." Raul shook hands. "I respect your decision and I really appreciate you telling me the truth. I wish you and my Eva many years of happiness."

Moved despite himself, Jesse managed a smile. "For you, I hope for beautiful women, umbrella drinks, warm sand and lots of sun."

"I'll drink to that." Raul's infectious smile warmed Jesse's heart. "Take care. Give my daughter a kiss for me."

With that, Raul turned and went up the steps to the jet, never looking back even once.

Jesse stayed by the car and watched the jet taxi onto the runway. He didn't move until he saw it take off and launch into the sky.

* * *

With her father gone for good, Eva felt the emptiness of the big house even more keenly. She longed for Jesse, even though she knew he'd be back soon enough. She missed Liam even more. She'd never been away from her son any longer than a few hours and this felt like an eternity. Though Marie and Mike made sure to call her at least once a day and let her Skype with Liam, she ached to hold him in her arms.

Yet she still didn't feel comfortable having him back here. While she'd considered the possibility of bringing him home, she couldn't shake the sense that the danger wasn't quite over yet. Her worry might have had something to do with the fact that Lori Pearson was out in the wind somewhere and Eva had no idea how much malice the other woman bore toward her. For all she knew, Lori could be involved with the cartel. If she could convince the wrong person that Eva had their missing money, they'd come after her. She couldn't risk exposing Liam to that kind of danger.

The thumb drive her father had given her felt as if it was burning a hole in her jeans pocket. Curious to see what it contained, she took it into Drew's office and plugged it into his computer.

Video files. Several of them, as well as data files. She carefully copied everything to the computer so she could make a second thumb drive and keep it safe.

Once she'd done that, she took a deep breath and clicked on the first video.

Though black-and-white, the quality seemed surprisingly good. While she wasn't sure how her father had obtained this footage or even if he'd been the one who'd planted cameras in Drew's office, when she heard the discussion between Drew and Lori, she actually gasped out loud.

Clearly in charge, Lori berated Drew, who looked frustrated and agitated. She demanded he tell her why there'd been a delay and asked if he didn't understand the cartel had been breathing down her neck.

The video ended abruptly and Eva clicked on the next one. This time, Drew outlined to Lori the ways campaign funds could and couldn't be used. Listening to Lori's replies, Eva quickly ascertained the two were figuring out ways to use that money without being caught.

But for what? Though she'd hoped for answers, this video provided none. So she checked out the next one.

Apparently, they got worse as they went on. There was one of Drew and Lori talking to Chris on speakerphone, as they all made plans to leave the country once they'd wired enough money to their individual offshore accounts. Judging by the amount of money they were discussing, the missing three million dollars seemed to be a mere drop in the bucket. In fact, the more she heard, the less the amount made sense.

Either way, just the first few videos were enough to convict Lori of several crimes. And Eva hadn't even watched half of them.

But she would. She clicked on the next one. This time, it wasn't just Drew and Lori. She was so engrossed in watching her husband and his campaign manager meet with three well-dressed politicians as well as two men who probably were part of the cartel, she didn't notice Shorty enter the room until he was right behind her. She smelled him before she saw him, recognizing the combination of cigarettes and beer and unwashed man.

"Hey." He greeted her, eyeing the computer screen with undisguised curiosity in his bloodshot eyes. "What's that?"

"Nothing." Hurriedly, she minimized the open page. "What's up, Shorty? Is there something I can help you with?"

"Um, yeah." He scratched the back of his bald head. "I'm wondering if you know when Raul will be back. We've got a bit of a situation that he needs to handle. One of his top lieutenants has been trying to reach him without any luck."

She shrugged, hoping like hell she appeared nonchalant. No doubt it had something to do with the big drug deal Raul had wanted to escape from. "I'm not sure. He and Jesse left a little bit ago. But I can tell him to find you when he returns."

Though Shorty stared for what felt like a bit too long, he finally nodded. "Thanks," he said, and ambled off.

Suddenly, she realized she didn't actually know whom in the club she could trust. Though Raul surely wouldn't have left her with someone who might be a danger, she still needed to be more careful. More than anyone, she knew how things could change on a dime.

She'd better quit wasting time. Heart pounding, she grabbed a blank thumb drive and copied the files to it. Now she had two extra copies—one on the computer and the other on the second thumb drive. She even had a good story to tell the sheriff on how she came to obtain all this information now—that she'd found the thumb drive in Drew's office.

The house seemed too quiet, as it did a lot these days. She truly was coming to hate this place, and as soon as she could, she planned to sell it and escape the bad memories.

When she heard the front door open, she knew Jesse had returned. Her father's loss hit her then, low and deep like a blow to the gut. Though tears filled her eyes, she refused to allow herself to cry. Raul had made his choice, just as Jesse had once when he'd chosen Brothers of Sin over her.

Despite that, despite everything, she slipped one thumb drive into her pocket and put the other inside the liquor cabinet behind a bottle of expensive Scotch and went to greet him.

Jesse looked as if he had been run over by a truck. Immediately alarmed, she went to him and touched his arm. "What happened? Is my dad all right?"

Slowly he nodded, his expression tortured. "He's fine."

"Then why—"

"I'm not." Interrupting her, he took her hand and gripped it tightly. "I have something I need to tell you."

For whatever reason, she hesitated. "I'm not sure I want to hear it. I can tell from your voice that it's bad news. I've had enough of that to last a lifetime."

"Please just listen. This is important." He looked around. "Where is everybody? I want to make sure we're not overheard."

"No idea. Shorty was in here a little bit ago, looking for Raul. I haven't seen any of the other guys."

"Do you mind if we go somewhere private? Like maybe Drew's office."

Though she really just wanted to be alone, she gave up. "Sure. We can close the door."

Once they'd done that, Eva perched on the edge of one of the expensive Italian leather chairs. "What's up?"

Instead of immediately answering, Jesse dragged his hand through his hair. Whatever he wanted to say must be bad, because he looked as if pain was eating him up from the inside out. Watching him, her heart ached. The last time she'd seen him like this had been when she'd given him the ultimatum and asked him to choose either her or the motorcycle club.

She didn't see how anything he could possibly say now would be worse than when he'd told her his choice.

"I've been lying to you," he began, his voice catching. She saw him visibly gather himself, his handsome face a study in torment. "I'm not at all what you think I am."

Studying him, she tried to make sense of what he meant. "I know you, Jesse Wyman," she said slowly. "You're loyal and dedicated and strong. No matter what kind of baggage we've had between us, I've always known I can count on you. My father thinks so highly of you, he trusted you to become my personal bodyguard."

"Not anymore." Expression grim, he swallowed hard, apparently struggling to find the right words to convey whatever he was trying to say. Finally, he shook his head. "Damn. I didn't expect it to be this difficult. Before I begin, know that I will always be there for you, no matter what you think of me."

A shiver ran up her spine. "You're beginning to scare me. I don't understand."

"I told Raul the truth about me earlier. I'm—" His cell rang, cutting him off. Swallowing hard, he checked it. "Sorry, I've got to take this." He flashed a clearly forced smile. "Looks like I've been granted a brief reprieve."

Then, to her disbelief, he stepped away and answered his phone, opening the door and walking out of the room, talking in such a low voice that she couldn't make out the words.

She sat frozen in the chair. What had he meant? He'd been lying how? She'd told him the truth—she considered Jesse one of the best men she'd ever known. Except for his unwillingness to leave Brothers of Sin, she honestly felt Jesse might be the most perfect man she'd ever met.

Right then and there, she decided she'd rather not know. Lies were lies and it didn't really matter what they were. Drew had lied, so had Lori. Of course, she herself had been guilty of lying when she'd hoped everyone would believe Liam was Drew's son.

No one was perfect. She could forgive a falsehood or two, as long as no one got hurt. What she honestly couldn't forgive was the awful, hurtful choice Jesse had made over two years ago. He might be an awesome specimen of a man, one with character and strength and integrity. But in the end, she'd had to face the fact that she'd never come first with him. Even now, she knew she never would. Damned if she'd let him unburden his conscience just to make himself feel better.

Decision made, she turned and eyed him outside on the patio, still deep in conversation on his phone. Perfect. She turned to leave the room.

And came face-to-face with Lori Pearson, holding a gun pointed directly at her.

Eva froze, her heart beginning to pound. "Lori? What's going on?" she asked, trying not to reveal her fear.

"You're coming with me," Lori said, her expression hard. "And don't try to alert that bodyguard of yours. I'd hate to have to shoot you like I did Drew."

Shaking, Eva swallowed. "*You* killed Drew? But why? I thought you and he were partners, both in his campaign and his legal practice."

"Partners." Lori spoke the word as if it was unfamiliar. "Maybe we started out that way, but partners don't screw over one another. Drew stole money and planned to leave me to take the fall. Those cartels don't mess around. They want what belongs to them and they have zero tolerance for waiting. I had to go into hiding so they didn't kill me. All because your husband ripped them off."

Eva took a deep breath, striving for the appearance of calm, though inside she was a mess. Did Lori truly intend to kill her? Why not, since she'd already killed once? All Eva could think of was her son. She couldn't die and leave little Liam an orphan. She had to figure out a way to outwit Lori. Staying calm and keeping Lori talking was all she could think of. That, and not revealing her terror. "That's what Chris said. Was he involved with the two of you in this money laundering scheme?"

Lori grimaced. "Of course not, you idiot. He's the entire reason that Drew decided to grab the cash and make a run for it."

Aware she had to keep Lori distracted, Eva nodded. "But why did you kill him? Wouldn't that mean the money would be lost forever?"

Eva's head was spinning. While she'd known from watching the videos how deeply Lori had been involved in Drew's illegal activities, she'd never in a million years suspected the other woman would go this far. Murder?

"I had to prove my loyalty to the cartel." Eyes gleaming, Lori spoke the words as matter-of-factly as if they were discussing the weather. "That got them off my back for a bit. Plus, I was super hopeful that I'd be able to dig up a clue as to where Drew stashed the money."

The money. All Lori really cared about was the money. Maybe Eva could somehow convince the other woman she knew where it was hidden, if only to buy herself time.

"Were you?" Eva tried hard not to sneak a look out the window at Jesse. Her one real chance at salvation. She hoped if she could keep Lori talking long enough, Jesse might be able to get in here and help her. If not, she'd have to figure out a way to help herself. Despite the way her knees were shaking, she couldn't think of a better time to reclaim her strength. For Liam.

Lori snorted. "I looked, believe me. Despite that, I still haven't a clue what Drew did with it, but I'm guessing it's sitting in some private offshore account right now. I would venture a wild guess that Chris knows exactly where it is, but I haven't had any luck in locating him." With her gun still trained on Eva, Lori squinted her eyes. "I don't suppose you know where he is, do you?"

For a second, Eva considered shaking her head. Instead, she decided to go with the truth. "He's in police custody in downtown Anniversary."

"What? Why?"

"He's been threatening me. He's the one who shot out my back window and sent a package bomb."

"No." Though the hand holding the pistol never wavered, Lori appeared on the verge of hysterical laughter. "Are you serious?"

"I am." Eyeing the gun, Eva decided she might as well ask point-blank. "What are you doing? Why are you holding a gun on me?"

"Tying up loose ends." Lori glanced around Drew's office. "You truly didn't have any idea about anything, did you?"

"You mean about Drew being in love with someone else? No. Or about you and him engaging in illegal activities like money laundering?" She thought of the video recordings that Lori didn't know she had. "I'm going to venture a wild guess that there's a lot more that I didn't know."

"Definitely."

Catching a glimpse of Jesse from the corner of her eye, Eva prayed he'd finish up his call. "Lori, are you going to shoot me?"

"Not yet." Lori's ambiguous answer didn't make Eva feel any better. "But I will shoot him, if I have to." She gestured toward Jesse with her pistol. "Just like what happened to the two biker goons outside. They were so busy smoking and shooting the breeze that they never saw what hit them."

"You *shot* them?" Pushing down the panic clawing at her, Eva tried to remain calm. "I didn't hear any gunshots."

"Silencers." Lori pointed toward some sort of attachment she'd put on her weapon. "They're very effective at keeping things quiet."

Plural. Which most likely meant Lori hadn't come here alone.

"What if I know where the money is?" Eva asked.

Lori snorted. "You don't though. Or you would have told me already."

Could Eva manage to convince the other woman? Or should she abandon this line of defense and try something else?

Carefully, heart still pounding, Eva began to look for something she could use as a weapon. "Please don't hurt Jesse."

"Aw, you care about him, don't you?" Lori sighed. "He's easy on the eyes, I'll give him that. But you know what? He's a Fed."

"What? No, he's not. He works for my father."

"You really *are* gullible, aren't you? I just found out from one of my contacts that Jesse Wyman—which probably isn't his real name—is an undercover ATF officer. He's been using you, honey."

"He's not." At least Eva could speak with authority. Though she remembered what Jesse had said earlier, when he'd tried to tell her about lying to her and how he wasn't who she thought he was. What if it was true? Devastated, she pushed the sense of betrayal away. "I don't know why your contact, whoever he is, would say such a thing, but Jesse is on my side."

"Right. At least until he's finished his job. I'm not sure what that is, but I can take an educated guess that it has a lot to do with the cartel, BOS and a large shipment of drugs."

"How do you know all this?" Eva asked, stunned and not sure what to think. "How reliable is your source?"

Now Lori grinned. "Pretty damn reliable. He works for the ATF too. Only he's in it for the money. And I can promise you, the cartel is going to pay a lot of money when we deliver you and your precious Jesse to them. Now move."

Aware she had to stall to at least give Jesse time to realize what was happening, Eva stood frozen. "Move where?"

"Here. In front of me. You're going to be my shield in case your bodyguard gets any foolish ideas."

Outside, Jesse appeared to be finishing up his call. Though he continued to talk, he turned and made his way toward the door.

"Now," Lori barked. "He's worth ten times more than you are, so don't make me shoot you."

Reluctantly, Eva moved closer to Drew's former campaign manager.

As Jesse reached for the door to come inside, he looked up, glanced through the window and locked eyes with Eva. His expression hardened as he caught sight of Lori and her pistol.

"He saw," Eva said, warning Lori. "He's not going to let you get away with this."

"Really? I'm willing to bet you'll be his first priority, Eva." Lori grabbed her arm, yanking her up closer and putting the barrel of the gun against Eva's temple. "I guess you'll find out quickly how much you actually matter to him. Will he rush in and try to save you or run off and alert his law enforcement coworkers?" Lori's savage grin made Eva feel ill.

"We'll know any second, won't we?"

Eva swallowed hard. "Yes, we will," she replied. In her heart, she had to believe Jesse would choose her. In her head, she wasn't entirely certain.

Chapter 16

As soon as he turned enough to see in the window, Jesse took in the situation in an instant. Lori Pearson, armed with what appeared to be a .38 with a silencer, had her weapon trained on Eva. Since she shouldn't have been able to gain entrance to the house with two biker guards on duty, and two more close by, he could only guess at what must have happened to them. Hopefully, that supposition would turn out to be wrong. He considered those guys part of his family. They had no part of the group working in drug trafficking. They were just bikers, loyal to the club and to Raul, not criminals.

He still had E.J. on the phone. Instead of hanging up, he murmured a request for help and dropped the phone, still connected, into his pocket. Hopefully, E.J. would be able to hear well enough to understand exactly what was going on and would send agents, as well as medical personnel in case the wounded bikers were still alive.

Either way, he couldn't afford to worry about them right now. Not with Eva's life in danger.

Moving slowly, keeping his hands in plain view, he opened the door and entered the room. "Lori. What the hell are you doing?"

"Exactly what I need to do," she replied. Her confident demeanor and tone should have warned him. Instead, he didn't turn until Eva squeaked out a warning, which came a millisecond too late.

Three men, cartel from the looks of them, stepped inside. They were all armed, with their weapons pointed at Eva and Jesse.

"Three cartel members," he said loudly, needing to make double sure his handler heard. "Why so many of you?"

The tall man in front sneered. "Because we couldn't afford to take any chances. We know what you are, Lawman. And you're going to be our insurance to make sure no one interferes in our business. Got it?"

Outed. Jesse didn't dare glance at Eva to see her reaction. He'd wanted to tell her himself, but now that choice had been taken away from him. But he couldn't allow himself to focus on that. Right now he needed to worry about keeping them alive.

Four armed against two unarmed. If Eva hadn't been there, Jesse might have taken a wild chance and tried to fight. As it was, he had to do whatever it took to protect her. Again, he thought of Shorty, Patches, Rusty and Baloo. Two of them would have been on guard duty outside. No doubt Lori had done something to neutralize them. However, the other two might still be upstairs safe, assuming Lori had no idea they were here.

His BOS brothers were now his and Eva's best chance. If only he could figure out a way to alert them. Even if E.J. could hear well enough to decipher what was going on, any assistance he could send would arrive far too late.

"Now what?" he asked, looking from Lori to the three armed men. "What's your plan?"

"You're coming with us," the man who'd spoken earlier declared. "You'll be our hostage until we've completed our transaction without interference by the police or DEA."

He noted they didn't mention the FBI. Minor detail, which could mean something or nothing at all.

"What about her?" he asked, jerking his head toward Eva.

The tall man laughed. "Lori here will take care of her. She's not our problem."

"No."

All four of them looked at him, clearly surprised.

"I'm not going anywhere until I know she's safe," he continued. "I mean it."

The three cartel guys shifted their weight, appearing uneasy. Finally, their spokesman replied, "Again, this isn't up to you. Now move."

"No. Go ahead and shoot me. I have a sneaking suspicion you need me alive, as hostages generally are. I won't be of much use to you dead."

He had them there. And relished the moment they realized it.

Movement behind them caught his attention. Lori opened her mouth to shout a warning, but by the time she got the words out, Shorty and Patches had already jumped in swinging.

Baseball bats? Though he couldn't be sure, he couldn't focus on that now. Instead, he leaped forward, intent on taking out the third cartel guy and hoping Eva could deal with Lori. Left hook to the jaw, and his opponent went down like a rock, dropping his pistol.

Jesse jumped on top of him, and a few more well-aimed punches knocked the guy unconscious.

Someone squeezed off a shot. Then another, a rapid volley that could come only from a semiautomatic or fully automatic weapon. Praying no one had been hit, he turned to look for Eva.

She was gone. Along with Lori.

Damn.

"Help, please," Shorty called. He'd grabbed one man from behind in a restraining hold and seemed to be struggling to hang on. Patches and his target were struggling. Jesse saw a spreading red stain on Patches's side and realized he'd been hit.

First, he helped Shorty. Once they'd used a lamp cord to tie the guy up, they joined Patches and tag-teamed the final cartel member.

"Round up all the guns," Jesse ordered. "Shorty, take a look at Patches's wound and call 911 if necessary. I'm going to find Eva."

Lori couldn't have taken her far. Praying they hadn't left the premises, he heard a feminine voice scream for help from what sounded like the backyard, near the pool.

He sprinted outside, skidding to a halt just as Eva broke free of Lori and shoved her in the pool, gun and all.

"Are you okay?"

Looking up, Eva exhaled, dusting her hands off on her jeans. "Yep. In fact, I'm better than okay. I've been wanting to push that witch in the pool for a good while now."

Damn, he loved her. No more unable to help himself than breathe, he crossed the distance between them and pulled her into his arms. She hugged him back for just a moment, before laughing up at him. "You'd best let me go or I might let you go swimming too."

He glanced at the pool, stunned to realize Lori hadn't surfaced. "Apparently she doesn't know how to swim," he commented, right before he jumped in to save her.

Later, after the sheriff and his men had arrived and taken the prisoners into custody, even though they'd only be holding them for the FBI, he checked on Patches. The other man sat perched on the back bumper of the ambulance, arguing with Shorty and two paramedics.

"What's going on?" Jesse asked.

"They fixed me up," Patches answered. "Right as rain. I'm fine now, but these fellers want me to go to the hospital to get checked out."

"Maybe you should," Jesse pointed out.

"He definitely should," Shorty concurred. "They say he lost a lot of blood."

"I'm fine." Patches stuck out his jaw. "I know my rights. They can't force me to go without my consent."

"He's right," one of the paramedics said, his tone glum. "So if you're not going to let us take you to the hospital, can you please get off the bumper so we can be on our way?"

"I'll move when I feel ready to move," Patches shot back. "And I'm not ready yet."

"He's dizzy from loss of blood," the other paramedic said with a sigh. "Sir, I really think you should let us take you to the hospital."

"I already told you..." Patches began.

"Enough." Jesse shook his head. "Patches, go with these men to the hospital. That's an order. Shorty, take the car and follow them so you can bring him home once he's done getting checked out."

"Fine," Patches mumbled. A bit of relief crept into his voice. "I'll go to the hospital."

Jesse watched until the ambulance had driven away and Shorty too, in Eva's car. Eva had taken a seat on the curb and put her head between her hands. Even as he debated whether or not he should, he approached her. "Are you all right?"

"I'm fine." Her dismissive look told him she was anything but.

"Do you want to talk?" he asked, still clinging to the stubborn hope that a future between them might be possible.

"Not now," she responded. "Not today. Maybe not ever. I'm not sure we have anything to discuss."

Though his heart sank, he managed to smile and nod. "I understand." And the sad part was that he did. Clearly, he needed to resign himself to a life bereft of her.

Despite trying not to watch him, Eva saw the myriad raw emotions cross Jesse's handsome face. For the first time since she'd met him, he appeared vulnerable. She shouldn't care—she *didn't* care—or so she told herself.

Her father had trusted him. *She* had trusted him. As had numerous other members of BOS. The thought that he could betray them made her feel sick to her stomach. Especially her father. With all her heart, she prayed Raul had made it out of the country. A horrible thought occurred to her. Had Jesse even let him go?

"My father?" she asked, pitching her voice low so that only he could hear. "Is he…"

"Gone."

She waited for him to elaborate. Instead, he turned and started to walk away.

"Wait." Without thinking, she reached out and grabbed his arm. "The thumb drive. I need to get the thumb drive to the authorities. But not them." She jerked her head toward the Anniversary sheriff's deputies. "Someone higher up the chain."

For a moment he only stared at her, his expressionless face matching the flat look in his eyes. As their gazes locked and held, she swore his softened.

"I can take you." His lopsided grin tugged at her heart, a reaction she ignored. "We can go to the FBI office in Dallas, if you like. Or the ATF office. Your choice."

"Which one is the one where you work?"

Something flashed in his eyes, gone too quickly for her to analyze it. "ATF. We're working in conjunction with the FBI on this, so either one is good."

"Your office," she answered. "Since you'll be with me, at least I know they'll take me seriously."

He nodded. "Let's get on the road. It's a long drive. Do you want to drive or should I?"

The thought of sitting beside him in a car for a couple of hours made her stomach hurt. "Let's take the bikes," she responded. "I need to ride after everything that's happened."

He nodded and turned to head for the garage. After a moment, she followed, grabbing her helmet along the way.

On the road, driving her Harley, she felt like herself again. With each mile the motorcycle ate up, she felt bits of her sorely flagging confidence return. Though just about everyone she'd known, loved and trusted had betrayed her with lies and avarice, she still had this. The strong part of herself that no one, not even Drew, had ever been able to completely destroy, though she'd allowed it to be banished temporarily.

By the time they reached Dallas, she felt centered and once again in control. Normally, the congested traffic on I-635 would have agitated her, but with her powerful bike rumbling underneath her, she hung on to her patience. Having Jesse with her helped. This was his world, his people. Her own would turn on him once they knew the truth. The Feds would probably regard him as a hero.

Again her stomach turned. She swallowed back her rancor and reminded herself to focus on the task at hand.

They pulled into a paid garage, got their tickets and parked. Removing her helmet, Eva combed her fingers through her hair while she waited for Jesse.

He left his bike and approached her. His expression seemed grim and she thought he might be slightly nervous. Even now, she knew him well enough that she could read him. She almost asked him why the nerves, but told herself it really was none of her business.

"Are you ready?" he asked, removing his riding gloves and shoving them into his jacket pocket.

She nodded.

They walked side by side toward the building, neither speaking.

Jesse pushed through the front door, greeting the security guard by name and heading toward the elevator. Eva kept close to him, noting how out of place he seemed in the professional building. Men and women in suits hurried past and one or two even gave them the side-eye, which meant they must look as out of place as she felt.

Luckily, when the elevator arrived, they were alone. As soon as the doors closed, she turned to Jesse. "You really work here?"

"I did." He shrugged, his hooded expression closed off and remote. "Though mostly I haven't spent much time here. As you know, I've been out in the field."

The doors slid open and they stepped out onto a small reception area. The perfectly made-up woman behind the desk jumped to her feet. "Jesse Wyman? I can't believe it's you."

She came around the desk, her heels clicking on the marble floor, and hugged him. "How have you been?"

"Not bad, thanks, Gloria." He turned toward Eva, as if he meant to introduce her, and then didn't. Eva and Gloria eyed each other while Eva battled a quick twinge of unwanted jealousy. Finally, she dipped her chin and waited while Jesse asked Gloria if someone named E.J. was in.

"Let me buzz him and see if he's available." Crossing back around her desk, she picked up the phone. A moment later, she nodded. "He'll see you in his office."

"Perfect." Jesse eyed the door. "Would you mind using your badge to let me in? I don't have mine on me."

"Of course." The door buzzed as she passed her badge across a sensor, and unlocked.

"Thanks, G," Jesse said. He took Eva's arm and shepherded her through.

As they moved down a hallway between cubicles, Eva eyed the crowded office area, watching as various people did a double take when they saw Jesse. They were interrupted several times while Jesse got handshakes, pats on the back or raucous comments about his time undercover. Since a few of the remarks referenced the motorcycle club, she kept her gaze straight ahead and her expression neutral.

Finally, they arrived at a corner office and Jesse rapped on the closed door. "Come in," a brusque, male voice ordered.

Inside, the stern-looking man with a lined, weary face stood. He smiled at Jesse and they shook hands. Finally, Jesse introduced her.

"This is Eva Rowson. Eva, this is my boss, E.J."

E.J. held out his hand and Eva took it. She liked that he kept his grip firm. She'd always hated men with limp handshakes.

"Why don't you both have a seat." Returning to his chair, E.J. waited. "Are you here to turn yourself in, Mrs. Rowson?"

Startled, Eva recoiled. "Not hardly. I came because I have hard evidence that implicates Lori Pearson and a few other local business leaders."

"But she'd like a written guarantee of immunity from prosecution," Jesse put in.

Eva hid her surprise and nodded. Until this very moment, she'd never even considered the possibility of being arrested for any crime. Drew's dealings had been his and his alone. She'd had no part of any of them.

E.J. looked from Eva to Jesse and back again. "This evidence you have. Will it exonerate you completely?"

Once more she had to consider. "I believe so. My father said it did and I trust him."

"But why should I trust you?" E.J. asked.

"I can vouch for her," Jesse interjected. "She truly had no part in any of Drew's business or political deals, I promise you."

E.J. narrowed his eyes. "I trust you, Jesse, but still, Drew was her husband. At some point, she had to wonder where all the extra cash was coming from, right?"

This time, Eva spoke up for herself. "There was no extra cash, at least that I was aware of. None of what Drew did ever made its way to me or my son."

Nodding, E.J. pushed up from his chair. "You two wait here. Let me check with my superior and see what I can do."

The instant he left the room, closing the door behind him, Eva turned to Jesse. "Why didn't you tell me there was a possibility I could face charges?"

He shrugged. "If I had, would you have come?"

She didn't even have to think. "Of course not."

"That's why. I figured you'd have a much better chance if you came to them, with me vouching for you, than if they'd come out and arrested you."

"You have a point," she said slowly. "And while I understand their reasoning, don't they have to have some sort of proof that I did something wrong?"

Jesse lifted one shoulder. "Don't panic, okay? Let's just wait and see what E.J. comes back with."

A moment later, the door swung open and E.J. returned. Eva's heart sank at the serious expression on the other man's face. This couldn't be good.

"We're willing to consider your request," E.J. said carefully.

Jesse snorted. "Come on. You know you don't have enough to charge her. From what I understand, she's got a ton of valuable information."

Carefully, Eva hid her surprise. Jesse had no idea what was on the thumb drive—she hadn't had a chance to tell him.

"I do," she said slowly. "Starting with a list of every buyer and distributor Drew set up within the last couple of years. And where he laundered the money, as well."

E.J. studied her. "If you know all of this, that would make you an accessory."

"Not hardly," Jesse interjected. "I was there when her father gave her the information. She knew absolutely nothing about any of this prior to that."

"And I brought it to you at the earliest opportunity," Eva added. "Do I get my immunity agreement or not?"

For a moment she thought Jesse's boss would continue to try to stall, but instead he finally nodded. "Agreed. I'm having someone draw it up as we speak. Now show me what you've got."

Not sure she should until she had the signed agreement in hand, she looked to Jesse. He slowly nodded. "E.J. gave you his word," he said. "He'll keep his promise."

While she wasn't sure she trusted E.J., she did trust Jesse.

"Okay," she said. Digging the thumb drive out of her pocket, she passed it over to E.J. "Here you go."

Both he and Jesse appeared stunned. "You had it on you?" Jesse asked. "What if they'd arrested you and confiscated all your belongings?"

Though she now felt slightly foolish, she passed it off with a shrug. "I haven't done anything wrong, so I didn't expect something like that to happen."

E.J. watched the banter between the two of them with a bemused look on his weathered face. Finally, he took the thumb drive and plugged it into his computer. A few clicks later and he sat staring at his monitor. "You weren't kidding," he said, clicking through file after file. "There's more than enough evidence here to not only put Lori Pearson away for years, but to completely shut down the cartel's operations here in north Texas. I believe we will get numerous arrests out of this."

Since she figured that was the closest Jesse's boss would come to thanking her, she grinned at him. "I told you it was worth it."

A soft knock on the door and a woman wearing a tailored navy suit entered. "Here you are, sir." She handed a stack of paperwork to E.J. "Everything you requested."

He thanked her. Once she'd exited, he passed the papers over to Eva. "Take a look at these. I think you'll find everything is in order. Once you've signed, I'll have copies made for your records."

She signed all the highlighted areas and passed the paperwork back to him. E.J. called his assistant and asked for photocopies. The woman nodded and carried everything away.

"Now that that's taken care of," E.J. began, steepling his fingers on the desk in front of him, "you should know Drew's assets will be frozen. Savings account, checking, credit cards—all of it. You won't be able to access anything."

"That won't affect me at all." She couldn't keep the bitterness from her voice. "Drew cleaned out everything a few days before he was shot. I haven't been able to figure out what he did with the money. On top of that, he apparently stole three million dollars from one of the cartels."

E.J. exchanged a look with Jesse. "So we've heard," he said carefully. "The FBI has been looking into that, as well as the attempts made on your life. I believe they have a suspect in custody."

Chris. "The Anniversary police picked up Drew's campaign manager earlier today. She came to the house with three cartel members and tried to take Jesse hostage."

E.J. gave her one of those benevolent, masculine smiles that she'd always found irritating. "I'm aware. Jesse's already made a full report."

"Oh." She didn't know what else to say. She still hadn't entirely adjusted to the fact that Jesse was a Fed.

"Now I have an important question for you," E.J. said, leaning forward. "Where might we find your father?"

Though Eva's heart skipped a beat, she shrugged. "I have no idea right at this moment. Why?"

"Because with the big bust going down, I've got agents out there looking for him. No one has been able to locate him."

"Since when?" Eva took care not to look toward

Jesse. "He's been staying at my house. He shouldn't be that difficult to find."

"But he is." The assistant special agent in charge turned his attention to Jesse. "You've been with him a lot lately. As a matter of fact, you were the last person seen with him. Any idea where he might have disappeared to?"

Eva braced herself. Here it came. The moment of truth. She knew hearing Jesse betray her father would break her completely.

"No idea," Jesse said, his easy tone sincere. "But he never goes far from his daughter. I'm sure he'll turn up. Especially once he hears about Lori Pearson and the cartel."

"Maybe so." E.J.'s expression turned stern. "We've taken the liberty of getting you a hotel room for the night."

Puzzled, Eva shook her head. "That won't be necessary. It's just a couple of hours from here to my house in Anniversary."

"My apologies, but we can't let you go home. We're also going to have to hold on to your cell phone. At least until the drug bust goes down. We can't allow anything to jeopardize that. My agents' lives are on the line."

"But…" She started to protest, but a quick look at Jesse's face told her he'd expected this. "How long will that be?" she asked instead, twisting her hands together in her lap. "I didn't bring a change of clothes or anything."

"Not very long." E.J.'s answer seemed deliberately ambiguous. "If you end up having to stay overnight, one of our staffers will take care of any clothing or toiletry needs you might have."

"We haven't eaten," Jesse put in, glancing at his watch. "How about you have someone escort us to a restaurant?"

She couldn't help but notice the way Jesse said *us*. As if they were a team. E.J. caught it too, she thought, guessing by the way he gave Jesse a long, considering look.

"We can't let you off the premises," E.J. finally said. "But we can send out for pizza or Chinese food if you'd like."

They ended up splitting a large pizza in one of the conference rooms. They'd barely finished eating when E.J. entered the room. "We'll be releasing you sooner than I thought. The drug deal went down and we were able to round everyone up without incident, along with several million dollars of drugs."

"Drugs?" she asked.

"Yes. Methamphetamine, mostly."

Drugs. The one thing her father had always refused to allow BOS to be involved in and the reason he'd left behind the motorcycle club he'd founded. "What about my father?" she asked, even though she already knew. "Is he all right?"

"He didn't show." E.J.'s expression briefly turned grim. "We're still looking for him."

E.J. took Jesse with him to congratulate the team, leaving her alone in the conference room. She wondered what would happen if she simply walked out now, went to the parking garage and got on her bike to head home. She actually pushed to her feet, half intending to do exactly that, when Jesse returned. He looked both jubilant and weary, angry and sad and something else that she couldn't identify. As if he'd just lost something or someone important to him.

"Are you ready?" he asked.

Unaccountably tongue-tied, she nodded.

Side by side they left the building and walked to the garage. When they reached the spot where they'd parked their motorcycles, he stopped and turned to face her. "It's finally over," he said. "Chris and Lori are in custody, as well as the BOS members who were instrumental in the drug trade. I heard they even arrested several key cartel guys."

"That's good. I wonder what's going to happen to BOS now."

"The club will survive. There are enough good guys. They'll band together and keep things going. I'm sorry you got dragged in the middle of it all."

"Me too." Tears stung the back of her eyes and she blinked them away. "Thank you for not betraying my father," she said, her tone formal. "I'll make sure to let him know if I ever hear from him again."

"I'm sure you will. Once it's safe to do so, he'll contact you." He looked down, then away, anywhere in fact, other than directly at her.

"I guess this is goodbye," Jesse continued. "I won't be going back to Anniversary with you."

She felt like he'd kicked her in the stomach. "You won't?"

"No. If you need any help picking up Liam, let me know and I'll see what I can arrange." His formal tone matched his distant, patently false smile.

Not again, not now. The depth of her anger surprised her. After everything she'd been through, everything *they'd* been through, she was done with falsehoods between them.

"Why are you acting like this?" She shook her head. "I've had enough of the subterfuge and BS. Seriously."

He looked at her then. Really looked at her. "I don't know what you want from me."

The rawness of his confession matched the way she felt inside. "Honesty, Jesse. That's all I ever wanted." Since that statement in itself was a partial lie, she amended. "One of the things I wanted from you."

"What was the other?" he asked, his dark gaze locked on her.

Since she had nothing left to lose now, she told him. "Your love, Jesse. I wanted your love more than anything."

He came closer. "You've always had that. Always. Even now, Eva. I love you just as much now as I did before. More, even. And you should know the entire reason I couldn't leave BOS and go with you was because of my job. I'd invested too much of my life and I couldn't let the ATF down. But if the choice had been mine to make, I would have chosen you."

"Your job." Blinking back tears, she shook her head. "While that's admirable, it still hurts. I wish you the best in your career with the ATF."

"I've quit." He swallowed hard. "I learned too late what really matters to me. I'll have to find another way to make a living. Either way, I couldn't leave without saying goodbye, Eva."

"Then don't." Suddenly, her entire world no longer felt as if it were tilted crazily on its axis. "I love you too, Jesse Wyman. I always have and always will. You showed me how much you care when you let my father go."

Jesse froze. "Are you sure?"

Slowly she nodded. "I am. But I need to know how you will feel about Liam if the DNA test reveals he's not yours."

"He's mine. You know it as well as I do."

Steadfast, she waited.

"Even if he's not mine by blood, Liam will always be my son, as far as I'm concerned." He kissed her then, the press of his mouth deep and full of love. She kissed him back, her heart singing, hoping he could feel her joy.

When they came up for air, she smiled. "Let's go pick up our son. Since it's a long drive to Oklahoma, we can talk about our plans for the future."

"And our life together as a family," he added. "That is, if you'll have me."

"Is that a question?" she teased gently, though she figured she already knew.

"It is." He kissed her again, a light press of his mouth. "I don't have a ring, but we can choose one together. Will you marry me, Eva?"

"Of course I will." As if there'd ever been any doubt.

His answering smile matched the glow of love in her heart. "Then let's go get our son. It's time he got to know his father."

Hand in hand, they headed for the door.

* * * * *

SPECIAL EXCERPT FROM

⬧ HARLEQUIN
ROMANTIC SUSPENSE

One night of passion results in a pregnancy, but Sophia doesn't tell Carter he's going to be a dad right away. Now she's back in town with his son, and someone is threatening them. Can he keep the woman he loves and his baby safe, despite his broken heart?

Read on for a sneak preview of
Ranger's Family in Danger,
the next thrilling romance in the
Rangers of Big Bend *miniseries*
by Lara Lacombe.

She shivered next to him, clearly upset as she spoke. He put his arm around her and pressed a kiss to the top of her head.

"It's okay," he soothed, stroking her upper arm. "I'm here now. I won't let anyone hurt you or Ben."

"I think he has a key."

That got his attention. He paused midstroke, digesting this bit of news. "What makes you say that?"

She told him about Jake Porter, the man who claimed to be Will's grandson. The way he'd visited her earlier, his displeasure at finding her in the house.

"We'll change all the locks," Carter declared. "I'll go first thing in the morning, as soon as the hardware stores open. We can even put some extra locks on, as additional deterrent. And I want you and Ben to stay with me until he's apprehended." His apartment wasn't large, but they would make it work. She could have his bed and he'd take the couch. The discomfort was a small price to pay for knowing she and the baby were safe.

"Oh, no," she said. "We can't do that."

Carter drew back and stared at her, blinking in confusion. This was a no-brainer. Someone was out there with an agenda, and it was clear they were after something inside this house. Changing the locks was a good first step, but he doubted the intruder was going to be put off so easily. Unless he missed his guess, this guy was going to come back. And the next time, he might not be content to simply ransack a few rooms.

Carter took her hand. "I'm not trying to be alarmist here, but he's probably going to try again."

"But the locks," she said weakly.

"I doubt he'll let new locks stop him," Carter replied. "And given the way he acted with you before, it's probably only going to escalate. If he finds you here, he might hurt you."

Don't miss
Ranger's Family in Danger *by Lara Lacombe,*
available February 2021 wherever
Harlequin Romantic Suspense
books and ebooks are sold.

Harlequin.com